MW01257825

An Illuminated Life

Corey Stewart

An Illuminated Life

Printed in the United States of America

Paperback ISBN: 978-1-965253-31-1
Ebook ISBN: 978-1-965253-32-8

For four who illuminated the world:
Joseph "Jay" St. John, 09.29.1948 — 05.14.2023
Fr. H. David Wilson, 10.25.1939 — 07.15.2023
Harry W. Lawrence, 07.27.1939 — 11.15.2023
Lynn W. Minasian, 10.28.48 — 11.15.2024
and for
Tariq Salam,
whose arrival in heaven in 2024 was—I can only assume— just
as eventful as his first trip to New York,
minus the money sewn into the lining of his coat.
"Take me to the Cape Kennedy!"

Thank you all for the color you added to my life.

One

When Porter was little, he had a teddy bear he took everywhere. He would clamp his grubby little hand around the bear's neck and drag it to preschool and the playground and the soccer field and the Episcopal church where the Haven family had worshipped since Jesus himself was a child, and eventually the fabric in the bear's neck wore through completely.

I know this because yesterday afternoon we dragged the boxes that Porter had shipped to Italy but never opened out of the upstairs closet and began sorting through them. We were picking through a box of musty-smelling soccer gear when Porter shouted, "Head Teddy!" and extracted the bear's head from a jumble of muddy cleats.

"What the hell is that?"

"It's Head Teddy," he said, holding up the decapitated bear head and tenderly brushing a cobweb from its ear. "I didn't know he was in here or I would've rescued him sooner."

"Did he used to have a body?"

"Yeah, of course," Porter said. "Delia was going to sew him back together but watch this." He tucked the bear's head into the crook of his arm like a football. "See how portable it made him?"

I'm not sure what Porter's devotion to a teddy bear's head says about him. Probably that he's much more into substance over style—which ought to thrill me as my hair turns gray and everything on my body heads south—and he's also far more sentimental than I'd ever realized, judging by the rest of the stuff in the boxes.

In addition to the bear head and the soccer paraphernalia, the boxes held a whole treasure trove of souvenirs from our relationship thirty years ago. Ticket stubs from Bruce Springsteen's 1992 concert in Chapel Hill, our third official date. Programs from a classical music concert series we attended on campus. Matchbooks from He's Not Here, our favorite bar, and from The Angus Barn, where we ate on the night he proposed.

"I had no idea you were such a pack rat," I said, inspecting a concert ticket. "Lyle Lovett at Wolf Trap, 1993. Geez, Porter! Did you keep everything?"

"That was a great show. Remember the woman who sang the song about San Antonio and brought the house down? Incredible."

"Francine Reed," I said, setting the ticket stub aside and pulling out a copy of *The Daily Tar Heel* from 1993.

Porter laughed. "How did you just pull that name out of thin air?"

"I had the live album, and Lyle Lovett introduces her at the start of the song. I've probably listened to it five hundred times." I put the newspaper announcing our alma mater's NCAA basketball championship on the floor and reached back into the box. "Plus, I knew who you meant," I said, extracting yet another pair of filthy cleats.

Porter pulled a blue leather folder from the bottom of the box, the kind that diplomas come in. "Or maybe your brain is just a bizarre Venus flytrap of random facts," he said, brushing dust off the cover. "Look at this. Senior Awards banquet at Forten Hall."

"Otherwise known as The Porter Haven Awards Show, if I'm not mistaken."

"This is the only one I kept. The Scholar-Athlete award. I was proud of this one."

"You're saying you actually did throw something out? Because I'm looking at these boxes and I don't believe you."

"Come on, Beth! You're making me sound like a hoarder. Everything in here means something to me. Do you see anything from anyone else I dated?"

"We're only on the second box."

"Well, you're welcome to keep looking, but I can assure you there's nothing." He dropped the folder on the ground and pushed himself to his feet, then put his hand on the top of my head. "These stone floors are killing my back. I'm going to take Head Teddy downstairs and make a coffee. Want one?"

"I'll come down with you. Help me up?" I said, extending my hand.

Porter put Head Teddy in a place of honor, right in the middle of the fireplace mantel in his living room. We decided to take a break on the boxes, so when Porter finished his coffee, he went out to the barn to check on his sheep and I walked across the field to my house.

Jenny FaceTimed while I was emptying the kitchen cabinets and stacking all of the glasses and dishes in precarious piles on the kitchen table. I hit the button to accept the call and propped the phone on the windowsill.

"What are you doing?" she asked as soon as the video connected. "Was there an earthquake I didn't hear about?"

"Very funny. No, I'm going to paint the kitchen cabinets," I said, standing on my toes to pull juice glasses down from a high shelf. "I thought I'd reorganize while I was at it. Do you have a cold? Your eyes are all red."

Jenny shook her head. "Scott moved out."

"What?" I set the glasses on the counter and picked up the phone. "When did that happen?"

"Almost a week ago. I'm so stupid, Bits. I've been expecting him to come back every day. I thought we'd laugh about it, you know? Like 'Ha ha, you won't believe what Scott did last week.' But now I don't think he's coming back." She sniffled. "He said he needs to find himself."

"What does that even mean?" I asked, leaning against the counter. "Has he joined an ashram? Become a Scientologist?"

Jenny snorted. "Not hardly. Apparently 'finding himself' means buying a cherry-red Ferrari and screwing a dental hygienist named Amber."

"You're not serious?"

"I had no idea anything was even wrong," Jenny said, dabbing her eyes with a wad of tissue. "He just announced over waffles that after thirty years of marriage and two children, he's not sure he still loves me and he needs some time to himself. He didn't mention Amber, of course. I had to find that out myself."

"God, Jen. I'm so sorry," I said. "I swear, you can't trust anyone. Do you think this is just a midlife crisis and he'll come to his senses?"

She shook her head. "He rented a place across town, in one of those old buildings they're converting to lofts."

"Where is he getting the money for a Ferrari and an apartment?" I asked.

"That's exactly what my brothers want to know," Jenny said. She shrugged. "I have no idea. Not from our joint account, which means he's been stashing money somewhere."

"Scott better watch out your brothers don't beat his ass," I said. "I know this doesn't help, but I'm honestly shocked, Jen. I never would have expected this from him in a million years."

"Right? I'm just floored."

"What can I do to help?"

"You're already doing it. I knew you'd understand, after what you went through."

"I definitely understand," I said. "This kind of shit is exactly why I'm not going to get married again. I don't want to spend one more minute of my life wondering what my spouse is doing behind my back."

"I keep asking myself what else I don't know," Jenny said, twirling a strand of hair around her finger. "How long has this been going on with Amber? Where's the money coming from? Why didn't he just tell me he was unhappy? I feel like he had this all planned out, and meanwhile, I was picking up his socks and cooking his dinner, totally clueless." She reached for more tissues and blew her nose. "The joke's on me, I guess. I thought he meant it when he said his vows."

"You're not a fool for trusting him, Jen. You're supposed to be able to trust your spouse," I said. "That's on him for breaking that trust."

"You may have to tell me that a few more times. I feel like an idiot."

"I know. I get it. But you're not an idiot. And trust me, you'll get answers to all your questions eventually," I told her. "Just try not to drive yourself crazy in the meantime. And whatever you do, don't start reviewing the past. You'll lose your mind if you start going backwards."

"I spotted them on Onondaga Avenue yesterday in that stupid car. She's tiny, with overfilled lips and boobs," Jenny said. "And please tell me who the hell drives a Ferrari in Syracuse, New York, the snowfall capital of America? I hope the bottom rots out from road salt."

"He's just such a cliché," I said. "Next thing you know he'll be getting hair plugs."

I glanced out the window above the sink. Porter was walking across the field toward my house, followed closely by Oliver, who had an enormous tree branch in his mouth.

"Nothing would surprise me. Oh, wait, Bits—get this. He wears pastel polos and skinny jeans now. He came over to fix the pilot light on the hot water heater and I about fell over."

I groaned. "I cannot imagine Scott in a pastel polo, much less skinny jeans. It's too gruesome. How are the kids dealing with all of this?"

"I don't talk to them about him. They're busy with their own lives, and I think they're just trying to ignore what's happening." Jenny wiped her eyes with her fingertips and forced a thin smile. "Let's change the subject. How's Italy?"

"It's good. You should come over. It would be good for you to get away."

Porter walked into the kitchen with Oliver on his heels. After several attempts to force the oversized branch through the narrow doorway, Oliver finally gave up. He dropped the branch in front of the door and ran inside to check his food bowl. Finding it empty, he came and sat on my feet.

"Oh, sorry," Porter whispered. "I didn't realize you were on the phone."

"I'm talking to Jenny," I said, reaching down to pet Oliver.

Porter leaned in front of me and waved at the screen. "Hi, Jenny."

"We were just talking about Jen coming for a visit," I told him.

"You really should," Porter told her. "This time of year is incredible. We're headed into a major food season—chestnuts, truffles, olive oil—and the weather is great."

Jenny wiped a tear off her cheek and nodded. "And we could finally meet in person. I can't believe I've never seen you in the flesh."

"Well, don't expect too much," Porter said, smiling. "But it would be great to have you here." He kissed the side of my head. "I'll leave you to it. Text me when you're free?"

I nodded.

Porter waved at Jenny, then whistled at Oliver, who followed him out the door.

"I still can't get over the fact that you and Porter ended up together after not talking for thirty years," Jenny said when Porter was gone, propping her chin on her hand. "Sometimes that's the only thing in the world that cheers me up. It's a love story for the ages."

"Yeah, well, I don't know about all that. But he's a good guy."

"Does he still want you to move in with him?"

I nodded. "He mentions it every once in a while. But I like having my own space. And if it all goes south, I don't want to have to move out."

"I thought things were good between you guys?"

"They are. But I don't want to depend on anyone like that again. It's too risky."

Jenny nodded. "Maybe I will come visit," she said. "No one will even notice I'm gone."

"Please do. I would love that."

"I think I will. I'll call you in a day or two."

"Hang in there, Jen. And call me anytime."

When Jenny and I hung up, I went back to emptying the cabinets. I was thinking about a girl who'd been in our class at Saint Francis de Sales Catholic school. Everyone, including me and Jenny, had called her Lovely Lacey. She had the most perfect life: a big brick house in Strathmore, two doting parents, and effortless beauty—the kind of girl who had a figure while the rest of us were still prepubescent blobs. On top of that, she was also intelligent and kind, which made her nickname both a truism and a mark of envy.

Lacey was, of course, the object of fervent male affection. You would think that the nuns holding her up as an exemplar of virtue might temper the boys' ardor, but it didn't. Lacey was the goddess everyone wanted, even though it was impossible to imagine her doing anything as crass as letting herself be felt up in the backseat of a Camaro.

Jenny and I often said, as we lay on her side-by-side twin beds thumbing through *Seventeen*, that if we could change places with anyone, it would be Lacey.

"I mean, does she even study?" Jenny asked, licking orange Cheetos dust off her fingers. "And who has skin that good?"

"She probably gets professional facials." I ripped the sample of Love's Baby Soft out of the magazine and held it to my nose. "Ew, gross. This smells like something a grandma would wear."

"What I don't understand," Jenny said, wiping her hand on her skirt and reaching for the perfume sample, "is how she makes that hideous PE uniform look so good." She held the scented paper to her nose. "That smells like baby powder and flowers. Nasty." She wadded up the perfume sample and tossed it in the general direction of the wastepaper basket. "It's just cruel that we have to wear those things in front of the boys. It's like they're trying to humiliate us."

"We're burning our PE uniforms the day we graduate," I said, flipping through the pages to find the next perfume sample. I tore it out, sniffed it, and handed it to Jenny.

"Ooh, Giorgio," she said, and rubbed the scented strip against her kilt. "Do you want some of this?"

I shook my head.

She dropped the perfume strip on the floor and dug in the Cheetos bag. "They're fire hazards to begin with. One match and it'll be an inferno."

Of all the injustices foisted on us at Catholic school, the PE uniforms were the worst. Three times a week, all the girls in our class filed like prisoners into the cinder block basement of the gym. There—beneath a toxic cloud of sweat, angst, and the Impulse Body Spray Sister Mary Michael expressly forbade—we swapped our plaid kilts and blue button downs for a zip-front, one-piece polyester abomination of navy-blue shorts and a horizontally striped blue and white top. But while everyone else tugged the shorts out of their crotch and yanked at the too-tight sleeves for the next hour, Lovely Lacey, who never broke a sweat, somehow managed to look like she'd just dropped in from Fashion Week.

"Do you think she had her PE uniform tailored or something?" I asked, leaning off the bed to retrieve my can of Tab from the floor.

Jenny nodded. "There's no other explanation."

To further compound the humiliation of being forced to wear a garment that was the love child of prison garb and Auschwitz pajamas, PE for the Catholic boys' school next door started ten minutes before ours did. Since the two schools shared the gymnasium and fields, this meant that we girls had to parade past the whole herd of leering, pimple-faced jackals on our way to PE.

The boys would stop shooting baskets or running sprints when we appeared and pretend to be judges in a beauty contest, calling out number scores as we walked by. Father Declan would blow his whistle and say, "Aye, c'mon, lads," but the boys ignored him and kept up their commentary as we scurried like cockroaches to pass without being noticed. Lacey, however, seemed oblivious. She floated above the fray on a cloud of untouchable perfection, immune to the testosterone fog of the gym and wholly uninterested in the consistent tens she received.

I never saw Lacey again after high school, but Jenny used to see her every Christmas when Lacey came home from Smith for the holidays. Every year, Jenny would report that Lacey had gotten more beautiful and was still dating the Harvard med student from the old money Boston family who'd swept her off her feet at the beginning of freshman year.

In late March of our senior year of college, though, Jenny called with a different kind of update. Porter and I weren't engaged yet, but we were serious, and he and my Honors thesis and grad school plans were taking up all of the space in my brain. I hadn't talked to Jenny in almost a month when she called, and she was breathing so heavily into the receiver that I thought something had happened to her. But no. She was calling to tell me that federal agents had swooped into Lacey's stately family home at dawn the previous morning.

"They arrested her father, and then went downtown and raided his office," she said.

"Why? What were they looking for?"

"I have no idea. The paper just says it was a federal raid. You should see the picture on the front page, Bits. Lacey's mom is standing on the porch in her bathrobe while about ten FBI agents carry boxes out of the house. I feel so bad for them."

I did too. When my mom and Aunt Celia were hit by a drunk driver our senior year of high school, the paper ran endless stories about it, each one accompanied by an unflattering yearbook photo of newly orphaned me. That had been mortifying enough, so I could only imagine how this felt for Lacey and her mother.

Eventually Lacey's dad was charged with possession and distribution of child pornography, and, after a trial that was front-page news in Syracuse for weeks, was sent to prison.

The next October, Jenny called me in Washington, DC, where I was attending grad school, with more news.

"Lacey's dad is dead," she said. "Sliced to pieces."

"Are you kidding?"

"Other inmates killed him. Don't these prisons have guards and cameras?"

"Jesus. Poor Lacey."

"I know. It's horrible."

"Who would have ever predicted this? Lacey's life always seemed so perfect."

"I remember being so impressed that they had a computer in their house," Jenny said. "First one I ever saw. I guess we know why now, huh? And Doctor Harvard apparently dumped her. I haven't seen her, but I heard she's back home with her mom."

"Remember how they used to go all out for Halloween? Her dad would make those apple donuts and cider—"

"And we had to come in and show off our costumes," Jenny said. "Kind of creepy to think of that now."

"Remember Lacey's birthday party at SkateTown? We thought her dad was so fun because he skated with us. She had that giant pink cake—"

"I gave her a Barbie Fashion Maker and she already had one and I really wanted to take mine back."

I laughed. "You should have."

"Anyway, it just goes to show that you can't judge a book by its cover. I thought Lacey had a perfect life and look how it's turned out? What a shit show."

Even though I'd had my own share of tragedies by then—both of my parents were dead by the time Jenny and I graduated high school—it took me a few more decades to realize that having your life go sideways isn't anything special. It happens every minute of every day to millions of people.

And more to the point, your misfortunes have nothing to do with what you deserve. You can be a good person and go out of your way to never hurt anyone and try to always do the right thing and still have your life skid into a ditch.

The only thing you can do is guard your heart.

I'd learned that the hard way.

Two

Earlier in the week, before the urge to reorganize the kitchen and paint the cabinets had taken hold, I'd started combing through the hundreds of documents stored on my laptop, looking for material that could be reworked into magazine articles and short stories. I felt certain I had pieces from my three months of work on a tourism project in Assisi that I could reuse, but I hadn't been able to find much of the material. After talking to Jenny and cleaning the insides of the cabinets with white vinegar, I left all the doors open so the shelves could dry and sat down at my computer. My plan was to search my documents by date to find everything I'd written during that time.

The tourism project had fallen into my lap when I was trying to recover from having my life go up in flames. My daughter, Mia, had been killed a year and a half earlier, and in the aftermath of her death, I'd discovered that my marriage was a total sham. I was paralyzed by grief and barely functioning when Porter—my former fiancé, whom I hadn't seen or spoken to in three decades—saw an article online about Mia's death. She'd been killed by a bicycle courier in central London who'd run a red light and sent her flying. The accident had received an enormous amount of press and ignited a huge firestorm about cyclists' rights and traffic laws.

After reading about Mia's death, Porter tracked down my number and called my house in London. And then he called back every day for weeks, patiently listening to me cry and telling me stories about his life in Italy. Eventually he invited me to fly down and visit him, thinking a change of scenery and some sunshine would do me good. I was half-starved and half-crazy with grief and barely functioning, but I flew to Rome. I stayed in Porter's guest room for four months, and then finally, when I couldn't put it off any longer, I flew back to England, confronted Crawford, hired a lawyer, packed my belongings, and fled to my uncle David's home in Chapel Hill to lick my wounds and try to imagine a day when I might want to interact with the world again. An editor I'd worked with several times over the years emailed out of the blue while I was still trying to figure out my next step. She offered me the chance to work on a three-month project in Assisi, Italy. The centerpiece was a new tourism initiative about the life of Saint Francis, but there were several side projects as well, writing about various places across Umbria and Tuscany.

Marco Mastropietro, a historian and Assisi native, was hired as my guide and driver for the duration of the project. He was a real character who became a good friend during the countless hours we spent together in the car. A lot of our adventures made their way into what eventually became my first book, so when the book was released, I mailed a copy to Marco at the tourism office. I hadn't heard from him in ages, but as I was dragging Word documents into file folders and searching for material to reuse, WhatsApp rang with a video call.

"Marco!" I said when his face appeared on the screen. "*Come stai*? I thought I'd hear from you months ago."

"*Bene, grazie*. I get your book a long time ago, is true. Is nice, this book. I am happy for you."

"Did you read it?" I asked, propping the phone against the lamp on my desk.

He shook his head. "I cannot read so much English. But I look for my name."

I laughed. "Of course you did."

"You are beautiful today. I like this color for you."

I looked down at Porter's faded Forten Hall sweatshirt. "Yeah? Do you like the coffee I spilled on it?"

"*Sei maldestra come sempre*. How you say this, *maldestra*?"

"Clumsy. I'm clumsy as usual."

"Clumsy." He nodded. "Is a good word." Marco held up a finger, silencing me, then called out, "*Ciao, Bruno*!" He waved and nodded, listening for a minute, before returning his attention to the screen. "Sorry. Was a friend of mine. I know everybody."

"You should run for mayor."

"No need," Marco said, shaking a cigarette out of a pack. "I will be famous from your book."

"I doubt that."

"Do you miss me, darling?" he asked, lighting the cigarette and inhaling deeply.

"I actually do! I think of you often."

"Say this in Italian. Is nice to hear," he said, then started coughing.

I waited for him to stop, then said, "*Ti penso spesso*."

"I think of you, too," he said. "But this is because I am curious about your life. That is not why you think of me."

"Oh, really? Why do I think of you?"

"Because you love me," he said, shrugging as he exhaled. "Don't worry, is normal. You are woman, I am Marco, is normal you should love me."

I laughed out loud. "I see your ego is still doing well."

He coughed again, then shook his head. "I am not well."

"I was talking about your enormous ego . . . Never mind. Maybe you wouldn't cough if you didn't smoke?"

"Is true, I am enormous, but how you know this? Who tell you?"

"Oh my God, Marco. Moving on."

"Tell me, *cara,* how is Pedro? You are still together with him?"

"I don't know anyone named Pedro."

"The man with the house where you stay."

"Porter? He's fine, he's good."

"You are married with him?"

I shook my head. "No. He lives next door."

"*Brava,*" Marco said, smiling. "Is not right to marry with him when you love Marco. When do you come to Assisi?"

I rolled my eyes. "Actually, I do need to come over. I'm writing about the church of Santa Maria sopra Minerva and I need some photos. Unless you want to take them for me?"

Marco shook his head. "Is not possible. I make photos always with this in the view." He held up his thumb and waggled it. "How you call this?"

"Your thumb."

"My *tum-ba.*"

"Close enough. I'm thinking of coming in a few days. Do you want to grab a coffee when I'm there?"

"We will have lunch together."

"Great! It will be good to see you."

"Is because I am beautiful like the *Davide* of Michelangelo." He smiled. "Try to control yourself. *Ciao, cara.*"

"We have new neighbors," Porter said, pulling up next to me on the long, cypress-lined driveway we shared a few hours later.

"Oh yeah?" I went around to the passenger door and freed Oliver, who was barking maniacally and trying to squeeze himself out of the half-opened window.

"They're coming over later for a drink. I hope that's okay."

"Sure, whatever." I shrugged. "You want to go for a walk? I was just heading out. I've been excavating the contents of my laptop and need a break."

Porter nodded and turned off the car. He grabbed the leash from the back seat and clipped it to Ollie's collar.

"How'd you meet the new neighbors?" I asked as we made our way down the drive. Oliver was zigzagging in front of us, dragging his leash behind him and investigating every tree trunk and shrub.

Porter said he'd been in the little hardware store in the next village over when he'd stepped in to help two guys who were having a hard time explaining what they needed.

"Are they American?"

"One. The other is Australian. They told me they'd just bought a house nearby and are renovating it and can't get the plumber or the electrician to call back."

"Sounds familiar."

"That's what I said. It turns out the house they bought is Villa Rosmarino. They moved in last weekend while we were in Turin, which is why we missed it."

"No way! I love that place. But boy, it really needs an overhaul. Are they nice? What are their names?"

"Dean is the American and Darren is the Australian. Or maybe vice-versa? Crap. Anyway, they're coming at five, just for a quick drink."

Porter whistled at Oliver, who had taken off across the field after a rabbit. Oliver ignored him.

"Oliver, come!" I shouted.

Oliver stopped in his tracks and turned to look at me. He glanced in the direction the rabbit had gone, then slowly began making his way toward us with his tail at half-mast.

"Thwarted again, huh, buddy?" Porter said, reaching down to scratch Oliver's ears when he rejoined us. "Should I be mad that he listens to you but not me?"

"It's all in the tone. Are the neighbors living here full-time? Are they retired? When did they buy the house? Do they speak any Italian?"

"We talked about nails."

"I better head back and take a shower," I said, glancing at my watch. "Want me to make olive tapenade? I got some bread this morning."

"That would be great. I've got a decent Tuscan red. If we like them, we'll move on to something better. I just invited them for drinks, so they won't be here long."

Those turned out to be famous last words.

Porter and I went to bed around three o'clock this morning, after the four of us killed six bottles of wine, including three bottles of very nice Barolo. Porter made omelets with fresh herbs—complete with showy pan-flipping and several rounds of applause—around midnight, after we'd polished off the tapenade and bread, plus a bowl of pasta with tomatoes, basil, and mozzarella that was left over from lunch and the almond cookies I'd made a few days earlier.

It was after two when we walked Dean and Darren—Double D, as we were calling them—home across the field using Porter's megawatt flashlight. Oliver was surprisingly spry, given the amount of table scraps he'd been fed over the course of the evening, but as soon as we got back to Porter's house, he curled up on the couch and fell asleep. Porter and I cleaned up the kitchen, crawled upstairs, brushed our teeth, and fell into Porter's bed. He was snoring before his head even hit the pillow.

I intended to stay in bed until at least noon, but just before eight, my eyes flew open. I was lying very still, hoping I could trick myself into falling back asleep, when Porter suddenly sat up and chucked a pillow at the window.

"Shut up, you goddamn birds!" he yelled, then turned to look at me. "Why are you awake?"

"Birds," I croaked. My throat felt like I'd eaten a bag of sand.

Porter groaned and lay back down, rolling onto his side and pulling the sheet over his face. I eased myself out of bed as he began snoring again and found my bathrobe, then brushed my teeth as quietly as I could before tiptoeing downstairs. Oliver was waiting by the bottom step, his tail beating a rhythm on the wall.

I let Ollie out and filled the bottom of the big Bialetti moka with water, scooped coffee into the metal basket, and screwed the pieces back together. I set the moka on the stove to percolate, then filled Oliver's water bowl and let him back inside. He drank like a dehydrated horse, sending water flying all over the floor and my bare feet as I leaned against the counter, yawning and looking out the window.

When the coffee was done, I divided it between two ceramic cups with lids that I'd found at the Leroy Merlin store and headed back upstairs. I put one cup on the nightstand next to Porter's head and made sure the lid was sealed tight, then took the other cup with me into the bathroom, setting it on the edge of the sink while I forced the ancient window up a crack and turned on the taps to fill the tub.

I was in the bath drinking the last of my coffee when Porter wandered in, stark naked but for one sock. His face looked like he'd done ten rounds with Muhammed Ali.

"Can I—" he said, gesturing towards the toilet.

I nodded and added some more hot water to the tub while he peed for what seemed like an hour. He pulled the chain to flush and went to the sink to wash his hands and brush his teeth.

"Is there more coffee downstairs?" he asked, looking at me in the reflection of the mirror. His toothbrush was sticking out the side of his mouth and there was toothpaste on his chin.

"I put it on your nightstand."

Porter rinsed his toothbrush and dropped it into a cup, swished water in his mouth and spit into the sink, dried his hands on his bare torso, then shuffled out. He returned a minute later with the coffee. "Any room?"

I nodded and pulled my legs into my body. Porter handed me his coffee cup and slid into the bathtub, sending water sloshing over the rim and onto the floor.

"Fuck," he said, then reached underwater to remove the sock he was still wearing. He dropped it over the side of the tub and settled himself, then reached for the cup of coffee. I handed it to him and stretched my legs out on one side of his body.

Porter pried the lid off his coffee cup, then leaned back, resting his feet on top of my thighs. "Thanks for the coffee. I'm worthless today."

"We need a bigger tub," I said, grabbing his toes.

He nodded but didn't say anything else until he had finished the entire cup of coffee and leaned over the edge of the tub to deposit the cup and lid on the floor.

"I feel like death," Porter groaned.

"Me, too. I thought a bath would rehydrate me."

He closed his eyes and leaned his head against the rim of the tub. "It smells good in here."

"Lavender." I closed my eyes too. I'm not sure we didn't both fall asleep because when Porter shifted in the tub, startling me, my hands were wrinkled like prunes and the water was noticeably cooler.

"I don't want to get out," Porter said. "But I'm starving."

"Me too. And Ollie's only had water this morning."

Porter looked down at Oliver, who was napping on the bathmat with his chin on Porter's wet sock.

"God, last night was fun, huh?" he said. "I don't think I've laughed that hard in a long time."

"We drank for almost ten hours. I feel lucky to be alive."

Porter yawned. "I'm not going to get anything done today."

"You told Double D we'd go look at their house."

"Surely they're suffering as much as we are?"

I pointed out the window where, across the expanse of fields, I could see a brush fire and two figures moving. "Looks like they're up and at 'em."

"Jesus."

"Come on, old man. I'm gonna pull the plug so we have to get out."

"Please don't."

"Too late. I'll make us something to eat."

Porter retracted his legs. I put my hands on the tub's edge and pulled myself to my knees.

"And more coffee?"

I nodded. "Move, Ollie, or I'm going to step on you."

"Careful," Porter said, leaning forward to grab my wrist as I got to my feet.

As I towel-dried my hair, I watched in the mirror as Porter stood up in the almost-empty tub. He was still muscular and lean, but where there used to be sharply defined ridges in his midsection, there was now just the slightest hint of roundness. I'd spent hours lying with my head in the crook of his arm when we were in college, running my hands over the topography of his torso while he sang to me, always a schmaltzy Dolly Parton-Julio Iglesias duet called "When You Tell Me That You Love Me." I have no idea why he chose that song or how he even knew the words, but almost twenty years later, I was traveling in the Netherlands when I heard the Dutch version and had to leave the shop I was in so I wouldn't start weeping.

"I'm getting old," Porter said, catching my eyes in the mirror. "You're going to trade me in for some young stallion with the body I used to have."

I shook my head. "Never. Who'd make my omelets?"

Porter laughed, then groaned. "Oh God. My head. Don't make me laugh."

"We'll eat Spididol for breakfast."

"What if we go somewhere instead of seeing Double D's house? We could go over there tomorrow instead."

"What did you have in mind?"

"We could take a ride to Gubbio to see the plates in the museum you wanted to see? I just want to do something that involves fresh air and walking. And no alcohol."

"Yeah, let's do it. I'll make us something to eat and feed Ollie, then we can go."

Three

We parked below the historic center of Gubbio near the ancient weavers' market and strolled up the Via dei Consoli.

Like Assisi, Gubbio is a medieval village made of stone and built into the side of a mountain, with a labyrinth of narrow alleyways branching off the historic center. There's also a fountain—La Fontana del Bargello—where, if you circle it three times in the presence of a Gubbio resident, you can receive a certificate declaring that you are certifiably insane. Porter and I agree we don't need a paper to tell us what we already know.

Porter was on the hunt for truffle oil, even though it was still very early in the season, so we ducked into a *tartufo* shop so he could sample a few. When he'd made his selection, I wandered outside while the shop assistant wrapped the bottle of oil in green tissue paper and chatted with him. When he finally came out, we went into my favorite ceramics shop across the street to look at the same green bowl I'd looked at the last two times we were in Gubbio.

"Beth, just buy it," Porter said. "We keep coming back to this same bowl. I don't understand why you don't just get it?"

"I have too many serving bowls. I don't need it."

"But you love it."

"I know. The color is amazing. But it's expensive and I don't need it."

Porter shrugged. "Suit yourself."

I tore myself away from the ceramics shop and we walked up to the grand piazza, which is flanked on both sides by palaces, one of which—the Palazzo dei Consoli—houses the Civic Museum.

"Remind me what we're looking at," Porter said as we walked up the stone stairs to the museum's entrance. "I know they're copper plates, but what's the story?"

"They're called the Iguvine Tables. They were found here in the 1400s."

"Why are they important?"

"Because they date to the third and first centuries before Christ. They describe an ancient order of priests and their rituals, so they're valuable from that angle too, but I think the main thing is that the oldest tables were written in the Etruscan alphabet that doesn't exist anymore," I said. "The newer ones from the first century BC use Latin characters."

"Got it."

"I think we need to see them at least once, don't you?"

"I don't know how I've lived this long without seeing them, to be honest," Porter said.

"Be as sarcastic as you want, Haven," I said, pushing my hip against his, "but don't forget how easily I can knock you off this mountain."

We paid the fee to get into the museum, then wandered through the displays of military artifacts, paintings, ceramics, and archaeological relics.

"How'd all this stuff from Tibet get here?" Porter asked, peering into a glass cabinet full of religious items from Nepal.

"It says an English colonel named Vivian Gabriel donated the collection," I said, reading off the plaque on the wall. "He was a descendant of a noble family from Gubbio and served in India."

"Ahh, the good old days when Vivian was a man."

"Evelyn too."

"What do you think of 'When Vivian was a man' as a band name? Should we add it to our list?"

"Massive merchandising potential. And very much in step with the times. I vote to add it."

Porter nodded and yawned loudly as we entered the gallery where the Iguvine Tables were displayed. Each of the seven bronze plates was set in its own wooden frame and suspended from a decorative arm attached to the wall.

"The etching is surprisingly clear for how old they are, don't you think?" I asked, leaning forward to squint at one of the larger tablets.

"Do they go left to right?"

I shook my head. "Right to left."

"Doesn't help," he said. "I still can't make out anything."

"The Etruscan alphabet doesn't seem to be related to any other language. It died out completely in the first century after Christ, which is why no one's been able to do much with these tables."

"Oh, good. I thought it was just me," Porter said, straightening up.

"Well, now we can say we've seen them."

He nodded. "I feel so much better about myself. Ready to ride up the mountain?"

I groaned. "Yeah, but I can't make any promises about my stomach."

We left the museum and crossed the wide stone piazza. Save for San Marco in Venice, which opens to the sea on one side, the majority of piazzas in Italy are enclosed by buildings for protection. The Gubbio piazza, however, is bordered on one side by a sheer drop into the streets below. There's a chest-high wall so you don't accidentally plummet over the side, but it's surprisingly open and feels spacious in a way the closed-in piazzas don't.

Porter took my hand as we continued down the main road toward the station for the *flunivia,* a stand-up cable car that looks like a bunch of giant metal birdcages hanging from a steel cable. The Basilica di Sant'Ubaldo sits above Gubbio, and to get to it you can either walk the steep, narrow road that twists and turns up the mountain or you can ride in the flunivia. I always choose to spare my quads and ride, despite my fear that one day the cable will snap and send the birdcages rolling ass over teakettle down the mountain.

Luckily, we made it to the top without incident. I jumped out of the birdcage and waited for Porter to step out, then we followed the dirt walkway up to the church and convent.

The Basilica of Saint Ubaldo is, by Italian standards, quite new. It was built on top of a medieval structure, like most everything in Tuscany and Umbria, but it wasn't finished until the early days of the sixteenth century. Once construction was complete, painters spent the next two hundred years adding scenes from the life of Ubaldo to the interior walls. My favorite painting inside the basilica isn't of Ubaldo, though. It's of Jesus Christ—but a bizarrely muscular Jesus who looks like he hasn't missed a workout in several millennia. Porter and I call it "Swole Jesus."

"Lamb of God, gettin' those gains," Porter muttered, high-fiving the risen Lord as we walked by the painting. "Remind me what I should know about Saint Baldy?"

Saint Ubaldo is the patron saint of Gubbio, I told him, as well as of demonic possession, obsessive-compulsive disorder, and migraines.

"That's an odd mix."

I shrugged. "I'm sure they thought OCD and migraines came from demons, like everything else."

"Is there a patron saint of hangovers?" Porter asked. "Because I will gladly prostrate myself in front of that guy today."

When I said I didn't know, Porter sighed. "Alright. Give me the highlight reel on Baldy then."

Ubaldo was born in 1084 and orphaned when he was very young, I told Porter. His uncle, the Bishop of Gubbio, raised him. Ubaldo was expected to follow in his uncle's footsteps and serve the church, but he came of age in the era of plenary indulgences and widespread corruption in the Catholic Church and was distressed by what he saw—as Saint Francis would be a century later. So after holding a couple of religious offices, Ubaldo gave up all of his possessions and tried to join the monastery of Fonte Avellana in the Marche region.

"The abbot of Fonte Avellana was this guy called Peter of Rimini who was really strict," I told Porter as we looked at the paintings of Ubaldo in the basilica. "The monks could only have bread and water, except on Tuesdays and Thursdays, when they could have a piece of fruit."

"And that's where Baldy wanted to stay?"

"Yeah, but Rimini Pete wouldn't let him. He sent Ubaldo back to Gubbio. Then the leaders in Perugia made Ubaldo their bishop."

"But I thought he wanted out of the church?" Porter said.

"He did," I said, nodding. "So much so that he promptly set out for Rome to resign in person to Pope Honorius the Second. It didn't work, though. Instead of letting him leave the church, they made Ubaldo the Bishop of Gubbio."

Ubaldo wasn't very popular in Gubbio until 1155, I told Porter. That was when he rose from his sickbed to reason with Emperor Frederick Barbarossa—the infamous Redbeard—who was ransacking his way through Umbria. Ubaldo convinced Barbarossa to spare Gubbio, then promptly went back to bed, where he stayed for five more years before dying.

"Five years in bed," Porter said. "Can you imagine?"

"Honestly, it doesn't sound that bad. If I had enough books and magazines, and the bed could be wheeled outside when it was nice out, and somebody brought tasty meals . . ."

Porter laughed. "You'd last two weeks, max."

Naturally, since he saved their village from Barbarossa, the good people of Gubbio revised their opinion of Ubaldo. When he died, they gave his corpse a nice spot in the town's cathedral, and that's where he stayed for three hundred years. But then it was decided that Ubaldo deserved better digs, so they built a basilica for him above Gubbio on Mount Ingino and hauled his carcass up there. That's where Ubaldo rests today—minus a finger bone that's on permanent holiday in France.

Every May, Gubbio has a wild festival called La Corsa dei Ceri, the Race of the Candles. Young men run up the steep mountainside carrying wooden pedestals topped with one of three statues—either Saint Ubaldo, Saint George, or Saint Anthony. Whoever gets to the basilica first wins.

"Let me guess," Porter said. "Baldy wins every year?"

I nodded. "Yeah. But it's his day and his basilica, so that only seems right."

"I don't think I could carry one of those ten feet, much less up the mountain," Porter said, eyeing one of the wooden pedestals that was leaning against the wall next to the painting of Swole Jesus. "And that's without the saint on top. Maybe that explains why Jesus is so jacked, huh?"

"No doubt. I wonder if anyone has ever dropped one of the saints?"

"It has to have happened at some point. They've been doing this race for what, several hundred years?"

"I read in the museum that the Iguvine Tables describe a ritual just like that race, so it may have even started before Christ, with pagan figures on top of the pedestals instead of saints."

"What do you think would happen if you dropped a saint?"

"Straight to hell," I said.

"Express train to *l'inferno*."

"Speaking of l'inferno, did you know Dante mentions Gubbio in the *Divine Comedy*? He talks about 'blessed Ubaldo's hill,'" I said. "Fonte Avellana is in there too."

Porter shook his head. "No, but I did see that there's a documentary about Dante coming out."

"Yeah, I saw an interview with the guy playing Dante. I definitely want to watch, and not just because he's smoking hot."

"He must be good looking if you're willing to watch a movie Robert Duvall's not in."

"Robert Duvall's about ninety now, but honestly, I'd still watch him play Dante."

"And gladly be his Beatrice?" Porter asked, grinning.

"Obviously. But I'd also gladly be Beatrice to the guy in the documentary. He's gorgeous."

"Poor you," Porter said, looping his arm around my neck as we left the basilica's courtyard. "You're stuck with me. You want to walk down or take the birdcage?"

"Birdcage."

The trip down the mountain in the birdcage was well worth the anxiety it provoked because as you descended from the basilica, the whole valley stretched out in front of you—endless terracotta rooftops, far-off fields, and mountains beyond. It was a gorgeously clear day, and the sky was a brilliant blue, making the entire scene look like a painting.

I pointed to some goats nibbling the shrubs on the slope of the mountain as we passed overhead. "Mia and I used to do an excellent rendition of 'The Lonely Goatherd' from *The Sound of Music*," I told Porter. "Complete with enthusiastic yodeling."

"I wish I could have heard it," he said, putting his hand on my back to steady me as the birdcage neared the station and began to rock. "I know you miss her."

As the cable car slowed at the bottom before turning and

heading back up the mountain, Porter hopped to the ground and held out his hand.

"Where to now?" he asked when I stepped out of the cage.

"Can we get a snack? I need some caffeine and fried food to keep going."

We stopped in a luncheonette and got Cokes and French fries, which we ate standing at a small table. As soon as the holy trinity of grease, salt, and sugary carbonation hit my stomach, I felt better.

"I can't remember the last time I was hungover like this," I told Porter. "What were we thinking?"

Porter popped the last few fries into his mouth and crumpled up our napkins. "We need to keep moving. Should we go see where Saint Francis tamed the wolf?" he asked. When I nodded, he said, "Let's do it," and arced the ball of napkins in the direction of the trash can. "Did you see that? Nothing but net, baby."

"Not bad for a soccer player," I said, and took his hand as we stepped outside.

All around Umbria, there are places where Saint Francis reportedly performed wondrous acts. Assisi, obviously, is the epicenter of Francis legends—it's where Francis was born and tore off his clothes and rejected his worldly possessions and heard the voice of God when he was praying in front of the San Damiano crucifix and amassed his first followers—but the whole countryside of Umbria is littered with miraculous sites. On the way to our favorite winery in Bevagna, for instance, is the spot where Francis preached to the birds, reminding them to be thankful for their lovely feathers and the gift of flight. The sanctuary of LaVerna, where Francis received the stigmata, is close too, only a two-hour drive from Assisi. Gubbio's claim to Francis-related fame is unusual, though, more like a Grimm Brothers fairytale than a story of faith.

Legend says that a large wolf was terrorizing the village, eating anyone who dared step outside the city walls. Francis, who was visiting Gubbio, went out to meet the beast in person. As soon as the wolf spotted Francis it lunged at him, but Francis made the sign of the cross and ordered the wolf to heel, which it did. Then Francis gave the wolf a little sermon and promised that if the wolf would come into town with him, he would broker a deal: The wolf would agree to quit murdering and whatnot, and the townspeople of Gubbio would feed him and try to forgive the fact that he'd eaten the neighbors.

The wolf agreed and followed Francis into town, where he put his paw in Francis's hand and they shook on their deal. After that, the wolf lived inside the city walls, sleeping in a cave and going door to door for food, successfully resisting the urge to murder. After the wolf died, his cave became the site of the Church of Saint Francis of Peace, La Chiesa di San Francesco della Pace, which was completed in the thirteenth century. The church's altar stone is the rock where Francis stood to pray after making the pact with the wolf.

"Apparently in the late 1800s, they were doing some renovations and found the skeleton of a really big wolf inside the church," I told Porter as we headed up the road. "On top of it was a stone with a cross carved in it, like the grave was something sacred and special. And they've found ancient maps that call this area *Trivio Morlupi.*"

"I get the *mor lupi* part—death of the wolf, right?—but what's *trivio?*"

"Crossroads, I think. You know how the Trevi Fountain is named for the three roads—the *tre vie*—that met there? I think *trivio* is the same thing."

"So much for four years of Latin," Porter said, sidestepping a group of pigeons clustered around the remains of a sandwich. "But I thought Francis met the wolf outside the city walls?"

I nodded. "He did, at the Church of the Vittorina, down by the nature preserve. This Francis of Peace church is where the wolf was buried," I said as we climbed the steps and ducked inside.

We took a quick look around the unassuming interior's stuffed wolf in a glass case, stone grave marker that once covered the wolf's remains, and statue of Francis with the wolf. After a few minutes, Porter asked if I was ready to go home.

"I think I've had about as much culture as I can take with a hangover," he said as we left the church and rejoined the sparse pedestrian traffic on the main road. "All I want to do is stretch out on the couch and watch some soccer."

"That sounds good to me."

"Are you going to let me buy you that green bowl on the way out?"

"Nah. I'll get it someday when I have something to celebrate."

"I can't get it for you as a gift?"

I shook my head. "No, but thanks."

Four

When we got home from Gubbio, Porter turned on the Juventus match and stretched out on the couch and I went to my own house, put on pajamas, and climbed into bed with a book. I think I was only four or five pages in when my eyes closed.

I slept for twelve and a half hours, which had to be some kind of personal best. But even with all that sleep, or maybe because of it, I still had to drag myself out of bed and into the shower the next morning. When I finally emerged—clean but still exhausted—I smeared moisturizer on my face, threw on a pair of jeans and a hoodie with only a few stains on it, then checked my email while I was waiting for the coffee to boil. Once I felt relatively alive, thanks to multiple cups of coffee and some toast with jam, I turned on a *Dateline* podcast and got to work.

As I wiped the kitchen cabinets down with white vinegar once more, I was listening with only half an ear as Keith Morrison narrated a gruesome murder. The rest of me was thinking about the email I'd just received from the editor of my first book. She wanted to know if I was making any headway on a second novel. The truth was that I'd made no progress whatsoever, so I needed to think of a way to be truthful about that while also keeping the hope of another book alive so she wouldn't drop me as a client.

My first book came together in a really nontraditional way—basically through no efforts of my own beyond the writing, although the writing itself was excruciating. I had just finished the Assisi tourism project and was renting the house next door to Porter—having lost my daughter, marriage, and life in London nearly two years before—when the pandemic hit and Italy locked down.

Some people made the most of being confined to their homes and learned to paint portraits and knit hats for preemies and make dolls for orphaned baby gorillas in Zimbabwe, but not me and Porter. Our only pandemic accomplishment was courageously drinking our way through his wine cellar and falling asleep on the couch every night to whatever disturbing documentary was on Netflix. It was not our most productive era, although I do think I could run a successful cult now.

The one upside to the pandemic was that when the world hit pause and our horizons were reduced to our own property lines, I suddenly had time to reflect on all that had happened in my fifty-plus years of life. I'd had a startlingly vivid vision one day, right after the stay-at-home orders were issued, of Mia looking down from heaven and saying, *Mom, what the hell?* as she watched me—or rather, a diminished, depressed, hollowed-out version of me—tie up grapes in the Italian countryside with a man she didn't know. That night I started writing her letters, trying to explain how I ended up here. I wanted Mia to understand how much I'd loved her and what my life had been like when I was her age, and how I'd reunited with Porter three decades after I swore I'd never speak to him again. I wanted her to know that her death had devastated me, but that I was trying my best to carry on in a way that would make her proud. In the process of putting all of that down in writing, I tried to find some logic in the twists and turns that had delivered me to a rural Italian village where Tuscany and Umbria meet on the map. Writing to my daughter was my way of taking ownership of the past, sorting through it and saying, *Right, this is how I got here.*

I'd been printing out the letters and putting them in a manila envelope as I wrote, but when I'd written everything I could think of, I compiled all the letters into one gigantic Word document and sent it to my uncle David. It had become very clear to me in the writing process that David's influence had shaped my life more than anyone else's. It was David, after all, who'd stepped in after my dad died when I was nine, and David who'd opened his home to me after my mom was killed when I was seventeen. As much as my letters were for my daughter to understand who her mother was, I also wanted my uncle to understand the critical role he'd played in my life and how grateful I was to him. And I suppose, as my only living family member, I also wanted him to say that my memories weren't entirely off-base.

I emailed the manuscript to him, and when he finished reading it, David wrote me a long reply saying that while he might have slightly different recollections here and there, he had no objection to anything I'd written and thought it was an honest, brave exercise and he was proud of me. And that was that. Or so I thought, until a few weeks later when David emailed again to ask if he could share what I'd written with a friend in publishing. I said no right away, but David pushed back, which was out of character for him.

Stories are how we make sense of our lives, kiddo, and there are thousands of other people who are struggling to put the pieces back together after a tragedy the same way you've struggled. It will help someone else to read your story. I feel strongly about this, Beth, or I'd never have asked. Can you trust me and just let my friend look at it?

I broached the idea with Porter, who was, of course, the other major stakeholder in what I'd written, and he said he'd like some time to think about it.

A few days later, Porter came over. As soon as he opened the door, Oliver pushed in front of him, did a quick drive-by check of his food bowl, and then—finding it empty—let out a sigh and came to sit on my feet.

"Let's do it," Porter said, taking off his sweat-stained Ajax Football Club hat and tossing it onto the table.

"Hi, Ollie," I said, leaning down to kiss the top of his head and inhale his delicious doggy scent. "Do what? Do you want some coffee?"

Porter shook his head. "No, thanks. I'll grab some water, though."

"Have you been up for hours?"

"Yeah, Brutus broke through the fence again." He opened the cabinet and reached for a glass. "I wanted to fix it before it got too hot."

"He's in love, poor dear."

"I don't think Clara wants anything to do with him," Porter said, filling his glass. He turned off the tap and joined me at the kitchen table. "What are you working on?"

"A little research about Saint Catherine. I'm looking for inspiration."

Porter drank his water in one gulp. "You could always write the love story of Brutus and Clara," he said, setting the glass on the table with a thump. "They're a modern-day Romeo and Juliet."

"That's an idea. I could have them exchange lusty looks over a bale of hay and lament that they're from opposite sides of the barn. You think it will sell?"

"There's a market for everything."

"Even sexy sheep shearing scenes?"

"Probably." Porter scooted his chair back from the table and crossed his leg over his knee so he could reach under his sock and scratch his ankle. "I've been thinking about what David said, about publishing your letters as a book."

"Yeah, well, I have mixed emotions."

"I know," Porter said. "You're a private person. I am too. But David's right. It could help other people who are grieving."

"I considered that. But doesn't it seem like I'm . . . I don't know . . . like I'm capitalizing on what happened to Mia? It feels dirty, like I'm trying to benefit from a tragedy."

Porter shook his head. "If that was the standard, no one would ever publish anything. What would there be to write about?"

"I don't know." I shrugged. "Happy stuff, I guess."

"What's the book that Dutch woman wrote, the one you were reading for the millionth time last week?"

"*The Hiding Place.* Corrie ten Boom."

"She was in Auschwitz, right?"

"Ravensbrück."

"Was she capitalizing on being in a concentration camp when she wrote her book? That was a tragedy."

"No, of course not. She was just telling her story. Sharing a message about remaining hopeful in horrible times. But war is a universal experience, Porter."

"And losing a child isn't?"

"God, I hope not." I pulled my feet out from under Oliver, who yawned and tipped onto his side, and stepped over him to get to the refrigerator. "I wouldn't wish it on anyone."

"But that's why you need to put it out in the world and let your story do some good, Beth. Because it does happen. Think how many people in the world are grieving at any given time. It doesn't matter what causes it. Sorrow is universal."

"What if people hate it?" I asked, reaching inside the fridge for a bottle of San Pellegrino.

"Some people will," Porter said, leaning over to inspect a bite on his leg. "Some people just enjoy making other people feel small. You can't live your life based on that."

"I'll think about it, okay?" I said, twisting the cap off the bottle. "But I've had enough conflict and drama to last a lifetime, and this just seems like asking for more."

"I know. I get it. But think about it."

"I will," I said. "I promise. But first I'm going to write *Clara and Brutus: the timeless love story of two Massese sheep*."

It took me several more weeks to decide, but eventually, with more encouragement from David and prompting by Porter, I agreed that David could share the manuscript with his friend. After that, things seemed to move very quickly. There were details to sort out—contracts to sign and typos to fix and fonts to choose and formatting to adjust and a title to select—and then we hired a guy with a drone to take a photo of Porter's house for the cover, and all of a sudden, the book was out.

I figured David would be kind enough to buy a copy and that would be it, but other people bought copies too, and the feedback was surprisingly positive. Complete strangers emailed to say that our story—my daughter's and mine and Porter's—did, in fact, help them. They found inspiration and hope and encouragement in the message that even if life doesn't work out the way you planned, you can still find peace and a way forward.

All the nice messages didn't stop me from aching with missing Mia, though, and I could never predict what would send me plummeting back into the pit of grief. Toto's *Africa* on the radio, a fluffy-tailed rabbit in the yard, the sharp scent of lemons on the trees on Porter's terrace . . . I'd be fine one minute and then not fine at all. Sometimes it wasn't a stabbing pain so much as the swelling ache of memories resurfacing, and when that happened, I'd have to resist the urge to call my ex-husband and ask, "Crawford, do you remember the time we . . .?" to fact-check my own mind. Had we really laughed ourselves to tears over Mia's first knock-knock joke? Was that really me flattened by a ten-foot wave in Cape Solander? Did we actually get looped on ouzo in that little taverna in Athens and spend three hours looking for our hotel? Was Mia's first ballet recital the disaster of toddler tears that I remember? But of course, I couldn't call Crawford. After more than twenty years of marriage and thirty years of friendship, he didn't care to speak to me anymore.

Thankfully, Porter seemed to understand the grief that cropped up unexpectedly; or at least, he tried to. And he wasn't threatened by my churning up the past, although he did tell me that he felt awful when he came to the part in the book about our breakup.

"Have I said how sorry I am about all of that?" he asked, setting the galley copy of the book on the table. "Young and stupid doesn't even begin to describe me at that moment."

"You've apologized."

"Okay," he said, running his hand through his hair. "I just wanted to be sure."

The nice comments from readers were great, but there were Internet trolls too, just as Porter and David had warned there would be.

"Don't be surprised by the things people complain about," David said on FaceTime a week before the book came out. "I could tell you stories from parish life . . ."

"Tell me."

"People will nitpick things you never anticipated. I had a parishioner once threaten to move his membership from my church because I mentioned Gandhi in a sermon."

"Is Gandhi offensive?"

"Anything is offensive if you're looking to be offended," David said. "But the specific complaint was that Gandhi wasn't a Christian, and thus was surely in hell and shouldn't be referenced in the church." He shook his head. "Oh, and every member of the vestry got an anonymous letter about me several years ago."

"What did the letters say?"

"Let's see . . . I think it was a complaint about a Bible study on biblical mistranslations. Somebody got their nose out of joint and decided I was being subversive."

"That's weird for Episcopalians. We're generally okay with questioning everything."

"Apparently not this parishioner. And who writes anonymous letters anymore? It reminded me of that story you wrote in college about the lady who wrote to the police chief every Tuesday to rat out her neighbors."

"Mrs. Hubert! I forgot about her. I wonder where that story is?"

"If you find it, send me a copy."

"I'll look for it. I've got a folder somewhere of college stuff."

David was right, of course. People on the Internet live to find things to be offended about, and it seemed I'd given them plenty of fodder. One troll slithered out of the bog to tell me that Crawford was going to hell for being gay, and another emailed that any father worth his salt would have shot the bike courier who killed Mia. *Womynfirst87* said I should have taken Crawford for every penny he had for lying to me all those years, and *JaydensMama2020* said that Porter and I would never be happy because I had sinned by getting divorced, which Jesus clearly said not to do. It got to the point that I was nauseous every time I opened my laptop.

Mostly I deleted the messages as soon as the writer's agenda became clear, but in a few instances, the emails were so offensive that I had to respond. I told *JaydensMama2020,* for instance, that Jesus lived in a world where men could divorce their wives for any reason at all, leaving the women to fend for themselves as beggars or prostitutes. *Given the context, Jesus isn't issuing an edict against divorce,* I wrote. *He's advocating for men to behave decently and consider the ramifications of their actions. He's taking a position that protects women in a world where they have virtually no agency and have to depend on a father or husband for survival.*

When a man from Alabama wrote, *You don't know shit about Holy Scripture, lady. Read Leviticus 18: A man shall not lie with another man. It's a good thing your kid is dead and doesn't have to see her mother whoring around with foreigners,* my fingers flew across the keyboard. I cited numerous scholarly works of socio-historical criticism arguing that the context of Leviticus 18 is incest, not homosexuality, and that homosexuality was commonplace in the ancient world, and that the words in 18:22 mean a young boy, not a man, and are therefore arguing against an imbalance of power . . . And then I just stopped.

I slammed my laptop shut and went to find Porter in the barn.

"You know, it's one thing to be willfully ignorant of everything we know about genetics and DNA and sexuality, but using religion to justify hatred and bigotry is just flat-out denying Jesus," I said, out of breath from stomping across the field. "It's ignoring every single lesson Jesus taught about loving all mankind, not to mention actual biblical scholarship."

"Hello to you too," Porter said, leaning his rake against the wall and pulling off his leather work gloves.

"Sorry. I just—"

"Are you crying? Come here."

"I'm crying because I'm frustrated, not because I'm sad."

"Frustrated with what, exactly?"

"Shouting into the void. Arguing that sometimes divorce is for the best and homophobia keeps people trapped in lies." I wrapped my arms around Porter's torso and breathed in the smell of laundry detergent and sweat and dirt.

"Ahh. You got more hate mail?"

I nodded. "It's always the same thing with these people, proof texting the Bible to justify oppressing and excluding others."

"What does proof texting mean?"

"Pulling a passage out of context to support your point of view. Like when someone says 'an eye for an eye' to justify revenge. In context, that's an argument for appropriate restitution, not vengeance." I let go of Porter and wiped my eyes. "I'm sorry. I don't know why I'm crying."

"Remember when I taught you to flip an omelet?" Porter asked, unsticking a strand of hair from my face and tucking it behind my ear.

I nodded, digging in the pocket of my jeans for a tissue. "I wasted about two dozen eggs."

"And you cried. I know you're frustrated, Beth, but you can't let people get to you like this," he said, pulling his work gloves back on. "Some people just aren't willing to accept new information."

"I know. But imagine how much arrogance is involved in declaring that millions of your fellow human beings are mistakes because of who they love? I mean, the hubris of assuming that you know what's divinely ordained and what's not is just staggering."

"I'm with you one hundred percent on this, you know that," Porter said, grabbing the rake. "But I hate seeing you so upset. These people aren't worth it."

"It makes me want to curl in a ball and stop engaging with the world. People are awful," I said. I lifted the hem of my T-shirt to wipe my face. "Do you want some help?"

"Nah. It's dirty work," he said, raking wet hay into a pile.

"And I'd be a fool to do it for you?" I asked, forcing a smile. "Name that tune."

"What's the wager?"

"I'll fix dinner for the song title and the band."

"The name's right there, *Dirty Work*. The band is Steely Dan. But I'll tell you the album and the movie it was in if you'll make some more of those almond cookies."

"Okay, go."

"*Can't Buy a Thrill* is the album. *The Kid Stays in the Picture* is the movie."

"I'm impressed."

"You gotta try harder than that to stump me," he said, leaning forward and planting a sweaty kiss on my cheek. "How about omelets for dinner?"

I laughed and pushed him away. "Fine, but we're using your kitchen and you have to clean the eggs off the floor."

"Deal."

I turned to leave, sidestepping the steaming piles of hay.

"Beth," Porter said as I reached the door.

I stopped and turned to look at him. "Yeah?"

"Not everyone is awful, you know."

I laughed. "Keep telling yourself that," I said.

Then I left, closing the barn door behind me.

Five

Alberto and Patrizio, the two old men who'd lived in my house for decades before I bought it, had apparently never cleaned the kitchen cabinets. As I pondered what I might tell my editor about my nonexistent second book, I wiped the shelves down with vinegar for the third time. I was rinsing out the rag and preparing to wipe them down for a fourth time when my phone chimed.

I grabbed my phone off the counter. It was Porter texting from the field, wanting to know if I was planning on having lunch.

Subtle, I texted back. *I take it you're hungry?*

Brutus is starting to look tasty.

Meet me on the terrace in 30. I'll do something with your meat.

I love it when you talk dirty.

I smiled and returned the phone to the counter, then went to the refrigerator to retrieve the remains of a steak and the ingredients for a salad. I threw together arugula and tomatoes while the steak reheated in a pan, then shaved thin slices of *parmigiano reggiano* off the giant brick I'd brought back from Parma and laid them on top of the arugula. When the steak was warm, I sliced it on top of Porter's salad, then loaded both of our bowls—along with bread, oil, vinegar, and a bottle of San Pellegrino—into one of the wooden wagons we used to cart stuff between our houses.

Oliver intercepted me midway across the field. After inspecting the contents of the wagon with his nose, he trotted next to me, his tail a golden flag in the breeze.

"Wouldn't this be much easier if we lived in the same house?" Porter asked, looking up from setting the table as I neared the terrace.

"The wagon works pretty well."

"What'd you make?"

"Salad. But don't worry, yours has steak."

"Is that the balsamic from Modena?" he asked as I offloaded the wagon's contents onto the table.

I nodded. "I need to write about that trip, don't let me forget. And the oil's what we bought in Bevagna. It's the last of it, though. We need to get some more."

"Will you do up my salad? It tastes better when you do it."

I nodded. "Crap. I forgot the salt and pepper."

"I'll get it."

When Porter returned from his kitchen with salt and pepper, he had a bottle of wine tucked under his arm and two wine glasses dangling from his fingers.

"I'm going to pitch a story about the church of Santa Maria sopra Minerva next," I told him. "Apparently not today, though, if we're drinking at lunchtime."

"I'm ready to call it a day," Porter said. "My shoulder is acting up and there's a match on at two that I want to see." He set the bottle of wine on the table. "May I interest you in a glass of rosagrà from your favorite winery?"

"Where have you been hiding that? I thought we finished it all."

"I like to pull a rabbit out of the hat every once in a while," he said, extracting the cork with a pop. "Give ya' the old razzle-dazzle. Keep the magic alive."

"Oh, I'm all in," I said, thrusting my glass towards him. "I can work tomorrow."

"That's the spirit."

I took a sip of the intensely pink wine as soon as it was poured and sat back in my chair. "If I'd known you had this, I would have fixed something better for lunch."

"No, this is good. I needed something green. Tell me about the church article."

I didn't really know much yet about the pagan temples that were converted to churches in Italy, I told Porter, but I did know that there were eleven just in Rome, plus the church of Santa Maria sopra Minerva in Assisi.

"They're living palimpsests," I said.

"I'm sure I'd agree if I knew what that word meant."

"Palimpsest? It's a manuscript that has a new text over an erased one. Back when parchment was hard to come by, scribes would reuse them, and you'd get manuscripts that had multiple layers of writing," I said. "But it can apply to pretty much anything where you can see the remnants of what used to be under what currently is."

"Like how you can see the formerly dashing and athletic me in the current rickety and gray version?"

"You look exactly the same to me, Porter. When I look at you, I see the same guy I met in college."

"You need new glasses. How about the side of the house where you can see the outline of the old door in the stones. Is that a palimajig?"

"Palimpsest. Sure, why not."

"Palimpsest would be a decent band name," Porter said, forking salad into his mouth. He leaned back in his chair and closed his eyes against the sun as he chewed. "We really missed the boat, you know. We should have started a band for our pandemic project."

"All we have is names, though. We don't have any musical talent."

"You can sing. And besides, no one's needed musical talent since MTV. Just Auto-Tune and a nice face."

"We should have started a fake band. Done a whole social media campaign, sent out press releases, hired an influencer. We probably could have moved a ton of merchandise before anyone found out the band didn't exist."

"There you go. Now you're using your creative powers for good."

I popped a tomato into my mouth and turned my face to the sun too, closing my eyes against the glare. "Or I can keep writing articles about musicians and churches that no one reads."

"You said that about your book too, and look what happened with that?"

"You're such a cheerleader."

"You're just saying that because of my giant megaphone."

I laughed.

"Seriously, Bethy, you've got to believe in yourself," Porter said, then leaned forward to finish his salad. When he'd stabbed the last tomato with his fork and popped it into his mouth, he sat back again with his eyes closed, enjoying his wine. When his glass was empty, he yawned and pushed his chair away from the table.

"Thank you for lunch," he said, standing up. "I've got to move before I fall asleep. Want me to take the dishes back?"

I shook my head. "Nah, I'll do it."

"I'm just going to check on the fence real quick before I close up shop. Come with me?"

I made a visor with my hand and squinted up at him. "I'm going to go home and see if the cabinets are finally dry enough to paint."

Porter held out his hand to help me up. "I'll come over later to help you finish that bottle of wine," he said. "Come on, Ollie."

Oliver opened one eye, emitted a yawn that sent his tongue rolling out of his mouth and ended with a squeak, then lumbered to his feet.

Porter's phone rang as they were walking away. I was packing up the remains of lunch and thinking about other things so it didn't even register when I heard him say, "I'm sorry, I'm not following. Who are you?"

When I'd finished unloading the wagon and had put the dishes from lunch in the sink, I wiped down the inside of the cabinets one more time and left the doors open so the shelves could dry. I decided to revisit an article I'd been working on before the pandemic hit while I waited. I'd come across the article while I was searching my laptop for reusable Assisi material, and thought it was probably worth the effort to revitalize.

The article was a profile of a man named Paolo Franceschini. The magazine it was originally intended for had stopped printing during the pandemic, but I'd seen that they'd moved a lot of content online recently, so I figured the time might be right to contact the editor.

I pulled the text up on my screen and scanned it, made a few minor tweaks, then leaned back in my chair, thinking about the day Porter and I first met Paolo Franceschini.

We were walking through the main piazza in Assisi one afternoon, meandering aimlessly towards the Basilica of Saint Francis, when we saw a group of musicians warming up in front of the church of Santa Maria sopra Minerva. Next to them was a small sign announcing a free concert, so we grabbed two chairs and sat down. While we were waiting for the program to begin, I wandered into the leather store to check out the purses, then popped into the bar next door to buy a couple bottles of water. When I returned to my seat, Porter was deep in conversation with a man who looked to be in his mid-sixties, with a gray beard and mustache and not much hair on his head. They were both laughing, and after Porter introduced me, the man said he needed to start the concert and hurried away.

"He's the conductor?" I asked once he was gone. "How did you end up talking to him?"

"He was muttering about the violins dragging—which they were—and when I turned around to see who was talking, he came over. Turns out he's a violinist himself. He's toured all over the world and runs a music school in Perugia." Porter lowered his voice to a whisper as the music started. "The guy's a riot. You'd love him."

At the end of the concert, after thanking his students for their work and the audience for listening, the conductor announced that the following weekend, he and members of his professional orchestra would perform Vivaldi's *The Four Seasons* at sunrise in front of the Basilica of Saint Francis.

Porter looked at me. "Oh, we're not missing that."

The following Saturday, we got up at four a.m. Oliver stood at the kitchen door of Porter's house, confused by the early morning hubbub, then stretched, yawned, and went back in the house as we piled into the car.

As Porter navigated the potholed country roads towards Assisi, I poured coffee from a dented metal Thermos onto my seat, my shirt, my linen pants, and finally, into a travel mug.

"I feel like there was supposed to be more?" Porter said, peering into the mug when I handed it to him at a red light.

The road smoothed out when we reached the autostrada, and Porter gunned the Fiat and zoomed down the highway. As soon as we exited towards Assisi, though, he had to slow down because of debris in the road from an overnight storm. He steered his way around branches and limbs, and by the time we finally parked in the public lot at Piazza Matteotti, we had to race across the historic center of town to get to the basilica in time. Luckily, there were two empty chairs in the last row. We collapsed into them just as the orchestra completed their warmup.

"I could really use a coffee and a bathroom," I whispered.

"Why didn't we park at the bottom of the basilica?" Porter asked. "It would have been so much closer."

"Because we're creatures of habit. Do you think there's any place to use the bathroom and get coffee? Maybe there will be an intermission."

Porter swiveled to look behind us. "The bar isn't even open yet," he said. "You may be out of luck on both ends."

"I'll just suck the coffee out of my shirt and hold it."

"Good plan." Porter reached into the side pocket of his linen blazer and extracted a CD and a black Sharpie. "I'm going to ask him to sign this after the concert."

"Who?"

"Paolo Franceschini. The conductor. Look," he said, handing me the CD. "This is my favorite recording of *The Four Seasons*. I've listened to it at least a thousand times, and it turns out he's the first violin!"

"You're such a nerd," I said, draping my arm across the back of his chair.

The predawn darkness lasted through the first and second movements of the music, but as the third movement began, the sun began to rise behind us, bathing the facade of the basilica in golden-pink light. The orchestra seemed to glow, and as the music swelled, I was totally overcome by the beauty of it all. Porter watched me dig a tissue out of my bag and dry my eyes and cheeks, then he reached over and took my hand, squeezing it as he leaned towards me.

"Who's the nerd now?" he whispered, making me laugh out loud.

When the concert ended, Paolo Franceschini thanked everyone for coming, and then the crowd began to disperse. A knot of people remained clustered around the conductor, though, and I shifted from foot to foot impatiently as Porter inched his way closer. When the elderly woman with a swipe of hot pink lipstick who had been clutching Franceschini's arm for ages finally let go and turned away, Porter swooped in.

I watched them talk, fearing for my bladder, until Porter finally shook the conductor's hand and started back towards me, grinning like a little kid.

"Look at this!"

Franceschini had signed Porter's CD "*Al mio unico tifoso vivente.*"

"You're his only living fan, huh?" I teased. "Are you going to start a fan club?"

"Yes, but obviously I will be the only member since everyone else is dead. Play nice and I'll let you send out the newsletter."

"Help me find a bathroom and I'll do it gladly."

We listened to the CD Franceschini had signed all the way home. That night, I put together a pitch for a travel magazine with Franceschini and his music school in Perugia as the centerpiece, and a few weeks later, the magazine accepted the piece on spec for a special arts issue. I tracked Signore Franceschini's email down and organized an interview.

On the day of our meeting, I bounced along the backroads to Perugia, then accidentally went the wrong way down a one-way street looking for the parking garage closest to the music school. I was ten minutes late when I finally arrived at Franceschini's office, but he just shrugged off my apologies and told me he'd just arrived himself. Our scheduled hour flew by, and then another, and I might have stayed all day had Signore Franceschini not needed to lead a rehearsal.

"I'm afraid the article is going to come off as fawning," I told Porter when I got home. "When he took out his violin and played for me in his office . . . I gotta be honest, I think I swooned. I'm a little in love with him, Porter."

"Seduction by strings," Porter said. "Add that to our list of band names in case we ever start an orchestra."

"I'm serious. He was so charming I could barely keep it together."

Porter's brow furrowed. "Should I be worried? Want me to fly into a jealous rage?"

"Would you? At least smash a glass or something. Although you were the one fanboying over him, so maybe I should be worried. This has happened to me before, you know."

Porter laughed. "Don't worry. I think he's great, but I'm not Crawford. I'm not interested in dating him."

I had nearly finished with the article when the pandemic hit and life as we knew it came to a screeching halt. I'd moved the draft to a Pending Projects folder on my laptop and pretty much forgotten about it, but reading over it now, I thought I'd managed to capture Franceschini's wit, charm, and talent, as well as his contagious love of music. I typed an email to the editor asking about the status of the arts issue, attached the draft, hit send, and went back to my kitchen cabinets.

I was standing in the middle of the kitchen about twenty minutes later, wondering if I had the energy to start painting the cabinets or should just leave it for tomorrow, when Porter poked his head in the kitchen door.

"Knock, knock," he said as Oliver pushed past him and galloped straight into my knees.

"Hey, champ," I said. "All good with the fence?"

"Yeah. I had to check Clara's leg too. I don't know what she cut it on."

"How's it look?"

"Okay, I guess. Brutus is driving her crazy, nipping at her. I put him in the barn to give her a break."

"Are you thirsty?"

Porter leaned against the wall to take off his boots. "Yeah," he said.

I opened the refrigerator and scanned the contents. "Water, beer, *succo di ananas*. We have the rest of the wine from lunch, but I forgot to put it in the refrigerator when I got back, so it's not cold."

"Beer, please. Where'd you get pineapple juice?"

I grabbed two bottles of Ichnusa beer, shook my head, and pushed the refrigerator door closed with my knee. "No idea. It's probably really old."

"I need to talk to you about something," Porter said, dropping into a chair and taking the beer I handed him.

"Sure."

"I got a phone call that's kind of weird." He removed his sweat-stained hat and ran his hand through his hair. His wavy light brown locks stood straight up, then fell into the kind of perfect swoop you see on male models. "Actually, you know what? Let's relax a minute first."

He popped the cap off his bottle and pushed it across the table towards me, then took the beer I was holding and opened it for himself. Oliver stood near the stove until I sat down, then he stretched himself out under the kitchen table, resting his chin on top of his neatly stacked paws.

"I really feel like we're sliding back into pandemic drinking habits," I said, taking a sip of beer. "It sucks the energy out of me to drink during the day. I don't get anything done."

"Yeah, I know. We gotta stop."

"I do love this beer, though," I said. "So, do you think he's going to run away with Clara?"

"Huh?" Porter asked.

"Brutus. Do you think he keeps breaking the fence so he can run away with Clara?"

"Oh. I don't know."

After a few minutes of silence, I said, "You mentioned you got a phone call?"

Porter upended his beer, drank all that remained in the bottle, and set the bottle on the table. "From a girl in the States."

"And?"

Porter exhaled loudly and scratched his forehead. "Stay calm when I tell you this, okay?"

I set my beer bottle down and reached for a napkin. "What's going on?"

"The girl who called . . . Well, she's not a girl, actually. She's a young woman, I guess. I don't know anything about her, except that she, uh, she said she's my daughter."

My gut clenched. "What?"

Porter dropped his head backwards and rolled it from side to side before meeting my eyes.

"She said she's my daughter." He cleared his throat. "She, uh, apparently did one of those ancestry tests and found out she has a first cousin. Lauren."

"Lauren, as in your niece?"

Porter nodded. "She tracked her down on Facebook or LinkedIn or something, and Lauren gave her my contact info."

"When was this? How old is she? What's her name?"

"She's about to turn twenty-eight. Her name's Sloan Miller."

"And you knew nothing about her?"

"Nothing," Porter said, shaking his head. "I promise."

I pushed myself away from the table, scraping the chair on the terracotta floor, and went to the sink.

"Can you just start at the beginning?" I said, smashing the stopper into the drain and turning the hot water on full force. "Tell me everything she said."

Porter exhaled loudly. "This girl, Sloan, took a DNA test and got an email that said she's Lauren's first cousin. I guess that means Lauren did the test, too. Then she tracked Lauren down and got my phone number."

"I meant the part where you somehow magically have a daughter," I said, dropping the plates from lunch into the sink.

"Remember when we broke up after college?"

I turned around and folded my arms over my chest. "Like it was yesterday."

"Right. And I told you all about what a shit show my life was then, all that—"

"Yes, yes," I said, making impatient circles with my hand. "Your dad was running a financial scam, your mom showed up looking for money, you got a DUI, Ford flew in, I drove down, we broke up. What does any of that have to do with your having a kid?"

"Ford bailed me out of jail, but my Jeep was impounded and—"

"I know all of that. Get to the girl, Porter."

"I will, if you'll let me get two words out."

I turned back to the sink.

"Remember that sketchy mall in Durham where we went to get that pill?" Porter said.

I nodded without turning around. We'd been seniors in college, and after a few too many drinks at a party, we'd decided—for reasons I couldn't fathom now—to sleep in the treehouse in Porter's backyard. It was too far to trek across the yard for a condom, so Porter promised he'd pull out, a plan that worked out about as well as you'd expect for a couple of inebriated twenty-somethings. The next morning, hungover and panicked, we'd driven across town to a seedy looking clinic that had the morning-after pill.

"There was another clinic over there too," Porter said. "A sperm clinic."

My hand tightened around the silverware I was holding. "A sperm bank? Where you donate sperm?"

Porter cleared his throat. "Yeah."

"What are you saying? You used to donate sperm?"

"They paid varsity athletes a hundred dollars a pop. More if you donated twice a week."

"You're joking." I dropped the silverware into the sink and turned to look at him. Hot, soapy water dripped down my arms and puddled on the floor.

"It was easy money, and a lot of us didn't have time to have a job during the season, with classes and practice and all. I did the testing and the paperwork and stuff before senior year, but then I, um, didn't do it. Not then, I mean."

"Why not?"

Porter looked sheepish. "I was dating that girl—"

"Stephanie."

"Right. Stephanie," he said, nodding. "And you can't have sex for a couple days before you donate. So I just, I didn't want to, you know, donate just then."

"Sure, right. And then?"

"And then I met you and broke up with her."

"And you went back to the clinic to donate because I wouldn't sleep with you right away?"

Porter shook his head.

I turned back to the sink. "Well, you could have," I said. "I made you wait a ridiculously long time, right? *Blue Balls Beth*, isn't that what your friends called me?"

"I didn't go back then because I didn't want to, once I met you."

"How gallant. Who says chivalry is dead?"

"It was supposed to be anonymous, you know. We were helping families who couldn't conceive, all that shit."

"And earning money."

"That too."

"But if she's only twenty-eight, the math doesn't add up, Porter. Wouldn't that mean we'd already graduated when you did this?" I said, scrubbing furiously at the residue in the bottom of a wine glass.

"I don't know how long they keep the donation," Porter said. "But yeah. I, uh, I did it after you went to grad school."

The only sound for a few minutes was me banging dishes around.

"And you're saying you did it because they paid you?" I asked finally.

"I needed money."

"But we'd graduated. You had a job."

"Yeah."

"But you needed money?"

"Well, you were in Washington, so I figured why not? I needed cash and we weren't having sex and—"

"For what?" I interrupted.

"Huh?"

"For what did you need cash? I mean, I know it wasn't to come see me. It wasn't for the long-distance calls you weren't making. It wasn't for the rent your trust fund paid. So I'm just curious what you needed cash for?"

I was making a mess, flinging soapy water all over the countertop like Big Bird on meth.

"Beth, come on." Porter got up and put his hands on my shoulders. "We're talking about ancient history."

I stiffened and let the wine glass I was holding slide under water. "I know."

"I needed some money, that's all. Who even knows what for? Weed, probably."

"And now you have a kid."

He let go of my shoulders. "Will you stop with the dishes, please?"

I grabbed a towel off the counter and turned around to face Porter, drying my hands.

"The point is, we need to figure out how to deal with this," he said, "in case she really is my kid."

"*We* don't have to figure out shit, Porter. *You* have to figure it out."

"Beth, come on."

"This is just perfect. I lost a daughter, and you magically gained one. Bravo. Mazel Tov. Well done, you."

Porter studied my face before dropping his shoulders and sighing. "C'mon, Ollie," he said, starting toward the door. Oliver lumbered to his feet under the table and followed Porter.

"Yeah, great, take the dog too," I yelled at his back. "Take everything. Who cares?"

As the kitchen door closed behind him, I grabbed Porter's empty beer bottle off the table and smashed it against the tile floor before sinking into a chair and burying my face in my hands.

Here's the thing.

Grief is a very unreliable narrator.

Sometimes it looks a whole lot like rage.

Six

For the next two days, I didn't cross the field to Porter's house. When he texted, under the pretense of asking if I had his mandolin slicer, I told him I was busy working on the Santa Maria church article. We both knew I was avoiding him.

I didn't fully understand my anger, to be honest. I believed Porter when he said that he'd had no idea Sloan existed, so it wasn't that I thought he had been hiding a secret daughter all along. And it wasn't jealousy, either—the only relationship he'd had was with a plastic specimen cup, so there was nothing to be jealous of. I didn't even blame him for having donated in the first place; it was his decision and his body, and no one could have predicted a time when genetic testing and the Internet made anonymity a joke. The fact that this girl had tracked him down through a DNA test pissed me off, but that wasn't Porter's fault. I knew he had donated with the understanding that he'd never be anything more than a number, and he wasn't to blame for the fact that there was now some living, breathing adult child busting into our lives like a pitcher of poisonous Kool Aid.

I did think Porter was being weirdly evasive about what he'd needed money for, but even that wasn't the real reason I was so upset. After tossing and turning about it for two nights, I realized there were two things about this scenario that enraged me. The first was how incredibly unfair it was that Porter now had a daughter and I didn't, and the second was that, once again, my life was being completely upended by someone else's choices.

Thinking about it made me feel sick, but I couldn't think of anything else. What sense did it make that my daughter—whom I'd wanted every single day of her life—had been taken from me, while Porter got saddled with a daughter he didn't even want? That's so far beyond ironic it's just downright cruel. And all I wanted—after losing Mia and discovering Crawford's decades of deception and moving from London to North Carolina to Italy and surviving the pandemic and spending the last four years getting back on my feet—was for things to be calm. Settled. Normal. Happy. Devoid of drama and bullshit. The timing of this revelation felt particularly cruel, coming just when the trauma was finally fading and Porter and I could enjoy our lives.

This girl obviously wanted a relationship with Porter; why else would she have called? And if she was going to be in his life, that meant I'd have to make peace with the idea of his having a daughter when I no longer did—not to mention making peace with the girl herself—if I was going to stay with him. Right now, that all seemed about as likely as traveling to the moon.

But I didn't say any of that to Porter. I couldn't. His face when I'd said he needed to figure it out without me looked like I'd slapped him.

So I holed up in my house and kept busy. I listened to *Dateline* podcasts and cleaned under the beds, over the door frames, along the baseboards and window ledges, and inside every closet. I scrubbed the corners of the bathroom floor with an old toothbrush, sanitized the inside of the refrigerator, and then, when I ran out of things to clean, I did what I always did when I couldn't sort out my feelings: I wrote to my uncle.

David,

Ciao from my little corner of the world.

How are things with you? I want to catch up with a video call, but I've also got something I really need your help with.

Are you ready for this? Porter got a phone call a few days ago from a girl—a twenty-eight-year-old woman, actually—who says that Porter is HER FATHER.

I wish I was joking, David. But thirty years ago, Porter—out of the goodness of his heart and the bounty of his testicles and a mysterious and pressing need for cash—was a sperm donor at some seedy strip mall in Durham. And now, through the glory of genetic testing, this grown-up child got linked to Porter's niece, Lauren, and Lauren put her in touch with Porter—without thinking to ask or warn him first.

I know this is not about me. It's about Porter and this woman, who deserves to know her father—I mean, she didn't ask to be born, and she has a right to know where she came from, etc. I want to be supportive of Porter and, if he finds out this actually is his daughter, help facilitate whatever relationship they're going to have—or at least not stand in the way of it. Goodness knows Porter has stuck with me through hard times.

But inside, I want to SCREAM. Throw plates, rend my clothes, smear ashes on my face, and punish someone for the utter unfairness of it all—the absolute injustice of losing Mia and this kid now parachuting in out of nowhere to turn the peaceful life we've managed to create completely upside down.

Does this make me a horrible person?

Don't answer. I already know.

Your small-hearted niece,
Beth

I hit send and closed my laptop.

I thought about whistling loudly enough to summon Oliver from wherever he was so I could take him for a long walk, but instead I decided to finally tackle the cabinets. I rummaged in the tiny closet where I kept tools and cleaning supplies and unearthed a small can of paint. I brought it, a stepladder, a stir-stick, and a paintbrush back to the kitchen and turned on *Radiolab*.

Hours later, I was still painting when Porter stuck his head inside my open kitchen door. He was holding four sunflowers and a bottle of wine.

"That looks really nice," he said. "How'd you think to put those colors together?"

"I wrote an article about color theory a hundred years ago. If you mix Kelly green and French blue, you get lavender, which is why the colors work together."

"Well, it's nice. Can I scoot by and get a vase?"

Porter rummaged under the sink, found a vase, filled it with water, and stuck the sunflowers in it.

"They're a peace offering," he said, putting the vase on top of the stack of plates in the middle of the kitchen table. He held up the bottle of wine. "And look what I found. A bottle of Montefalco Sagrantino from Cantina Dionigi. The last one in the cellar."

"Thanks."

"I made some soup for dinner."

"I'm not really hungry."

Porter was quiet for a minute, watching me paint. "Do you mind if I stick around for a bit?"

I shrugged. "Suit yourself."

"Anything I can do to help?"

"Just talk. Not about her, though, please."

I turned the podcast off and went back to painting while Porter leaned against the refrigerator, crossed his arms over his chest, and told me about a trip he and Ford had taken in the late '80s. Porter was a senior in high school and Ford was at the University of Virginia and their spring breaks overlapped, so they rented a bright yellow 1964 Impala convertible from a guy named One-Armed Jack and headed to Florida.

"Jack had two arms, so I'm not sure how he got that nickname, but we got this car for about twenty bucks a day. We called it the She-Cougar," he told me. "The She-Cougar didn't cruise down the road so much as chew up the asphalt and spit it out the exhaust pipe. We rode all the way to St. George on the back roads listening to the Allman Brothers eight-track that was stuck in the tape player," he said. "Stayed on the island a week, fishing and eating oysters right out of the water. Ford had to force me to get in the car and go back to Forten."

"You would have missed out on being Hottest Senior, Best Athlete, Most Likely to Succeed, and Second Coming of the Messiah if you hadn't gone back," I said, concentrating on the straight edge I was painting along the inside of the cabinet door.

"I never should have let you see my yearbook."

I didn't answer.

"The soccer season was over and I'd already committed to Carolina. I just wanted to be done with Forten."

"I get it," I said, dipping my brush in the paint can. "I would have gladly skipped the end of my senior year."

"I can imagine, with your mom's accident."

"Even before that. I wanted to get out of Syracuse more than anything." I dabbed paint into the back corner of the cabinet. "Jenny never understood why. She was happy there."

"Yeah?"

"Content, anyway."

"Are they different, happy and content?"

"I think happy is being pleased with how things are, and content is just not wanting more."

"Which one are you?"

"At the moment? Neither." I shook my head. "Of course, Jenny wants to get out of Syracuse now too. Scott announced he doesn't love her anymore and went off to find himself, so she'd rather not stick around."

Porter pushed himself off the refrigerator door and walked over to the kitchen table. "Jesus. How's he finding himself?" he asked, pulling two wine glasses out of the jumble.

"With a dental hygienist and a Ferrari. And skinny jeans." I finished the cabinet I was working on and propped the brush on top of the paint can while I scooted the stepladder across the floor.

"The keys to male enlightenment," Porter said, looking for a wine opener. "Tried it myself. Well, not the skinny jeans. That would have been my rock bottom."

While Porter uncorked the bottle of wine, I thought about what I wanted to say about Sloan.

"I'm sorry about the way I reacted about your daughter," I said as he cleared a space for his wine glass and sat down at the kitchen table. "It wasn't supportive. Or helpful."

"We don't know she's my daughter yet."

"We should probably assume she is. How else could she be genetically related to Lauren? Besides," I said, "it doesn't feel right to hope that she's not. None of this is her fault."

Porter made a face. "But do you? Hope that she's not?"

I sighed. "Of course I do. I don't know her. I don't know what her agenda is. I mean, the deal was that it was supposed to be an anonymous donation, right? It pisses me off that she can just track you down and barge into our lives. But then again, she has a right to know where she came from, so I see that side of it too." I used the back of my hand to brush a strand of hair out of my face.

"I just want things to be calm, Porter. I feel like you and I are still finding our way forward and I don't want anything to ruin that."

"Nothing's going to change between us, Beth. I promise. You're my priority and you always will be."

"You're only saying that because you don't have kids," I said, using the edge of my T-shirt to wipe a smudge of paint off the glass front of the cabinet. "You don't know what it's like. If Mia was alive, she would always be my priority."

He was quiet for a second. "You wouldn't be here if Mia was alive?"

"That's not what I said. I might still be here, if you and I had reconnected some other way, but she would always . . ." I shook my head. "Look, I'm just saying that if you and Mia didn't get along or something, that would be a problem for me. Maybe it's different for men, but for—"

"Why wouldn't we get along?"

"I'm sure you would, Porter. All I'm saying is that I don't think it's possible to be a parent and not prioritize your kid. I never did anything without first considering how it would impact Mia. Maybe fathers can do that, but mothers can't."

"Micheline managed it."

"You're right," I said, nodding. "I'm sorry. You had a horrible mother. But Micheline wasn't normal, and I don't think you're anything like her. And if Sloan is your daughter, it will change things. It will change *you*. And that means it will change *us*. I don't know how exactly, but it will."

Porter started to say something but then seemed to think better of it. I turned back to the cabinets and dunked the brush in the can of paint. I could feel him watching me.

"All right, so it's going to change us somehow," he said finally. "Are you willing to find out how? That's the real question, isn't it?"

I turned to look at him, the paintbrush suspended in mid-air.

I started to reply—to tell him that the only thing I wanted in the entire world was for my life to be so boring that all I did was take long walks and write articles and bake bread and enjoy the miracle of my relationship with Porter after thirty years of no contact—but instead I said, "Look, I know this is huge for you. I know you weren't expecting to suddenly have a kid, and I know you must be freaking out. I want to support you, Porter, I really do."

"But . . .?"

I shook my head. "No but. Let's have a drink. I can finish painting when I come back."

"Come back from where?"

I set the paintbrush on top of the can and stepped off the ladder. "I'm going to Assisi tomorrow."

"What for?"

I wanted to say, *Because I desperately need to get away from you so I can think.*

"I need to finish the article and take some photos of the church. Let's just put a pin in this until I get back."

Seven

When Porter finally left, my mind was racing. I needed a distraction, so I cleaned up the paint supplies and went back to my desk to work on the article I'd started about pagan church conversions.

The church I wanted to photograph—Santa Maria sopra Minerva—is in the Piazza del Comune, Assisi's main square. The building dates back to the first century BCE and is fronted by six tall Corinthian columns, which the Romans appropriated from the Greeks and used extensively in the centuries before Christ. To get inside the church, you climb steep marble stairs that have been worn down by thousands of footsteps and are wedged between the columns, forming a passage too narrow for two people to pass.

The name of the church means Saint Mary over Minerva, but there's not much evidence to support the idea that it was originally named for Minerva, the goddess of wisdom and war. Instead, all the evidence points to it having been originally dedicated to Hercules, the archetype of masculine strength and bravery. Somehow Santa Maria sopra Hercules just doesn't have the same ring to it.

I worked on the article for a couple hours, then went to bed, where I tossed and turned all night. Around five I gave up on sleeping and dragged myself into the shower, and after a cup of coffee, hit the road for Assisi.

When I exited the highway just past Perugia onto a rural road, I stopped for another cup of coffee and a *cornetto con crema*, the cream-filled croissant sold at virtually every roadside bar and gas station in Italy. When I got back on the road, I got stuck behind an enormous piece of farm equipment whose wheels took up all of my lane and half of the other one. Normally I would gun the Panda and pass, but it was too foggy to see much beyond the back end of the combine, so I had to be content to just follow its taillights and putter along, thinking about how I might shape my article. I was convinced there was something to be learned from all the transformations the church had undergone in its lifetime, but I wasn't quite sure yet what that was.

Whether Santa Maria sopra Minerva was originally dedicated to Minerva or Hercules, what's certain is that the building was a pagan temple before becoming a Christian church. When the Christian church was no longer useful, the building was turned into private houses and public shops, then a municipal building, then a prison, and finally, in the 1500s, it became a Christian church again. That's when the inside was demolished and replaced with the Baroque interior you see today.

It feels rude to say this about a church, but I'm not a fan of the interior. It's so at odds with the austere facade that it's a bit jarring when you first walk in, and compared to other churches around Europe—especially St. John's Cathedral in Malta, which out-Baroques all other Baroque churches—the interior of Santa

Maria sopra Minerva looks like leftovers from a rummage sale, a hodgepodge of secondhand gold leaf and gently used statues. But the fact that the physical space served so many different purposes in its lifetime was fascinating to me, and I was determined to craft an article around its evolution.

Maybe the takeaway is that places are what you make them, I thought, creeping into the left lane to see if I could pass. *After all, it's humans who decide what meaning a place will have. Before we arrived, the whole world—from Jonestown to Waco to the killing fields of Pol Pot—was Edenic.*

I scooted back behind the tractor to avoid an oncoming car and forced myself to be patient.

David would remind me that the reverse is true too—sometimes humans make plain places holy. When Mary and Joseph went to Bethlehem for the census, for instance, the Bible tells us they found no room in the inn—which wasn't an inn at all, but rather a room in a relative's house, a *kataluma*. Given the emphasis on hospitality in their culture, Mary and Joseph would have expected to be welcomed and given a place to sleep, but because of the census requiring everyone to return to their hometown, they were probably beaten to Bethlehem by a bunch of Joseph's relatives who snagged the guest room. Mary and Joseph had to sleep in the only space available—a room on the lower level that housed the animals. But because of what happened there, that unassuming space became sacred.

I smiled to myself, thinking how much less gripping the story would be if Jesus had been born in an actual inn. The first witness to the birth of the Savior could have been somebody from housekeeping wanting to refill the minibar.

I decided that would be the through-line of my article: far from being static and unchanging, a physical place could go through endless iterations. Just like every other facet of life, a place is what you make of it, and the varied life of the church of Santa Maria was a great example.

As I puttered behind the combine in the fog, I thought about the first time I visited Assisi.

Mia had only been gone a few months, and I'd come to visit Porter from London. He'd taken me all over Tuscany and Umbria, trying to jar me out of the profound funk I was in. Even though I was a zombie, Italy still got under my skin, and Assisi really hooked me. After only one afternoon there, all the places I'd previously claimed as my true loves—Vienna and Prague and Amsterdam—slid down a notch in the rankings.

When I finally left Porter's house after my four-month stay and went back to London to face the demise of my marriage head on, I figured I'd never see Assisi, or Porter, again.

London was a disaster. My first day back, I was cleaning the top shelf of the closet in our bedroom when I found photos of Crawford and his boyfriend. I confronted Crawford and we fought, I cried, we fought some more, and I quickly realized that I needed to get out of London and unravel my married life from a safe remove. So I flew to David's house in North Carolina. Communication with Porter dwindled to nonexistent while I was there, but when the Assisi tourism project fell into my lap, I couldn't turn down the chance to return to Italy and the town that I'd fallen in love with.

That's when Marco entered my life like some kind of philosophy-spouting, espresso-drinking, cigarette-smoking Tasmanian Devil. He was a good tour guide with a contagious love of history, but even more than that, he made me laugh so hard I couldn't breathe, which I desperately needed then. Of course, he also made me furious by being very critical and rude—sometimes due to speaking in a language not his own, and sometimes because that's just how he was, an entitled man in a society that was still very patriarchal. I'd called him out on his misogyny early on, but he never stopped marveling at the fact that I was on my own in the world, as if my extra X chromosome depended on a man for its survival. As aggravating as that was, he also encouraged me to prioritize myself and what I wanted from life. He urged me to take some risks, and in a weird way, it was because of Marco that I'd rented the house next door to Porter's and given our relationship—and life in the Italian countryside—a fighting chance.

I was looking forward to seeing Marco and Assisi again as I crawled along in the combine's exhaust. As we neared Petrignano, the fog lifted. I saw my chance and gunned the Panda into the other lane, then swerved onto Vialle Michelangelo and headed up the mountain towards Assisi. I downshifted and steered with my knees while I tapped out a WhatsApp message to Marco to let him know I was almost there, then shifted gears and picked up the pace.

When I finally pulled into the lot at Piazza Matteotti where I always parked, Marco was leaning against an Alfa Romeo smoking a cigarette. He dropped the cigarette and ground it under his foot, then loped towards me as I pushed the car door closed with my hip.

I slung my purse over my shoulder and launched myself at his midsection. "Ciao, Marco!"

He wrapped his arms around me briefly, then pushed me away and looked at my face.

"You look beautiful, *mia cara*. Not too old," he said. "Did you miss me?"

I nodded. "I worried about you the whole pandemic."

Marco shook his head. "Is not necessary. I am strong like Etruscan warrior."

"Okay, but I still worried."

"Is because you love me," he said, shrugging. "But don't worry, darling, is our secret. Come," he said, grabbing my elbow.

"Where are we going?" I asked as we waited to cross the street that ran between the parking lot and the historical center of Assisi.

"Where do you think?" Marco said. "To the bed. We make love and then we make photos of the church."

"Nice try," I said, pulling my arm out of his grasp as we crossed the street. "I will buy you lunch, though."

"*Va bene*," he said. "It will give me energy for the sex."

We walked downhill towards the main piazza, stopping in the church of San Rufino where both Saint Francis and Saint Clare had been baptized in the 1200s. The museum in the basement had been closed the last time I was in town, so I paid ten euros for me and Marco to go inside for a look.

After perusing the vestments and monstrances and ancient tombstones in the museum, we left the church and went for a long walk through the residential streets on the upper end of Assisi's historic area. There was a house up there that I loved, owned by an old man who forged his own decorative iron plant holders in the shape of vines. He attached the plant holders to the stone facade of his house and filled each one with a terracotta pot full of colorful flowers, which made the house look like it was in bloom.

After I snapped a few photos of the house, we walked back downhill to a small restaurant on a side street very close to the apartment I'd rented when I was working on the tourism project. There were four tables outside under a low stone arch and Marco pointed to one with a *Riservato* sign on it before ducking inside to speak to the owner.

"So, when do you come back?" he asked when he returned, sliding into the chair opposite me.

"To Assisi? I don't have any plans to come back. I bought a house last year, you know. The one next to Porter that I'd been renting."

"Next to who?"

"Pedro. I told you all of this."

"I am old and have dementia," Marco said. "I remember nothing. Do you love him? More than you love me?"

"The last time I checked, you had a wife, Marco."

Marco shook his head. "Is not like that," he said. "I am not married. I share a house with the mother of my son, but right now she stay with her sister. I tell you this in continuous, but you do not want to hear me."

A waiter appeared before I could answer. He set a bowl of olives and a bottle of Sagrantino from my favorite winery in Bevagna on the table in front of us, took a wine opener from the pocket of his apron, and began uncorking the wine.

"You remembered my favorite wine!"

Marco made a face. "What I am, a monster? Of course I remember."

"So you only have dementia when it comes to Porter?"

"Who?"

I laughed and picked up my glass. "I said yesterday that I wasn't going to drink during the day anymore."

Marco looked at me like I was speaking Vietnamese, then turned his attention to the waiter.

As soon as the waiter walked away, I clinked my glass against Marco's and took a sip. The wine was just as delicious as the first time I'd had it, when Marco and I sampled all sixteen labels at the small, family-owned winery. When we'd finally stumbled out of the tasting room, both of us listing significantly to starboard, Marco walked straight into a ditch and I started laughing so hard that I fell to the ground and had to be helped up by the owner.

"I want to know everything that's been going on with you," I said, forcing myself to put my glass down rather than empty it in one sip. "What did you do during the lockdown?"

"I read many books," Marco said, tossing an olive into his mouth. "I study. I make a garden. I dream of American writer who love me."

"And now? Are you working again?"

He nodded. "We start again with the tourist plan and the

show about the life of Saint Francis." He spit the pit of the olive into his napkin and took a sip of wine. "But why do you stay with Pedro all this time? You say to me you will never marry again. You want to be free. *Elisabetta libera*, you say."

I did not want to discuss my relationship with Porter, especially on the heels of the news about Sloan, so I just shrugged and deployed the surefire way to change topics I'd learned during the many hours I'd spent with Marco.

"How is AC Milan doing this year?" I asked as if I hadn't heard his question. "I hear they suck."

I sat back and sipped my wine, listening with half an ear as Marco defended his favorite soccer team.

As I nodded along, I thought about how Marco embodied that acceptance that so many Italians seem to have—that life is difficult and painful and the goal is to find the good moments and make them count. Marco drove me nuts, but the truth was, I was incredibly grateful for my time with him. I could never tell him that, since he was convinced I had a secret, salacious plan to seduce him, but I agreed with what David had always maintained: Marco came into my life at the exact moment I needed him. David claimed this was evidence of a benevolent God acting on my behalf, but I had a very hard time seeing Marco—a self-proclaimed Casanova and God's gift to women—as an instrument of the Lord. Nevertheless, I was very grateful I'd met him, no matter why it happened.

The food arrived and Marco and the waiter had a brief conversation in rapid-fire Italian that I couldn't follow and then we started eating. Marco continued to talk, bringing me up to speed on local politics and the possibility that the tourism plan would finally get off the ground.

"*Quindi vedremo come va*," he said finally, forking a piece of beef into his mouth and setting his knife and fork down on his plate with a clatter. "We see how it go."

When we had polished off the bottle of wine, Marco pushed

his chair back from the table. I told him to stay seated, that I would pay since I'd invited him to lunch, but Marco steepled his hands in front of his chest and moved them up and down in that decidedly Italian gesture that meant that only God could protect me from my own stupidity.

"What you think I am?" he asked. "Saint Francis of poverty?"

"Well, thank you. But if we make it until aperitivo time, that will be my treat, okay?"

"Why we would not make it?" Marco asked. "Today is not the day I kill you," he said, then stepped inside the restaurant.

After he'd settled the bill, Marco and I walked to the Piazza del Comune and took the pictures I needed of Santa Maria. Afterwards, I looked into a few shops while Marco stood around chatting with people I didn't recognize, and then he suggested we get a gelato. I said sure, thinking we would go to the *gelateria* that was about four steps away from where we were standing, but Marco shook his head.

"No. Is for tourists. The best gelato is in Saint Mary of the Angels. We cannot go by feet."

"We don't need to go all the way down the mountain," I said, pointing to the shop. "Look how convenient this gelato place is."

His mouth twisted with displeasure. "Is American idea, *convenient*. Gelato is not convenient. Gelato is delicious or is shit. Here is shit. In Santa Maria, is delicious."

"So you want to walk all the way back to my car and drive down the mountain?"

"No." He pointed across the piazza to a small alley where a motorcycle was parked next to the wall. "Is mine."

"Oh."

"Come," he said, walking across the square. "We must be fast before anyone see me." When we got to the motorcycle, he unstrapped a black helmet from the back of the seat and handed it to me. "Can you push the hairs up and look like a man?"

I twisted my hair into a rope and tucked it up under the back of the helmet, then waited for Marco to get on the bike before climbing on behind him. As he started the engine and we lurched forward, I resisted the urge to hold onto him and kept my hands on my legs, gripping the seat with my thighs as hard as I could.

Marco sped downhill on the cobblestoned streets, swerving around clusters of tourists. As we neared the basilica, he aimed the motorcycle at the steep ramp that ran down the left side of the church and then, at the bottom, whipped the bike around the corner so fast I nearly went flying into the monastery courtyard.

"Shit!" I shrieked, grabbing the sides of the seat.

He didn't slow down at all as we zoomed through the streets below the basilica and raced across the parking lot where several tour buses idled. He zipped out the exit and joined the two-lane road that headed downhill from the historic part of Assisi, careening into the roundabout and nearly colliding with a truck before shooting out the other side.

I was pretty sure all that delicious wine from lunch was going to reappear, but finally, as we headed into the suburb of Saint Mary of the Angels, the road straightened out. I let go of the seat and allowed the muscles in my back to relax, anticipating a more civilized ride into town. But instead of continuing straight at a leisurely pace, Marco took a left turn without warning, and I nearly flew off the back of the bike again.

He slowed the motorcycle and leaned back to shout at me. "Is okay, you can hold now."

I wrapped my arms around his midsection. "You said you weren't going to kill me today! Where are we going?"

"Is better gelato in Spello than Saint Mary. We go there."

I started to suggest that we just stick with the gelato in Saint Mary, but then I remembered how futile it was to argue with Marco, who had a black belt in selective hearing. I decided to just enjoy the ride. I tightened my arms around his torso and leaned my helmeted head against his back, turning my face to watch the scenery go by.

The sky was bright blue and cloudless, and I breathed in deeply as we passed a succession of olive groves and stone houses. I knew this road well from walking the trail between Assisi and Spello several times and I was keeping my eye out for Villa Costanzi, a private home Marco and I had visited. It was built on what used to be—four or five hundred years before Christ—a shrine to Jupiter and Venus.

Marco pointed to the yellow villa as we passed. I nodded and shouted, "I remember," and he picked up speed to swerve around a three-wheeled truck loaded with lumber.

As we passed under the stone arch that marked the entrance to Spello, Marco slowed to a crawl, threading his way along the cobbled streets and skirting clots of pedestrians. He finally stopped the bike next to a butcher shop and I slid off the back with all the grace of a tranquilized hippo.

"Oh, thank God," I said, pulling the helmet off. "I thought I was going to hurl."

"What means this, hurl?"

"*Vomitare.*"

"Hurl," Marco repeated. "Is a good word." He took the helmet and strapped it onto the back of the motorcycle, then grabbed my elbow. "Come," he said, steering me around a group of women who were window shopping. "We go up the hill. The best place for gelato is *nascosta*. I don't know how to say this."

"*Nascosta* means hidden," I told him. "The best ice cream shop is hidden."

"Hidden," he repeated. "Is a new word for me. Now I practice this word."

"Okay, go ahead."

"You love me, but you hidden this."

"Not quite," I said, shaking my head. "Hidden is an adjective. I *hide* my love for you; my love for you *is hidden*."

"I know. Is why I say it," Marco said, grinning down at me. "You should not hide your love for me, *mia cara*. Is not right."

We passed several stores I would have happily popped into if my elbow wasn't firmly in the grip of the gelato mission leader. I loved Spello and its quaint shops selling Umbrian olive oil, olive wood spoons and bowls, and lavender-infused lotions and creams. One of the storefronts was completely covered by flower garlands that were draped in graceful swoops across the windows, and I was able to stop and marvel at it for a split second before Marco tugged on my arm.

Spello is famous for its flower festival every June, when the townspeople get together and create amazing mosaics out of live blooms. This event is called the *infiorata*, which means "the flowering"—a word I'd pronounced as *inforiata*, which means "enraged," before Marco corrected me.

"Is hilarious, to think of a village *inforiata* celebration," Marco said when he finally pointed out my mistake. We were at lunch near the sea and he was laughing so hard he could barely talk. "*Inforiata* festival! All the people of Spello are furious so they make a festival to scream and beat the neighbor."

"Hilarious," I said, poking at the eyeball of the fish splayed on a platter between us.

"We make a sign for tourists. 'Come to Spello festival to beat the neighbor!'"

"Ha ha. Very funny."

"Is hilarious!" Marco said, dabbing at his eyes with a napkin.

"How many times were you going to let me say it wrong before you corrected me?"

"You are *inforiata* because I do not correct you?" he asked, grinning. "Come, everyone! Welcome to Spello to beat the neighbor!"

"It's beat off. Beat *off* the neighbor, not beat the neighbor," I said. "Whenever you're talking about another person, you say beat off."

"Beat off," Marco repeated, nodding. "See? We learn each other. 'Come to Spello to beat off the neighbor.'"

I'd never told him the truth. There was no telling how many people he'd threatened to masturbate in the past couple of years.

Eight

When we finally arrived at the *gelateria* at the top of Spello, only a few people were in line, and luckily Marco didn't know any of them, otherwise he probably would have shoved me behind the potted tree in the corner.

I couldn't imagine living like he did, under the controlling thumb of his girlfriend. She called and texted him nonstop all day long and monitored his every move, and at some point, I'd started calling Marco *l'ostaggio*, the hostage, until I realized how sad it made him. I'd once heard his girlfriend screaming down the phone at him and was still traumatized by the rage in her voice and the horrible things she said. If Porter ever yelled at me like that, it would be the very last thing he did.

"What kind of gelato are you getting?" I asked as we stepped up to the counter.

Marco looked down at me. "First I try yours, like always. Then I choose."

I ordered a cup of lemon and basil gelato.

"You eat everything *limone*," Marco said, grabbing a napkin from the stack on the counter.

"Lemon is my favorite. I've never had lemon and basil gelato, though. Do you think they're going to just put a basil leaf on top, or what?"

Marco shrugged as the girl behind the counter took the three euros I handed her and gave me the paper cup of gelato and a small pink spoon. We went outside and perched on a low stone wall where we could watch the few people who had ventured that far up the hill go by.

I took a bite of the gelato and moaned with pleasure. "Wow. This is incredible."

"See? I tell you is better than Saint Mary gelato. Why you don't believe me?"

"It's so lemony. And look at all the little pieces of basil chopped up in there," I said, tilting the cup toward him. I took another bite and moaned again. "Oh wow."

"It sound like you make love with this gelato."

"This is better than sex."

Marco laughed. "Only because you make *sesso* with Pedro and not me."

"Here." I shoved the cup at him. "See for yourself."

"I use your *cucchiaio*," he said, loading the little plastic spoon with gelato.

"That's fine."

I'd shared many spoons, as well as several other things, with Marco while we were working together. Early on, we'd been driving to Ravenna to see the mosaics in the church and had become desperate for a bathroom. We finally spotted a gas station and wheeled into it at top speed, only to find an entire tour bus of Japanese people already in line for the single toilet. In pain and truly afraid I might pee on the floor, I'd ignored the handwritten *Vietato Entrare* sign on what I suspected was the employee bathroom and opened the door a crack to peek in. When I saw a toilet, I slid inside—followed by a loud chorus of protests from the Japanese tourists and by Marco, who pushed in behind me and locked the door.

"What are you doing?" I asked him, already unbuckling my belt.

"You hear this people?" he said. "They want to kill us! Make *pipi,* then is my turn."

After sharing a bathroom, forks and spoons had never seemed like a big deal.

"Isn't it good?" I asked Marco, who was digging into the cup of gelato for a second spoonful.

He nodded. "I only show you the best of Umbria."

"Do you want me to get you your own?"

Marco shook his head, licking the spoon clean. "No. Yours is better."

"That's what Porter always says."

Marco rolled his eyes. "Forget Pedro. When you are done, I have a surprise," he said.

"I have to get back on the road."

"It will not take long."

I took the spoon back from Marco and scooped the last of the ice cream onto it, then tossed the paper cup into a trash can as we started back downhill. The foot traffic had picked up considerably and we had to squeeze past a crowd of people gathered in front of a wine bar. Marco nearly collided with a tiny old lady wearing a silk scarf and an elegant chignon who stepped off the sidewalk directly in front of him.

She looked up at him towering overhead and gasped. "*Oh! Pardonnez-moi.*"

"*C'est entièrement ma faute, madame,*" Marco said, bowing slightly. Then he put his hand on her frail, birdlike arm and guided her back to the safety of the sidewalk.

"Sometimes I forget how sweet you can be," I said when he rejoined me.

He slung his arm around my neck. "Did you see how she look at me when I speak her language?" he asked. "She want me badly. Behave, Grandma."

When we got back to the butcher shop where Marco had parked his motorcycle, he unsnapped the helmet and handed it to me.

"Thanks," I said, setting it on my head and reaching behind me to twist my hair into a knot. Marco smacked the top of the helmet, causing it to drop onto my skull with a thud. I pushed the coil of hair up under the back rim of the helmet and fastened the chin strap, then waited for Marco to climb on the bike.

When I was settled behind him, he pushed the throttle, making the bike lurch forward. My helmeted head collided with his back.

"Hold to me!" Marco yelled.

I gripped the sides of his shirt in my fists and squeezed my legs around the frame of the bike as we roared down the street and back under the marble arch that marked the boundary of Spello. I thought we'd take the same two-lane road all the way back to Assisi, but before we got to Villa Costanzi, Marco turned off onto a tightly packed dirt path in the middle of an olive grove. The bike wobbled as we took the corner, then righted itself, and we continued uphill.

After several minutes on the increasingly narrow track, Marco suddenly made another abrupt right turn, then stopped in a clump of trees.

"We are here," he said, shutting off the engine.

"Where are we?" I asked, managing to get off the motorcycle with slightly more grace than before.

"Is a surprise. No one knows is here."

I followed him through the olive trees to a small clearing. On the back edge was a small stone structure. Not a house, exactly; more like a hut or cabin, blending seamlessly into the olive grove around it.

Marco pushed against the wooden door of the hut and ducked inside. He turned and beckoned me to follow him. "Come inside, darling."

"What is this?" I asked.

"*È il mio refugio.*"

"Your refuge?"

He nodded. "I come here to be in peace."

"Whose place is this, though?"

"These are trees of my family, and this was the place for olive men to rest from the sun. When I was small, I play here."

Marco went to the corner and dragged a large steamer trunk forward. He lifted the lid and showed me what was inside: a few books, a radio, a flashlight, two bottles of wine.

"Doesn't anyone use this place? Like when they're picking olives?"

"No," Marco said. "My sister own these trees now. She send the machines only and she never come." He shook his head with disgust.

I nodded. I knew that every fall, Marco spent weeks picking olives by hand from his own trees and the groves of his neighbors and thought the machines that shook the fruit off the trees were a lazy and disrespectful way to get olives. I also knew there was no love lost between him and his sister.

He pulled a thin blanket from the trunk, then closed the lid and slid the trunk back into the corner. "Come, we sit outside."

Marco spread the blanket on the ground outside and we eased ourselves down onto it, settling our backs against the stone wall of the hut. The stones and the ground were warm, and the fading sunlight was shining directly on us through a small gap in the trees.

"This is nice," I said, closing my eyes. "Very peaceful."

"Is because the trees are *alberi pacifici*. How you say this?"

"Peaceful trees? You mean because they're olive trees?"

"I mean because they have seen all things—Saint Francis, Saint Clare, invasion by Goth people, war with Perugia, war with Pope, war with America, war with Germany. They see all but stay in peace because they know these things do not belong to them. *Capisci?*"

I nodded without opening my eyes. "They're just observers."

"You understand me perfectly, darling. *Non pensano alla futura ma solo a ciò che esiste nel presente.* How you say in English?"

"They don't think about the future, just what exists in the present," I said, my eyes still closed against the sunlight.

"*Brava.* The trees only give energy to grow, to survive. They do not give energy to worry about war or who steal the body of Saint Francis or what is happening in the government. They only welcome the sun and rain and think to enjoy today."

"I get it," I said, then stifled a yawn. "I just need to rest for a minute, okay? I haven't been sleeping well."

"Make a little sleep, *mia cara.* I do not talk," Marco said, putting his arm around me so I could rest my head in the crook of his shoulder.

In the hundreds of hours I'd spent with him, I don't think I'd ever known Marco to be quiet for more than two or three minutes, and even that was rare. But he must have kept his word and held his tongue, or maybe he fell asleep too, because when I woke up, the sun was gone and Marco was extracting his arm from underneath me.

"*Buongiorno,*" he said when I startled awake. "Is a new morning!"

For a minute I believed him, and wondered how I could have possibly slept through the night sitting upright in an olive grove.

I rubbed my eyes and looked at my watch. "Oh my God. It's eight o'clock. I still have to drive home! We gotta go, Marco."

"I put the blanket away and we go. Is five minutes."

Marco folded the blanket and returned it to the trunk, then closed the door of the hut behind us. He reached for my hand as we walked back to the motorcycle.

"Relax," he said, gripping my hand tighter when I tried to pull away. "Is not because I love you. Is because there are rocks and you do not know this place."

The drive back to Assisi and up to Piazza Matteotti where I'd parked was only a few minutes once we rejoined the paved road. Marco dropped me right where you pay for parking and I fed the ticket and a couple of euro notes into the machine, got my exit ticket, and walked over to my car. Marco pulled his motorcycle up next to me and turned the engine off.

"I hope you enjoy today," he said.

"I did. It was really good to see you."

"I want to tell you something, but I am too tired to speak in English."

Marco had shown me the refuge, he said in Italian, because he sensed I might need it. He wanted me to know that I was free to go there if I ever needed some time and space to be alone and think. No one would bother me, he said, or even know I was there, including him.

"Thank you, Marco," I said, opening my car door. "But I'm fine, really. I appreciate the offer, though."

Marco shrugged. "Okay. We see each other soon, yes?"

"Of course." I slid into the driver's seat and put the key in the ignition.

Marco put the helmet on, leaving the chin strap dangling, and started the motorcycle. He revved the engine once, twice, then leaned over and rapped on my window.

"Yes?" I said, rolling the window down.

"*Ricorda gli alberi*," he shouted over the engine, then headed for the exit. He steered around the electronic barrier and roared off down the street.

Remember the trees.

I had no idea why he'd said this to me, but Marco had an uncanny ability to laser in on something I didn't even know I was struggling with. He'd done it several times before, offering up seemingly random—but somehow spot-on—advice from the cluttered circus of his brain, like some kind of intuitive idiot savant.

I pondered his strange statement as I stopped for gas and then merged onto the autostrada. Somewhere around the second exit for Perugia, it dawned on me that what Marco was saying might be the exact position I needed to take for dealing with the news of Porter's daughter. If I just observed and didn't get involved, then I couldn't get hurt. If Porter decided to have a relationship with Sloan, it wouldn't be my problem, and if he decided not to have a relationship with her, oh well. I wasn't about to invest myself in someone else's kid.

Shit! Porter.

I moved into the right lane, downshifted into third, and held my right knee against the steering wheel as I tapped out a text.

On my way back, I wrote, then tossed the phone into the passenger seat and turned on the radio.

Nine

"Have you ever walked into a place and actually felt its spirit?" I asked Porter the next morning.

I should have been putting the ruins of my kitchen back together, but the paint in the cabinets was still tacky when I touched it, so instead I'd wandered over to Porter's terrace and stretched out on the lounge chair next to the one he was occupying.

"Sure," Porter said. "That's a big thing in restaurants. You want a customer to walk in and feel good. It's all about lighting and colors and smell."

Oliver waited patiently until I was settled on the chair, then jumped up to join me, turning in tight circles before stretching his long body next to mine with all four paws sticking straight out towards Porter.

"I went to look at an apartment in DC once and just

immediately walked back out again," I told him, stroking Oliver's ear. "The rental agent tried to sell me on what a great location it was and how many amenities the building had, but there was something . . . I don't know, evil is too dramatic, but *off* with that place. You know what I mean?"

He nodded. "Yep."

"I was thinking about Santa Maria sopra Minerva—"

"What? I'm shocked."

"I know, I know. But I read this article about genetic memory and savants when I got home last night that was really interesting."

Porter reached over and shook Oliver's paw. "Wake up and learn something, dog."

Oliver yawned and stretched, then went back to sleep.

"There are people who know things they've never been taught, right?" I said, shifting my hips so I could face Porter. "Children with incredible musical talents, or artists who've never had a lesson in their lives."

"Like Mozart."

"He started composing when he was, what, four or five? I don't think I could even use scissors at that age."

"Having seen you with power tools, I would say that's probably true."

I reached over to swat his arm. "Brat."

Porter leaned away from me and laughed.

"But how do these savants know what they know?" I asked, petting Oliver, who had raised his head in concern when I tried to whack Porter. "Maybe we're not born as blank slates. Maybe our brains are born with infinite knowledge, and we spend our lives unlocking that knowledge, not acquiring it."

"How would that work?"

"I don't know," I said, shrugging. "But maybe that explains people who have a head injury and wake up speaking fluent French. Maybe a physical injury can unlock stored knowledge."

"Then hit me, please," Porter said. "I would prefer to never think about the Italian subjunctive again."

"I had a dream once that I was on a submarine reading a book in Arabic. I could see the pages, I could read the words, and the story I was reading made total sense."

Porter looked over at me, narrowing his eyes. "Anything else you want to tell me, Mata Hari?"

"It was weird and I wish I could remember what I was reading. But seriously, if there's knowledge stored in our memories, maybe there are other things too."

"Like what?"

"Experiences, maybe. Like have you ever had a really deep reaction to someone or some place that you couldn't explain?"

"I felt like I'd known you my whole life when we met. Does that count?"

I glanced over at him. "Yes, that counts. Absolutely."

"What were you thinking of?"

I told Porter about the odd feeling of recognition I'd had in parts of England. "Canterbury, in particular, felt like home in a really bizarre way. I was walking along some side streets on the way to the cathedral, looking at the brick walls, and I felt like I knew my way around and had seen it all before."

"But you hadn't?"

I shook my head. "No, never. It was the first time I'd been there. But some of my ancestors were English masons. Maybe there was something sparking in my genetic code, some sort of cellular-level recognition."

"Hmm," Porter said, his mouth twisting in thought. "Maybe. I've never thought about it."

"I remember hearing a story once about a man who received a heart transplant and started taking on the donor's personality after the surgery. All of a sudden, he hated broccoli and liked heavy metal music and was afraid of flying, stuff like that," I said. "But he also became very depressed and ending up committing suicide, which is how he'd gotten the donor heart in the first place."

"Geez."

"And I've read about twins who were separated at birth and adopted out to different families and ended up with the same first and middle names, the same career, wives and pets with the same names . . ."

"I heard about that in psychology class. The Jim twins, right? Didn't they show up wearing the same thing when they were finally reunited?"

"I think so," I said, scratching Oliver's snout. He raised one lip like Elvis, baring his teeth, but didn't wake up. "And if there's memory stored in our DNA, or knowledge waiting to be unlocked in our brains, maybe there's also memory stored in physical places?"

"Aha! Like Santa Maria sopra Minerva. I see what you did there. Tricky."

"Think about it, though. What kind of suffering went on when Santa Maria was a jail? What happened there when it was a pagan temple? What happened during the Goth War, and the wars with Perugia?"

"Enquiring minds want to know."

"Well, I do, anyway. When I was writing the piece about the 1997 earthquake in Assisi, it was very obvious to me that the past isn't really gone there. The whole medieval world is lying just under the surface, waiting for an opportunity to re-emerge. And if that's true of the physical past, then maybe it's also true of the emotional past," I said.

"What would that mean in practical terms?"

"Maybe the things that happened to the people whose DNA we inherited are encoded in us too. They know now that mothers retain cells from their babies in their brains. What else do we retain?"

"I have a feeling you're talking around something," Porter said, reaching into the beat-up cooler he'd found in the barn and now kept beside his lounge chair. He pulled out a beer and offered it to me.

"So much for not day drinking," I said, taking the bottle. "Is it even noon yet? We've really got to stop, Porter."

"Tomorrow's another day, Miss Scarlett."

Oliver woke up to inspect my beer. When he was satisfied it was nothing he wanted, he yawned and went back to sleep.

"Maybe I am talking around something," I said. "I didn't mean to. But I can't pretend I'm not concerned about whatever Pandora's box Sloan might open. There's a reason sperm donation was supposed to be anonymous."

Porter made a face. "No kidding. It was supposed to be like giving blood. No strings attached."

"I wonder if this has happened to any of your teammates?"

"I don't know. There's a Facebook group for soccer alumni, but I never go on it."

I took a sip of beer, then wiped my mouth with the sleeve of my hoodie. "A marriage could get turned totally upside down by this kind of news," I said.

"That's the problem, Beth. I don't want things to be turned upside down."

I was quiet for a minute, drinking my beer and trying to loosen a knot of curly fur at the base of Oliver's ear.

"I don't either," I said finally. "I know it doesn't make sense to you, Porter, but I just can't handle any more upheavals. I really can't. I've used up all the forgiveness and understanding I have and just don't have it in me to deal with anything else."

He didn't respond.

After a few minutes, I gave up on Oliver's knot and said, "I saw a video the other day of someone's pet beaver."

"There's a lot I want to say about that."

"The beaver was gathering up everything it could get its little paws on to build a dam in the hallway of their house."

"Why?"

I shrugged. "Because it's instinctual. It's what beavers do," I said. "Like Oliver chasing rabbits and barking at strangers and bringing us socks and doing all of the stuff he does, I guess." Hearing his name, Oliver lifted his head and looked at me. "You said he wasn't more than a couple of weeks old when you found him."

Porter nodded. "I had to feed him disgusting wet food every four hours. He smelled horrible and was full of worms."

"Don't listen to him, Ollie," I said, scratching his head. "He doesn't mean it." Oliver sighed and rolled onto his back so I could scratch his belly. "The point is, he spent little or no time with his parents, but he still knows how to do all of that stuff."

"It's in his DNA."

I looked over at Porter. "Exactly. It's strong stuff, DNA. I think you need to be prepared that if you meet Sloan, you may want to keep her in your life."

"And what if I do?"

I took a sip of my beer and stared off into the fields. Someone had a fire going across the valley and I could see the smoke curling into the air, but I couldn't smell it.

"Beth?"

I looked back at Porter. "I don't know," I said.

I managed to hold myself to one beer and went to get my hair colored at the little *parruchiere* in the village after lunch. The salon was hopping, as always.

I'd been too intimidated to go to the salon my first couple of months in Italy, even though my hair had begun graying at an alarming rate. I bought home hair color kits at the beauty store instead and did my best, but after I got comfortable speaking rudimentary Italian, I made an appointment and ended up staying for so long that Porter came looking for me, fearing I might be dealing with a hair catastrophe.

The truth was, every appointment took far longer than was necessary because the salon functioned more like a social club than a place of business. Women rotated in and out, sharing tidbits of local news and gossip and grabbing a coffee from Enzo—Roberta the owner's twenty-something nephew—whose main job was to keep the customers caffeinated and complimented. Even in the dead of winter, Enzo wore only tight jeans and a skin-tight T-shirt that strained to cover his bulging biceps. When conversation lagged, Roberta would bark at him to sweep the floor, which he did with a great show of rippling muscles, bumping and grinding against the broom like a Chippendales dancer while the women in the salon clapped and hollered.

After conferring with Roberta about what we were going to do to my hair—which was the exact same thing we did every time I came in—she mixed up a batch of chemicals and applied them to my head. As I was waiting for my color to set, I leaned back in the salon chair and thought about Marco. He'd sent me an audio message when I got back from Assisi, saying it had been good to see me and that he hoped I'd gotten home safely and I shouldn't forget that the hut was available to me whenever I needed it. The funny part of his message—what really stuck out to me—was that he'd used my name, which he absolutely never did.

For the most part, aside from some short-lived arguments that usually ended in laughter, Marco and I had gotten along famously from the moment we met. But we'd had a huge fight one day when Marco was still under contract as my tour guide. He'd been in a foul mood from the moment he picked me up that morning, correcting my pronunciation and needling me, and when we finally got to La Scarzuola—the site of a thirteenth-century convent where Saint Francis reportedly planted a laurel tree that gushed fresh water—I truly thought he might blow a gasket.

The owner of La Scarzuola, a man named Buzzi, had turned the entire property into a bizarre, surreal, architectural acid trip. There were sandcastle-looking structures at odd angles, whacky mosaics, a Tower of Babel, a whale, a labyrinth, a musical staircase and—Marco's favorite—an enormous statue of a nude woman with extremely prominent nipples.

What we had come to see, though, was a fresco of Saint Francis that was supposed to be one of the oldest in Umbria. It was inside the convent at the top of the property, but no matter how much Marco pleaded with him, the site manager refused to let us go into the convent, which had been off-limits to the public for ages.

"I tell him is a holy place," Marco said, turning to me and switching to English in the midst of making his case to the site manager. "It should not belong to one man who lock the door."

I nodded but didn't say anything. I agreed with Marco completely, but even if I'd had the language skills to do it, there was no way I was going to join the fight.

Marco continued to argue with the site manager for several more minutes, then finally shook his head, threw his hands in the air, and pronounced the entirety of La Scarzuola *un abominio ed un profanazione*—an abomination and a desecration. At that, the site manager went berserk.

"Jesus, Marco!" I said, tugging on his arm as every vein in the manager's neck popped out and his face turned purple with rage. "Let's get out of here."

As I dragged him to the parking lot—with the manager shouting at top volume about the various implements we might use to fuck ourselves on the way out—Marco corrected the way I said *Scarzuola*.

"Is not difficult," he said, opening his car door and shaking his head like he was suffering physically from my mistake. "Say again, correctly."

That did it. I got in and slammed the passenger door shut. When Marco slid behind the wheel, I told him his English pronunciation sucked just as bad as my Italian. And then, as we made our way out of the Orvieto hills, I set out to prove it to him. I drilled him on every "th" word I could think of—*thumb*, *math, theater, thimble, thermal, teeth, leather, moth, thread, bath, thump, thug*. Every time he messed up, I shook my head and said, "Is not difficult. Say again, correctly."

When I told him to say *hither and thither*, he told me he was going to drive us off the side of the mountain if I didn't shut up. I retaliated by making him say "Beth" over and over again, all the way from Lake Trasimeno to the Assisi exit and up the mountain to Via Sermei, where he told me to get out of the car before he killed me.

After that, whenever he had to introduce me to someone, he defaulted to *Elisabetta*, and when it was just us, *cara*, sweetheart. Hearing him say my name always gave me a start, because he only said it when he really wanted to get my attention and make a point.

Roberta came over as I was deleting Marco's message and putting my phone away. She lifted the plastic cap to peer at my hair and told me I could go to the sink, where Enzo washed my hair and gave me an excellent head massage. Then Roberta gave me a quick trim, dried my hair, pronounced the whole effect *bellissima*, and hurried off to rejoin the gossip.

I stopped in the grocery store to pick up a few essentials before heading home. Porter's car was still gone when I arrived and there was no sign of Oliver, so I put the groceries away and sat down at my laptop to do some more work on pagan church conversions.

As my computer came to life, the email notification dinged.

Dear Beth,

I'm sorry for the delayed response to your email. I've been consumed with a project here, but you've been in my thoughts, as always.

Wow.

That was my reaction to the sudden appearance of this young woman who claims to be Porter's daughter. "Wow" is hardly an original response, but it's an honest one, and I certainly understand your feelings. It doesn't make you a bad person to have a hard time adjusting to something so big and potentially life changing. You're still grieving Mia and the loss of the family life you thought you'd have, and suddenly more chaos arrives in the form of someone who will certainly impact your life with Porter. Frankly, I'd be more concerned if you blithely accepted this as good news.

Yet it does have the potential to be good news! It may be that this young woman will bring a tremendous amount of joy to your life. And so while I'm in no way advocating that you bury your head in the sand or disingenuously claim to be thrilled without reservation, I do think it's appropriate to voice your concerns to Porter and then wait to see what happens.

As we've discussed many times before, one of the follies of being human is our tendency to write the end of the story before the story has actually played out. We conjure up all of the possible negative outcomes and think we can accurately project what's going to happen in the future, but in doing so, we close ourselves off to the possibility of things working out and being much better than we anticipated. What if you grow to love Sloan? What if she ends up being a wonderful part of your life? Don't react to a problem before it actually exists, kiddo. That's my advice.

For what it's worth, I suggest you make a conscious choice to accept this situation with a mind and heart that are open to the possibility that—as unlikely as it may seem in the present moment—this young woman may prove to be a blessing. Choose the path of acceptance, stop putting up walls, and see how the situation develops. As you well know, sometimes the best course of action is to get out of our own way and let events unfold. After all, if you're not open to the possibility of being pleasantly surprised—of receiving blessings you couldn't possibly have anticipated and for which there is no appropriate response but delight and gratitude—then what's the point of being alive?

Stay in touch, please. You're in my prayers, kiddo.

As ever,
Your favorite uncle,
David

When I was finished reading David's email, I took off my glasses, set them on the desk, and closed the lid of my laptop.

I knew David was right, and I loved Porter and wanted to support him.

But I wanted my own daughter back, not to make room in my life for someone else's kid.

Ten

Porter texted while I was out for a walk this morning and asked if I would go over to Dean and Darren's with him. We hadn't seen them other than to wave since the marathon of debauched drinking, so I reluctantly agreed to go.

I came home and filled up Oliver's water bowl, then turned on a TV show called *Il Contadino Cerca Moglie* about farmers looking for wives. Oliver loved that show because there were often farm animals or other dogs on it. He stood in front of the TV watching for a second, then jumped up onto the couch and stretched out, let out a loud sigh, and propped his head on the arm rest so he could see the television.

Porter and I walked over to Villa Rosmarino by way of the road. It nearly doubled the distance when you added in our long driveway and theirs, but Porter said he needed the exercise, and I wasn't in any hurry.

Darren and Dean were outside putting down a layer of weed barrier fabric in the planting beds closest to the house. Porter muttered, "Top priority" as we walked up the drive and I knew exactly what he meant because the one time we'd been inside Villa Rosmarino, there were at least a hundred critical repairs that needed to be made. But I couldn't blame the guys for wanting to be outside on such a beautiful day.

"Hello, hello!" Darren said when we walked up, shaking Porter's hand and clapping him on the shoulder.

Dean kissed my cheek. "Don't mind the sweat, angel face. I'm a dirty boy today."

I laughed and turned to hug Darren. Porter started to shake Dean's hand, but Dean sidestepped his outstretched arm and placed a loud smack on Porter's cheek.

"Hello, delicious," he said. "My God, you're gorgeous. What's it like to wake up looking like that? I told Darren I might need to reconsider my hall pass list after the other night."

"Sorry it took us so long to come over," I said. "I had to go to Assisi for some research."

"We went to Perugia on one of our house-hunting trips, but we haven't made it to Assisi yet," Darren said. "Have you spent much time there?"

"Oh, Beth knows every nook and cranny," Porter said, shooting me a look.

I pretended not to notice. "We were dead the other morning," I said. "You guys were out here working and we were so hungover we could barely move."

"Years of training," Dean said, puffing out his chest. "Plus a bit of the hair of the dog. First order of business when you wake up. That's the key."

"We had dry toast and Spididol for lunch," I said.

When they looked puzzled, I explained that—next to olive oil, cheese, wine, coffee, fashion, cars, art, architecture, literature, music and pasta—Spididol was Italy's greatest treasure.

"It's just ibuprofen with some sort of salt in it," Porter said, "but it's amazing." He looked at me. "What's the magic ingredient?"

"I think it's arginine? It's a lifesaver. We take it for everything."

"We had a dram of whiskey and steak and eggs for brekkie," Darren said. "I can't get over the meat here."

He and Porter started discussing the local Val di Chiana beef cows, so I drifted away to look at the gardens, followed by Dean.

"We had a great time the other night," Dean said as we walked towards the olive trees that stood on the edge of their property. "Darren thought we might have made a mistake, buying this place, but he's completely changed his tune after meeting you guys."

I nodded. "I get it. Italy's a really hard place to live sometimes. But then you look at all this," I said, gesturing at the rolling hills that surrounded our little valley, "and somehow the insane bureaucracy and endless bullshit seem worth it. Good neighbors certainly help."

"We've been looking for a place for years," Dean said, reaching in front of him to pull an olive leaf off a branch. He lifted it to his nose and sniffed, then let it fall to the ground. "Every time we got close to making a purchase, some dying grandma would miraculously recover and decide not to sell or the bank would cob up the paperwork."

"I lucked into my place, but I've heard plenty of horror stories from other expats."

"How'd you find your house?"

"I stayed with Porter for a few months and got to know his neighbors. When they moved, I was able to rent the house from them, and then I ended up buying it."

"How long have you two been together, anyway? Darren asked, but I didn't know."

"Me and Porter? Not so long, this time around. But we were engaged in college, so we knew each other before."

"I love that you live next door to each other instead of together. I told Darren one of you must be a slob. He's super messy and I'd love to not have to share a bathroom with him."

"Neither of us is particularly messy. It's just that after I got divorced, it was really important for me to be financially independent and have my own space. It worked out really well to live next door to Porter because I could be near him without the pressure of living with him. We were just friends then," I said. "Now we're just used to it."

"I'm sorry if we came off a bit nosy the other night," Dean said. "Sometimes we ask too many questions."

I knew what he was referring to. While I was dishing out pasta, Darren had asked whether Porter and I had any children. I'd frozen in place, then set the bowl on the table and walked out of the kitchen, leaving Porter to explain. When I came back, having gone upstairs to wash my face and spend several minutes holding onto the sink and taking deep breaths, the conversation had moved on to property taxes.

"It's okay," I said.

Dean patted my arm. "We're sorry about your daughter."

"Tour time!" Darren called from the house before I could respond.

The inside of Villa Rosmarino was in worse shape than I remembered. There were brown outlines of water damage on the ceiling and peeling plaster in almost every corner, plus wires protruding where light fixtures should have been in three of the rooms. The stove looked to be World War II era, complete with what may well have been bullet holes, and the tiny washing machine chugging in the corner of the kitchen emptied into a cracked sink and sounded like it was tumbling rocks. The only room that was actually put together was the bedroom, which had a large tribal-looking carpet on the floor and a sleigh bed against one wall.

"We're a work in progress," Darren said when we came back downstairs. "Obviously."

"There's great potential here," Porter said. "A little elbow grease and a few repairs and it will be great." He met my eyes and raised his eyebrows.

"Guys, I think we better get home," I said. "I've got some work to finish up."

We exchanged hugs. Porter promised to bring over the name of a stone mason he knew and invited Darren and Dean to come for dinner later in the week, and then we left.

"It's nice to have neighbors, huh?" I said when we were walking down the driveway.

"They don't have a clue how long it's going to take to get that place in shape. Or how much money," Porter said. "Some of that water damage looked pretty fresh. I wouldn't be surprised if the roof is still leaking." He sighed. "I should send Tomasso over to take a look. There's no use making any other repairs until that's fixed."

"I'm just glad we have nice neighbors. They'll figure out the house."

Porter was quiet until we were almost to the road, then he asked, "So how was Assisi?"

"Good," I said. "I got the pictures I needed and had lunch with Marco."

"You were gone a long time."

"Yeah, well, you know me and Assisi. I had to visit all my favorite places."

Porter took my hand as we turned into our driveway. When we got to my house, he gave my hand a gentle tug. "Spend the night?"

I shook my head. "I need to do some work and then I'm going to turn in early and read."

"Oh."

"Somebody wants his dinner," I said, pointing at Oliver, who was standing on the couch and barking. I wrapped my arms around Porter in a quick hug. "I'll see you in the morning, okay?"

He didn't let go when I tried to step backwards.

"Porter?" I said, laughing and pushing against his hips.

He let go and I turned away. I could feel him watching as I walked up to the house, so when I opened the front door, I turned around and waved. "Have a good night."

Porter started to walk away, then stopped. "Beth?" he called.

"Yeah?"

"We're okay, aren't we?" he asked. "I know we still need to talk about the whole Sloan thing, but we're okay, right?"

"Yeah, of course." I leaned down to pet Oliver, who had come running when I opened the door. I looked back up at Porter. "Get some sleep, okay? Everything's fine."

When I got inside, I fed Oliver, then poured myself a glass of water and sat down to read over the pagan church research. I still needed to think of how I wanted to shape what I'd learned about the conversion process into an article.

Of any European city, Rome had the most pagan temple conversions—eleven, including the Pantheon, which, in the seventh century, was given to the Catholic Church and renamed St. Mary of the Martyrs. Now it's back to being called the Pantheon, of course, although it does still function as a Catholic church when it's not full of tourists.

For decades, archaeologists who excavated the remnants of pagan temples in Italy maintained the idea that these sites—devoted to the gods of the Greeks—had been destroyed in violent demonstrations of Christian superiority. Reading their accounts, you get a vivid picture of sandal-stomping, sledgehammer-wielding, medieval Christian mobs marching across the Greco-Roman Empire, smashing pagan temples and erecting churches over the rubble while orchestral music swells, the gods weep, and a glowing white cross appears in the sky.

As usual, the truth was something else entirely.

It turns out that pagan temple conversion wasn't nearly as big a thing as those early archeologists imagined. Even in the fourth and fifth centuries, when Christianity was spreading like wildfire and churches were springing up everywhere, the pagan temples were largely left alone. No one seemed to feel the need to destroy them; in fact, in the fourth century, the Roman emperor issued an edict saying that while paganism should be wiped out, the temples should be allowed to stand.

After the Goths wreaked havoc across the Italian peninsula from 535 to 554 AD, however, many cities were left without the materials and manpower to build the new churches their citizens required. That's when the idea of converting pagan temples actually seemed to take hold—a matter of necessity and convenience more than religious fervor. Scholars now think that, as Christianity's popularity rose and the pagan temples fell out of use, some of the temples' building materials were carted off—a pillar for Giacomo's house here, some marble for Giuseppe's villa there—and what was left was fixed up to meet the demand for Christian churches. The whole process was a lot less about rampaging and a lot more about recycling.

I sat back in my chair and propped my feet on the desk, drinking San Pellegrino straight from the bottle. I still had to figure out how to frame up the piece. It made sense that the transition from pagan temples to Christian churches had been less of a radical redeployment than a gradual repurposing, but that wouldn't make for a very interesting magazine article.

My phone dinged and I pushed myself away from the desk and let the chair roll backwards until it bumped into the bookshelf behind me. I was surprised to see a WhatsApp message from Marco with no context, no greeting, and no punctuation. Just a string of words: *gira su via degli ulivi e percorre quasi un chilometro cerca una sedia di legno sotto un albero e gira a destra.*

The message made no sense and I figured Marco had sent it to me by mistake. He was probably arranging a rendezvous with his latest side piece.

I put the phone back on the bookshelf and decided to give the pagan church article a rest. I wandered into the bathroom and left my jeans and T-shirt in a pile on the floor, then stood in my underwear and squeezed toothpaste onto my toothbrush, steadily avoiding my reflection in the mirror.

As I was brushing my teeth, it dawned on me that what Marco had sent were actually directions to his hut in the olive grove. *Turn on the street of olives and go for almost a kilometer look for a wooden chair under a tree and turn right.* He knew, of course, that I had walked the road between Assisi and Spello several times and was very familiar with it, but he'd also correctly surmised that I wouldn't have noticed—as I held on for dear life on the back of his motorcycle—that the street into the groves was called Via degli Ulivi or that there was a wooden chair under the tree at the turn into the clearing.

I stopped brushing for a minute, my toothbrush poised in midair. Why was he sending me directions to his cabin?

I spit a mouthful of toothpaste froth into the sink, rinsed my toothbrush and mouth, then clicked off the bathroom light and got in bed to read. Oliver jumped up and stretched out beside me, his head on my arm.

I had no clue why Marco thought I needed those directions. He probably used the hut as a sex den, and I shuddered to think what I might walk in on if I actually went there.

Eleven

A few nights later, Double D and three of their Australian friends came over for dinner. Things had been weird between me and Porter for days. He had broached the topic of Sloan again mid-morning, when we were outside digging a channel to direct water away from a corner of the barn, but I hadn't been in the mood to talk about it and refused to be dragged into a conversation. I could tell Porter was annoyed because he started issuing orders in a really patronizing tone of voice, and after half an hour, I propped my shovel against the side of the barn and went home. About two hours before they were supposed to come over, I texted Porter that I really wasn't in the mood to host a dinner party, but he insisted it was too late to cancel.

We had vowed that this dinner would not be a repeat of the drinks debauchery, so I baked bread and made pappardelle with lemon, ricotta, and butter as the starter to go with the chicken piccata Porter was making, the idea being at least there would be food to soak up the wine if things went off the rails again. For dessert I made a tiramisu that turned out surprisingly well.

Dean, Darren, and their guests showed up at seven with two bottles of wine and a bouquet of flowers, plus a tray of cookies. It was chilly outside on the terrace and I thought about asking Porter to roll the heater out of the barn, but once the second bottle of wine was uncorked, I didn't feel the cold anymore, and no one else seemed to, either.

"Did you make the pasta?" Dean asked me, dragging the last of his noodles through the sauce on his plate.

I nodded. "It's easy. I just crank it through my little machine and let it dry."

"See?" he said, turning to Darren. "I told you we should have bought a pasta machine." He looked at me. "There was a gorgeous one at Williams Sonoma I wanted to ship over, but someone"—he jerked his chin in the direction of Darren—"said no."

"I'm sure they're easy to find here, Dean," Nicolette said. "Anyone can make pasta."

Nicolette was from Byron Bay and apparently made a living as some kind of social media influencer. When Porter asked her exactly what that meant, she said her life was aspirational to the people who followed her online.

"So you just post stuff about your life?" he asked. "And people are interested?"

"Her fabulous life!" Naomi, Nicolette's assistant, interjected. "Nicolette knows everyone and goes everywhere. She is an inspiration to women around the world."

The only thing I felt inspired to do was knock the phone out of her hand, but I kept that to myself. From the moment they'd arrived, Nicolette had been taking photographs of everything: Oliver, the house, the trees, the terrace, the food, and especially Porter.

"She never stops with that fucking camera," Dean had said before dinner, sidling up next to me and muttering so that only I could hear him. We were milling around the terrace, having a first glass of wine. Porter was gesturing towards the fields and giving everyone an abridged version of how he'd ended up living in Italy, and Nicolette was hanging on every word.

"She might want to ask Porter before she posts anything," I said. "He's a pretty private person."

"I don't think she knows the meaning of the word 'private.'"

"What's her angle?" I asked. "Why does anyone care about her life?"

Dean laughed. "Oh, girl. She's one of the Byron babes."

"I don't have a clue what that means."

"You know that place in Malibu where everyone lives in three-million-dollar Airstream trailers and eats organic food and talks about how down to Earth they are? That's the American version of Byron Bay. It's a beach community outside Sydney. Very hippie chic, but with gobs of money and gorgeous scenery. Everyone there is a candle maker or a chicken herder, and it's all on social media."

I rolled my eyes. "Sounds hideous. Her husband seems nice, though."

"Gus is a doll. I have never been able to figure out what he sees in her. I think he must be whipped," Dean said, then mimed cracking a whip. "You get my drift."

"I do indeed. What's Naomi's deal?"

"She has her nose so far up Nicolette's ass she can't even see. Personal assistant is her official title, but she's really just Nicolette's bitch."

I laughed. "Well, sit next to me at dinner. I may need more info."

"I'll sit on your lap," Dean said, clinking his wine glass against mine.

Dean wasn't sitting on my lap, but he was sitting so close

that I had to be careful my elbow didn't knock into him as I ate.

"Pasta machines are everywhere here," Porter said, "but you have to get a good one. Beth's is a Marcato something or other."

"Marcato Atlas," I said. "It's pretty reliable."

"Nicolette has a very nice pasta maker," Naomi said.

"No, I don't," Nicolette said, then turned to me. "I think it's nice that some women still cook," she said, baring her shockingly white teeth at me in what I assumed was meant to be a smile, "but we have a live-in who does all of that." She glanced at Naomi. "Maybe you meant Annisa has a pasta machine?"

"I gave you a pasta machine for your birthday," Naomi said to her lap.

"Poppet, don't lick the dish," Darren said to Dean. "Our new friends will think we're savages."

I handed Dean the basket of bread. "Here you go. I take it as a compliment."

Dean made concentric circles on his plate until he had a tiny lake of sauce in the middle, then dragged the bread through the sauce several times before shoving the whole thing into his mouth.

"That's called *fare la scarpetta*, what you're doing," Porter told him.

"What does that mean?" Nicolette asked.

"Making the little shoe. That's what it's called when you mop up sauce with a piece of bread," Porter said, shrugging. "I have no idea why."

Nicolette beamed like he'd just explained the origins of the universe. "Fascinating," she said, touching his arm. "It's so nice to meet someone so worldly and knowledgeable."

Porter gave her a quick smile that didn't touch his eyes, then stood up to refill everyone's wine glass. "So, Gus, what line of work are you in?" he asked as he poured.

"Private banking," Gus said. "But I'm going to retire as soon as possible."

"Where are you from?" I asked him. "I've been to Australia a couple times. It's so beautiful that you can almost forget that everything there will kill you."

Gus laughed. "I work in Sydney, live in Byron, but I was born and raised in Melbourne."

"I was born in Byron Bay," Nicolette told Porter, who looked confused about why he should care.

"I had a good friend from Melbourne," I said. "I've never been there, though."

"Ooh! Is there a handsome Aussie in your past?" Dean asked me. "Tell Uncle Dean everything."

"Just a good friend from graduate school."

"Maybe Gus knows him," Darren said.

"Yeah, right," I said, smiling. "You know how that is when you travel and somebody's like 'Oh, you're from New York—you must know John!'"

"I actually do know John from New York. I gave him a handy in the bathroom at CBGB!" Dean said, then cackled with laughter.

Darren reached across the table for Dean's wine glass. "Okay, we're going to drink some water now."

"Weren't the bathrooms at CBGB horrible?" Porter asked Dean. "You had to go while you were still sober; otherwise, you might accidentally touch something."

"I didn't know you were a New York club kid," I said, looking across the table at Porter.

"A surprise after all these years," he said, winking at me.

"Lots of them lately."

"Are you from New York?" Nicolette asked Porter.

He shook his head. "Richmond, Virginia. I had a summer internship in Manhattan one year and we went out a lot."

"What's your friend from Melbourne's name?" Gus asked me.

"Mac Martin. I don't remember what part of Melbourne he

lived in, but he went to an all-boys school that everyone called a castle."

"Melbourne High School," Gus said. "The castle on the hill. We played footy together, me and Mac."

"You can't be serious? You actually know him?"

Gus nodded. "I do. Saw him last year at our thirty-five-year reunion. We're on a group text, all the footy boys."

"Incredible," Nicolette said, beaming at Porter. She leaned toward him and put her hand on his leg. "Isn't it such a small world?"

"What's this about playing footsie?" Dean asked.

"Footy. Australian rules football," Darren said. "Keep your pants on."

Dean rolled his eyes and reached across the table for his wine glass, but Darren pulled it just out of his reach.

"I can't believe you know Mac! We used to be really close."

"Tell me you weren't one of his conquests?" Gus said.

"No, no. He was, uh, he was a friend of my, uh . . . He was a friend of a former friend of mine in Washington, and we went to grad school together at American University."

Porter shot me a look, his brow furrowed.

"Crawford's friend," I told him.

"Well, that clears it up," Nicolette said, rolling her eyes at me and turning back to Porter. "Is she always this mysterious? Who's Crawford?"

"I'm ready to make the chicken," Porter said, pushing his chair back and standing up. "Beth, will you help me bring in the dishes?"

I nodded and stood up and started gathering plates. Naomi and Darren both offered to help, but we told them to stay put. As we walked across the terrace toward the house, Porter whispered, "You okay?"

"Yeah, of course," I said, nodding. "That's incredible, though, isn't it? I mean, Mac was one of my best friends."

"I know."

"How can I help with the chicken?"

Porter held the door to the kitchen open for me. "I don't need help. I pounded the chicken earlier and everything's sliced. Lemons are juiced, capers are drained. All good in here."

"Should I come back to help carry the food out?"

Porter nodded. "Give me about fifteen minutes. You can go ahead and take clean plates now, though. I'll put it on a serving dish."

As I turned to leave the kitchen with a stack of dishes in my hands, I nearly collided with Nicolette.

"Oh, hi," I said. "Are you looking for the bathroom?"

She shook her head and held up her phone. "Nope. Just came in to get some shots of the chef in action." She craned her head inside, scanning the kitchen. "And maybe get a tour of the house from the owner?"

"Maybe later, huh?" Porter said. "I need to get dinner out the door."

Nicolette looked at me. "Gus is calling your friend."

"He's calling Mac?"

She nodded. "I told him I'd send you out."

Porter looked at me, his eyes widening briefly. "Go," he said. "I can handle things in here."

Gus was standing on the edge of the terrace shouting into the screen of his iPhone. When he saw me come out the kitchen door, he waved me over.

I set the stack of dishes on the table, my stomach in knots at the thought of seeing Mac's face again. I'd lost so many things when Crawford and I split up, but Mac and Hugh—Crawford's best friends from his undergrad days at Georgetown—were near the top of the losses I grieved. The four of us had been a tight quartet in Washington, DC during and after grad school; a 1990s version of *St. Elmo's Fire* minus the cocaine and saxophone. But they were Crawford's friends, and for the last four years, every time I thought of Mac or Hugh, I heard James Taylor singing "Her Town, Too," in my head, with that line that says, "She gets the house and the garden, he gets the boys in the band." I didn't care about not getting the house or the garden, but I definitely missed the boys in the band.

"Sorry, I don't know your last name," Gus said as I approached.

"Steeler. Beth Steeler."

"Right, mate, so I'm in Italy with someone you know," Gus shouted at the phone screen. "Beth Steeler. Does that ring any bells in your dense noggin?"

He turned the phone towards me so I could see Mac's expression. It was the Mac I remembered, a little bit rounder in the face and with almost completely gray hair, but the same mischievous grin and twinkling eyes.

I couldn't help it. I started sobbing.

"Am I that ugly?" Mac asked, laughing.

"No, the opposite," I said, wiping my eyes. Gus handed me the phone and walked away. "I'm really happy to see you. I've missed you so much, Mac."

"I've missed you too. Hugh and I both have. He'll be mad as a cut snake that he didn't get to talk to you."

I smiled and nodded, trying to stop the tears.

"But how do you know Gus?" Mac asked. "That's incredible. He was only a year ahead of me at school."

I wiped my eyes with my sleeve. "He's a friend of a friend. They came for dinner and when he said he was from Melbourne, I mentioned you. I can't believe this, Mac! It's so good to see your face."

I walked away from the terrace where Double D and Gus and Naomi were talking and leaned against Porter's car. I stayed on the phone with Mac for almost half an hour. He didn't mention Crawford or Mia's accident, which I was grateful for, and he didn't pry about my life; we mostly just grinned at each other like window-licking simpletons.

"Mac, I better let you go," I said finally, watching Porter come out the kitchen door bearing a tray of food. Nicolette was close on his heels, filming him with her phone. "They're putting food on the table and I'm being a terrible hostess."

"I'm absolutely rapt to see your face, beauty. Will you get my number from Gus and keep in touch?"

I nodded. "Definitely. And please give Hugh my love. Tell him I miss him."

"I'll ring him now and do it," Mac said. "Hey, before you go, I just want to say that me and Hugh were gutted by all the . . . by everything that happened. We didn't know, ya know, about Crawford." Mac made a face. "We're still mates, but he kept that secret from us too. Even from Hugh. That hurt."

I nodded. "Thanks, Mac. I appreciate that. I really love you guys, I hope you know that."

"Aw, don't have a sook, darling. No more tears. Old Mac is still devoted to you and if it doesn't work out with this Italian fellow, you know where to find me." He gestured behind him at the trappings of domestic life. "We'll do one of those Mormon arrangements. My old lady won't mind."

I was laughing and crying at the same time when we hung up. I wiped my eyes as best I could, took a few deep breaths, and went to join the others at the table. Porter looked up as I approached, and I nodded in response to his unasked question.

I tried to follow the conversation over dinner, but after talking to Mac, my mind was back at Vito's Pizzeria in Georgetown, a neighborhood spot Crawford and Mac and Hugh and I had treated as our personal flophouse and food trough for years. On this particular night, Mac had just been released from the hospital and we were celebrating with—what else?—pizza and beer.

"Want me to ask for scissors?" I asked Mac. Hugh was bent over Mac's extended arm, trying to remove the white plastic identification bracelet on his wrist with a pizza cutter. "It might be safer."

Mac shook his head. "Nah. I trust him." He reached up with his free hand and tousled Hugh's hair. "He saved my life."

"How could you not have known your appendix burst?" Crawford asked. "Weren't you in pain?"

Mac shrugged. "No more than usual. And I had something important to do."

"Something or someone?" I asked.

Hugh laughed. "Someone. Stacey."

"I thought her name was Tracy?" Crawford said. "The girl from the library? Her name is Tracy."

"It's actually Casey," Mac said. "And she's a lovely sheila."

"She must be, if you didn't even realize your insides were exploding," I said.

"He thought it was gas," Hugh told me. "He asked me to step on him, which usually works, but this time it didn't help at all. I took him to the doc-in-the-box and they called an ambulance."

"Wait. You step on him when he has gas?" Crawford asked. "What is wrong with you two?"

"They put the lights on and everything," Mac said proudly. "I said I was in agony, just like Hugh told me to, and got the good drugs."

"Tell them about your roommates," Hugh prompted, still sawing away at the hospital bracelet.

"After they picked all the pieces out of my gut, this bloke came in and pushed me up to a room," Mac said. "It's a nice way to travel, wheeled around in bed. I highly recommend it."

"Jesus Christ, Mac," Crawford said. "Did the doctor say why your appendix burst? Are you on antibiotics?"

"I go up to his room, and it's full of these huge, terrifying men," Hugh said, still bent over Mac's wrist. "They were all sitting around the other bed, where this enormous guy was propped up with—"

"Tyson, his name was. Like the fighter," Mac said.

"Tyson had been shot several times," Hugh said, pausing in

his efforts to free Mac's wrist. "Mac and I couldn't even hear ourselves talk because of all the *motherfucker* this and *motherfucker* that. The nurse kept coming in and—"

"He was a teddy bear, really," Mac said. "We talked later, when his friends left. He grew up in one of the states I didn't think was real—"

"Rhode Island," Hugh said, hacking away with the pizza cutter again.

I tried to think of how I was going to describe this injury to 9-1-1. *My friend's artery has been severed with a pizza cutter, but he'd like to finish his beer before the ambulance comes, so don't hurry. But please do turn the lights on and bring the good drugs.*

"I tried to call Mac's mom," Hugh said, "but I couldn't hear a thing."

"Mum would have loved Tyson's tattoos," Mac told us. "She's got a good friend who's aboriginal and he's got a—"

"One guy had his whole face covered," Hugh said, looking up at Mac. "Remember? He had that design on one side and on the other side was—"

"Is there a point to this story?" Crawford interrupted.

"They were making plans to murder the guy who shot Tyson and now Mac knows too much and needs to disappear," Hugh said. He tossed the pizza cutter onto the table, sat back in his chair, crossed his arms over his chest, and glared at Crawford. "Happy now, Counselor?"

I started laughing. "You're involved in gang warfare now, Mac?"

"You won't be laughing when I'm chopped to bits and tossed in the Potomac, love," Mac said. "You'll wish you'd given ol' Mac a chance."

"I suggested he go stay with the Feds at the Watergate," Hugh said, turning to Mac. "Mère adores you, and they won't squeal. I don't think they even know anyone in a gang."

"That would last about five minutes," I told Hugh. "I don't think your parents and Mac keep the same schedule."

"Hold up," Crawford said. "Let me get this straight, Hugh. You're not sure if your parents—two economists for the federal government—know anyone in a gang?"

"You can't be sure," Hugh said, shrugging. "Mère has a very diverse friend group."

"You're right," Mac said to me. "I'm a creature of the night. I'll come bunk with you, instead."

"In my twin bed?" I shook my head. "I think not. But Crawford's got a big place."

Crawford shook his head. "Nope. No gang warfare in my house."

"Some friend you are," Hugh said. "We'll both go to the Watergate." He bent down and tore the partially severed plastic bracelet apart with his teeth. "There," he said, handing it to Mac. "Run free, stallion."

The friendship between Mac, a black belt womanizer, and Hugh, a serial dater of frivolous men, had always fascinated me. They were completely devoted to each other and not at all shy about showing it. Mac once took a swing at a guy who called Hugh a faggot in a bar in Adams Morgan and had nearly been beaten to a pulp as a result. When I went to see him the next morning, he was totally unfazed by the whole thing, lying on the couch in Hugh's sunlight-filled apartment holding a bag of frozen Tater Tots to his face.

"Good grief, Mac," I said, trying to hide the shock I felt. One of his eyes was full of blood, giving him a creepy cyborg look, and his face was swollen in vivid shades of purple, blue, and yellow. "Did you really need to fight the guy?"

"Of course I did," Mac said. "That faggot's my best mate." He smiled up at Hugh, who had come into the room carrying a bag of frozen vegetables.

Hugh bent down and kissed Mac on the top of the head. "I'm going to cook the Tots for breakfast. You can use these instead," he said, dropping the bag of vegetables onto Mac's crotch and holding out his hand for the Tater Tots.

Crawford had always been a bit on the outside, the responsible adult to these two overgrown puppies. He acted as though their antics exasperated him, but I think he actually envied their closeness. And once I discovered the truth about Crawford's sexuality, I figured he must have also envied the way Hugh lived—honestly and openly—and the fact that the Feds accepted their gay son without reservation. Hugh was very close to both of his parents, sharing both his dating exploits and the contents of his mother's closet.

Crawford's parents, on the other hand, were like twin icebergs. When his father—whom we'd always called "Three" after the numbers behind his name—keeled over with a massive heart attack on the Bedford Hills golf course, I remember having the distinct impression that Crawford was relieved. It struck me then that had his parents been more concerned with their son's well-being and less consumed with their social standing, Crawford might have felt free to be honest about who he was, and both of our lives would have been very different.

The sound of Dean's water glass shattering on the stone table interrupted my thoughts.

I looked around.

Nicolette had her thin, tanned arm with its enormous stack of silver bangles draped across the back of Porter's chair and was speaking to him in a low murmur. Porter was turned towards her, his body angled so that their knees were touching, nodding as if they were sharing secrets. Darren was picking up pieces of broken glass, while Dean was taking advantage of the distraction he'd created to free his wine glass from captivity. Gus had his arms folded tightly across his chest and his head down and seemed to be snoring, and Naomi was watching Nicolette and Porter with a bizarrely intense stare.

"What do you think they're talking about?" I asked Dean, who had dropped back into his chair and was downing his wine in one gulp. I jerked my chin towards Porter and Nicolette.

Dean wiped the back of his mouth with his napkin, dropped it onto his lap, and yelled, "Nicolette! Nicolette!"

When she reluctantly dragged her eyes away from Porter's face and fixed them on Dean, he asked, "What are you two talking about that's so fascinating?"

"Porter is telling me about his daughter."

Porter sprang up and grabbed two empty wine bottles off the table. "I'm going to swap these out," he said, and started towards the kitchen.

"I'll help," Nicolette said, leaping to her feet and following him.

"I'm going to find the bathroom," Naomi said, and took off after Nicolette.

Darren had finished picking up the pieces of broken glass and piled them on his plate and was mopping up the spilled water with a dinner napkin.

Dean looked at me, his empty wine glass in midair. "I thought you guys didn't have kids?" he said. "I mean, I know you did, but I—"

"We don't," I said. "Porter does."

Dean started to speak again, but Darren cut him off.

"Dean, weren't you saying you wanted the recipe for those almond cookies?"

Dean cocked his head and looked at Darren for what seemed like a year before he recovered. "Oh, yes, I did say that." He turned to me. "Can I get the recipe from you?"

I nodded, suddenly too exhausted to speak.

I didn't want to watch Nicolette hit on Porter or Naomi obsess over Nicolette or Gus sleep at the table. I didn't want to hear Darren and Dean bicker. And I sure didn't want to talk about Porter's newfound daughter.

I just wanted to go home.

I thought about what Marco had said about the olive trees—about how they only concern themselves with the present moment—and about how often he had encouraged me to put myself and what I wanted first. "It is not possible to always be last in your own life," he'd told me on several occasions. "When children are small, yes, is necessary. But no more. Now you must change how you are thinking. Now you are first."

I looked down at Oliver, who was stretched out under the table, and poked him with my foot. Ollie looked up at me, tilting his head sideways and perking his ears.

"You ready to go, buddy?" I whispered.

I pushed my chair backwards and got up, telling Darren and Dean I needed to run home for a minute and feed Oliver. And then I walked away. Someone called my name, probably Dean, but I didn't look back.

When I got to my house, I filled Oliver's water bowl, brushed my teeth, and stretched out on the couch to watch TV. Oliver joined me, curling himself into the triangle of my bent legs and propping his head on my thigh so he could see the TV.

Next thing I knew, it was morning and Porter was standing in front of me.

Twelve

"Who gets up and leaves a dinner party they're hosting without saying a word?"

Porter was standing in front of the couch, his arms crossed and his face contorted with anger. Oliver was sitting next to him, pawing at his leg.

"Good morning," I said, yawning.

"I'm serious, Beth. Have you lost your mind? I told them you hadn't been feeling well, but they didn't leave for two more hours!"

"I'll come do the dishes," I said, pushing myself upright. "Let me just take a shower."

"I don't give a fuck about the dishes," Porter said. "We did them last night. I just want to know what's going on with you?"

"Did Nicolette get some great footage of you all soaped up?" I asked, then laughed—an abrupt snort that sounded almost as sarcastic as I'd intended. "That will make a great Instagram story, I'm sure."

Porter glared at me, then turned and went into the kitchen. I could hear him banging the Bialetti around as I went into my bedroom to grab some clothes. I carried them into the bathroom and turned on the taps, letting the water heat up while I brushed my teeth, then dropped my dirty clothes in a heap on the floor and stepped into the shower. The hot water felt amazing on my throbbing head, and I closed my eyes, letting the heat and steam bring me back to life.

I had to force myself to get out and dry off. When I'd dressed and combed my hair, I went into the kitchen. Porter was sitting at the kitchen table drinking coffee.

"On the stove," he said.

I poured myself a cup of coffee and joined him at the table.

"Let's start over," he said. "Good morning."

I nodded but didn't say anything.

"I was really surprised that you left last night."

"Yeah? How long did it take you to notice?"

"What's that supposed to mean?"

"Nothing. Just that you looked pretty occupied with Nicolette."

Porter rolled his eyes. "She's a pain in the ass."

I didn't answer. We sat in silence for several minutes until I finished my coffee and got up and opened the fridge. "I'm going to make myself some breakfast. Are you hungry?"

Porter shook his head.

He didn't say a word as I heated a small skillet, added olive oil, and laid two thick slices of bread in the pan. I dug in the kitchen drawer for the small metal ring I used for just this purpose and pressed it against each piece of bread, then removed the circles of bread I'd cut and tossed them to Oliver, who snapped them out of midair. I cracked an egg into each of the circles, then added salt and pepper and fresh parmesan and leaned against the counter while they cooked.

Porter looked up as I slid one of the toast and egg combos onto a plate and set it in front of him. "Thanks."

"Yep." I put the other piece of bread on a plate, grabbed two forks out of the drawer, and sat down across from him, sliding a fork toward him.

We ate in silence. When we were both finished, Porter grabbed the plates off the table and took them to the sink.

"Just leave them," I said.

He set the dishes down and turned to face me. "You know, nothing happened with Nicolette. And nothing was going to happen, either."

"Okay."

"So why did you leave?"

I considered how I might explain to Porter that throughout dinner, I'd sat looking at the scene in front of me—at Darren and Dean bickering because Dean once again had too much to drink; at Gus nodding off, oblivious to his wife hitting on Porter; at Nicolette and Porter's bodies angled towards each other, swapping confidences; at Naomi's unsettling interest in Nicolette—and all I'd been able to think about was how much I missed Mac and Hugh and how much I didn't want to be at that particular dinner party. And then it had dawned on me that I didn't have to be there. So I left.

"I was bored," I said, shrugging. "And tired."

"Oh, well then. By all means, get up and leave."

"What were you two talking about, anyway?" I asked, twisting the cap off a new bottle of San Pellegrino.

Porter's eyes shot around the room before meeting mine. "Sloan."

"I know that. She announced that to the table, remember?"

"She asked if I had kids and I told her about the situation with Sloan. That's it."

I pushed my chair back from the table. "Okay. Well, I guess we don't need to talk about it then. Nicolette has it all sorted."

"Where are you going?"

"For a walk," I said.

"I'm coming with you."

I thought about saying no, but instead I just grabbed Oliver's leash from the hook on the wall and clipped it to his collar. Oliver started spinning in wild circles, making the leash whip my legs.

"Good Lord, dog. You act like you've never gone for a walk before," I said, grabbing the end of the leash off the floor. "Calm down."

The three of us headed out. Oliver carried his leash in his mouth until we got close to the end of the driveway, then I took it from him. Without a word, we turned to the right, away from Villa Rosmarino. Porter had his fists stuffed in the pockets of his threadbare Carolina Soccer fleece and his irritation was palpable.

"I'm dying to hear what wise counsel Nicolette had about Sloan," I said.

Porter looked away from me. "She said I didn't owe Sloan anything. That the donation was done anonymously and should stay that way."

"It's a little late for that, isn't it? Sloan knows who you are."

"That doesn't mean she has the right to contact me."

"I thought you already agreed to another phone call?"

"I can un-agree."

I didn't respond immediately. We were walking at a pretty good clip along the shoulder of the road. Oliver strained against the leash, stopping to nose at things in the underbrush, and I had to constantly tug the leash to keep him moving.

"That seems kind of foolish," I said finally. "I think you want to meet her. And you should."

"I thought you didn't want to meet her?"

"We're not talking about me. She's your daughter, not mine."

"So you won't meet her if I decide to?"

I shrugged. "I'm not involved in this."

Porter shot me a withering look. "Oh, right. I forgot. Little Miss Independent will do her own thing, and everyone else can go to hell."

"I have to be independent, Porter! It's not a choice. I've had my life turned upside down several times, you know, and it's taken me years to recover. I can't afford to let that happen again."

"Try to hear me when I say this, Beth," Porter spat. "I am not Crawford Campbell."

"I know that."

"So stop treating me like I am."

We came to a small path that led into a grove of olive trees. Porter turned right and I reluctantly followed him. After a few minutes of walking, he bent down and unclipped Oliver's leash from his collar, then took the leash from me.

"I'm not going to let this girl mess up my life," he said, slinging the leash over his shoulder. "I told you that."

"Okay."

"And there was nothing going on with me and Nicolette last night. I couldn't care less if I ever see her and her stupid phone again. She's obnoxious."

"Then why the hell did you talk to her about something so personal?"

"Like you don't tell Marco everything?" Porter snapped.

"That's ridiculous. And even if I did, it's totally different. I actually *know* Marco. He's my friend, not some random stranger I met five minutes ago."

We walked in silence for a few minutes.

"I wish I'd never done it, you know," Porter said. "The donation, I mean. I wouldn't have done it if I'd thought for a second it wouldn't be anonymous."

"I still don't get why you did it."

"I told you. I needed the money."

"Um hmm." I glanced at him. "Something about that just doesn't make sense and I'm having a hard time figuring out what you're not telling me."

"What difference does it make why I did it? It's done. Now I have to deal with the consequences."

I nodded. "That's true. But I have to deal with them too, don't I? And it would help if I didn't feel like I was being made a fool of right out of the gate."

Porter sighed. "How long am I going to have to pay for Crawford's lies?"

"This has nothing to do with Crawford. I know you, Porter. I know when you're dissembling. I know when you're being evasive. You can't expect me to get involved when my gut is telling me that you're hiding something."

We walked for a few more minutes, not speaking, then Porter whistled for Oliver, who came bounding out of the trees. Porter clicked the leash onto his collar and handed it back to me.

"I've got things I need to do today," he said. "I'm going to head back."

He turned and walked back towards the road.

I watched him go for a second, then turned and kept going in the other direction.

Away from Porter. Away from home.

Thirteen

When Oliver and I finally got back, it was early afternoon. I hadn't intended to stay out that long, but the more we walked, the better I felt, so we just kept going until we got to the olive mill, then I made myself turn around.

Oliver stood panting in the kitchen while I filled his water bowl and set it in front of him. I got myself a glass of water and leaned against the counter to drink it while Ollie submerged his whole snout into his bowl and blew bubbles. He lapped half the water down, then raised his head, water dripping from his chin, and looked at me with his head tilted and his ears up.

"What is it, buddy?"

He put his foot in his empty food bowl.

"Oh my God, Oliver! I'm so sorry, pup. You didn't have any breakfast, poor baby."

I filled his bowl with kibble and set it on the floor in front of him. Oliver ate it all in about three bites, then stood looking at me, licking crumbs off his whiskers.

"Still hungry, huh?"

In the refrigerator there was a hunk of mortadella Porter had brought over one night when we were watching a movie at my place. I pulled it out of the fridge, unwrapped the wax paper it was in, sniffed it twice to make sure it wasn't rancid, then got a knife out and cut off hunks, tossing them to Oliver. When it was gone, I chucked the wax paper in the trash, washed my hands, and told Oliver that was all. He belched, sighed, and stretched himself out on the tile floor for a nap.

I grabbed my phone off the bookshelf and turned it on. Marco had sent a photo from Rocca Maggiore, the castle where the tourism group was planning to stage part of the show about the life of Saint Francis.

David had sent a message too. *Call me when you're free to talk, kiddo.*

I sat down on the floor next to Oliver, my back against the kitchen cabinets, and called David. He answered on the second ring.

"Hi. Let's switch to video," he said.

"Okay, but I'm a sweaty mess."

He smiled broadly as the cameras on our phones connected. "There you are! You're not a mess at all. How are you, kid?"

"I'm good. How about you?"

"Hi, Oliver."

Ollie thumped his tail on the floor and put his head on my leg so he could look at the phone.

"We just went for a long walk," I said.

"Anything new on the surprise offspring front?" David asked. "I started to write you more about it and then I thought it would be easier to call."

I shook my head. "Not really. Porter's kind of all over the

place. He was going to talk to her again, but now he's apparently decided not to," I said, shrugging. "The whole thing makes me nauseous. And Porter and I just keep fighting, which is horrible. I don't even know what to say about it all."

David nodded. "We can talk about it when you're ready."

"The only other news on this end is that we have new neighbors," I said, then gave him a quick rundown on Dean and Darren. I left out the dinner with Gus and Nicolette and Naomi. "How about you? How's retired life?"

"Ah, it's fine. I'm teaching a class at a church in Durham that's going well—very intelligent and engaged congregation—and I'm still running the book club at my old parish. We're reading *Revelations of Divine Love* at the moment. Julian of Norwich."

"'All shall be well and all manner of things shall be well.' That's all I remember about her, other than she compared the universe to a walnut or something."

"A hazelnut, but very good. I'm going back out to the coast to do an interim gig in a couple of months, but there's nothing much else on the horizon. A few repairs around the house. I've got to replace some of the fascia board where the gutter came loose."

"Are you still going to come visit?"

"Yes, I wanted to talk to you about that. I was thinking late spring, before the crowds come?"

"That would be great!"

"I thought maybe if you could arrange your schedule and Porter didn't mind too much, I could steal you for a bit of traveling? I'd like to go to Belgium and the Netherlands. I want to see Bruges, and I also want to go to Ghent and see the Mystic Lamb altarpiece. It would be a lot more fun with you."

"Absolutely! Oh, this makes me so happy, David. I'd love to do that."

"I've had a rather sharp reminder that I need to do these things before it's too late. Do you remember Neil Roberts over at Duke? Good friend of mine, New Testament scholar?"

I nodded. "He came for dinner and the electricity went out, right?"

"That was Neil," David said, nodding. "I went to his retirement party a couple weeks ago. He stayed on for the summer to finish the book he was working on, so they waited until the fall semester was in swing and his colleagues were back on campus to throw him a lovely retirement party. Lots of champagne and fond memories," he said, smiling. "Neil said he was finally going to travel. He'd always wanted to, but with Betty being ill for so long and the demands of his teaching schedule, it just hadn't happened. Now he had his tickets booked, some new luggage, and he was finally getting on a plane."

"Oh God, David. What are you about to tell me?"

"He went to bed that night and died of a massive heart attack."

"No!" I said, clapping my hand over my mouth. "Oh, that's awful. I'm so sorry. I know how much you loved him."

David sighed. "I did. He was a scholar and a gentleman, cut from a cloth they just don't make anymore. But the point is, that's a really common story. Don't wait for your life to start, kiddo. We spend our lives worrying about things that won't matter in five weeks, much less five years. Stop worrying and start living, that's the lesson today. And when the chance to have fun comes along, grab it by the balls."

I laughed out loud. "Did you really just say balls to me?"

He smiled. "I'm losing my filter in my old age."

"I like it. And your advice is duly noted," I said. "Fun seems to be in short supply around here lately."

"You're too old for me to tell you what to do, but I would suggest you find a way to make peace with Porter and start enjoying your life again as soon as possible. Life is short, kiddo, and most of the battles we fight never needed to be fought in the first place. Make every day above ground a good day."

Oliver was on my heels as I pulled on a jacket and left the house to find Porter a little while later.

I'd been pondering David's advice, and I knew he was right. I needed to extend an olive branch to Porter so we could reach a consensus on how to move forward. My plan was to apologize and go from there; together, we'd figure out what to do about Sloan.

Oliver and I walked down my driveway until it merged with the cypress-lined lane, and then we turned towards Porter's house. The sun was starting to go down and the valley was bathed in golden light. Porter's car was next to the barn, so I figured that's where he was, but when I went inside to look, there was no sign of him.

I walked over to the house and stuck my head in the kitchen door and hollered for Porter while Oliver checked his food bowl, but he wasn't there, either, so we headed out to the fields. I didn't hear the tractor, but I figured he must be weeding or something. I was being careful not to step on any of the newly planted vegetables and herbs, so it wasn't until I was midway across the field that I looked up towards Villa Rosmarino. Porter was standing in the rows of rosemary bushes the house was named for. About two inches in front of him, with her manicured hand resting on his midsection, was Nicolette.

I stopped in my tracks. Porter was talking to Nicolette intently, his head bent toward hers. She answered him and moved her hand up to rub his bicep. He nodded and began talking again.

Oliver got tired of sniffing the plants and looked around. He caught sight of Porter and took off galloping towards him. The movement must have caught Porter's eye because he turned to look and saw me. He immediately stepped away from Nicolette and waved.

I couldn't hear what he said, but I saw Nicolette throw her head back and laugh in response. She patted his shoulder as if to console him, then turned and headed back to the house as Porter began walking towards me.

I froze for a second, then turned and walked as fast as I could, cutting diagonally across the field toward my house, not caring what plants I trampled. When I got to the house, I banged open the front door, snatched my car keys and purse off the table in the entryway, and went back out to my car.

Porter jogged up as I slid behind the wheel.

"Where are you going?"

"What difference does it make?"

I closed the car door, cranked the engine, and took off.

I didn't know where I was going, but I knew if I didn't get out of there, I was going to say something I'd regret.

Fourteen

I didn't intend to see Marco; in fact, I hadn't planned on going to Assisi at all. I just drove blindly, wanting to get away from Porter. It was only when I saw a sign for Perugia and noticed I was passing the stores that lined the autostrada to Assisi—the cashmere outlet, Leroy Merlin, the pottery store, the gas station I always went to—that I realized where I was headed.

I was driving on autopilot, but as I passed through Saint Mary of the Angels, rather than heading up the mountain to the historical center of Assisi like I usually would, I made a right turn toward Spello. And then, as if guided by some internal compass, I took a left on Via degli Ulivi without even having to look for it. Branches scraped the sides of the Panda on the narrow track and my wheels spun a few times in the dirt, but I downshifted and kept going up until I spotted the wooden chair Marco had mentioned and made a hard right into the trees. Still not really thinking about what I was doing, I shut the car off, went inside Marco's hut to retrieve the blanket from the wooden crate, and spread it out on the ground in front of the hut, just as he had done. Then I leaned back against the stones and closed my eyes. I needed peace and quiet so I could think.

Less than an hour later, I heard a motorcycle coming up the lane. I figured it was someone out joyriding, so I went inside the hut, hoping that whoever it was would keep going. But the motorcycle turned into the clearing, and then Marco was off the bike, helmet in hand, grinning and waving.

"*Ciao, cara*!" he shouted.

He didn't press me about why I was there or act like it was strange at all, and just shrugged when I apologized for intruding.

"Is why I tell you how to come here."

"Shouldn't you be home for dinner?"

"Vittoria stay at the house of her sister in Fano, near the sea," Marco explained. "Is no sport tonight, so I think I will come here and talk to the trees, smoke a little, relax."

"Do you want me to go? I know you weren't expecting company."

Marco shook his head. "No. Is beautiful to find you here." He slung his backpack off his shoulder and laid it on the blanket, then knelt beside it to unpack cigarettes, bread, cheese, sausage, wine, olive oil, matches, a small plate, and a paring knife. "We make picnic."

"No, it's okay. I know you didn't plan on sharing your meal."

Marco stopped what he was doing and looked at me. "Why you say this? We share everything—gelato, pasta, even toilet. Tonight we share picnic."

While he sliced the cheese and sausage, Marco updated me on the various people I'd met while I was working on the tourism project.

"Did I tell you about Pepe Bear?" he asked.

Pepe was the caretaker for an estate on the edge of Assisi. We called him Pepe Bear because the first time I met him, Pepe was standing on a ladder, clipping vines off the top of a stone wall. He didn't have a shirt on and was sweating profusely through his copious body hair and I'd stopped short and gasped, thinking I was looking at an actual bear. Marco, of course, found this hilarious.

"He go in hospital for *chirurgia* on his *fianco*," Marco said, patting his right hip. "They make for him a new one."

"Hip replacement surgery."

"Yes. Now he can walk, but only like this." He jumped to his feet and lurched around the clearing. "Like a drunk."

"But he's okay?"

Marco nodded. "I take him to hospital. We pack all what he need—bear pajamas, book about bears, telephone for calling other bears, olive oil."

"He took olive oil to the hospital?"

"Yes, of course," Marco said. "Olive oil in hospital will kill you."

He rejoined me on the blanket, lit up a cigarette, and told me about a friend of his who had a drone and was convinced there were medieval buildings buried outside the walls of Assisi. He was continuously hounding Marco to come dig with him after midnight, when they wouldn't be seen by the authorities.

"I say to him, what I am?" Marco said, handing me the cigarette. "A dog who look for a bone? No, I do not go to dig in the dark. But he ask me in continuous."

I took a deep drag, trying to remember the last time I'd smoked a cigarette. Porter and I occasionally smoked a joint that he got from a farmer down the road, but I couldn't remember the last time I'd had a cigarette.

Marco took the cigarette from my outstretched hand and let it dangle from his lips as he uncorked the bottle of wine.

"Tell me, *cara*, do you remember when we go on the raft at Norcia?"

I nodded and started to laugh. I remembered the rafting trip in Norcia very clearly for several reasons, the primary one being I'd honestly thought I was going to die.

Marco and I had gone to Spoleto to visit an archeological museum, and then we'd continued on to Ferentillo to see the mummies that were preserved in the bottom of a church there. Afterward, we wound our way on twisty mountain roads to a little camp where a rafting company had their base. We changed into the wetsuits they gave us and joined four other people for what was supposed to be a pleasant rafting trip down the Corno River.

Along with me and Marco, there was a German couple on the raft, plus a beautiful brother-sister pair from the States. The guide, who was from Peru, seemed terribly annoyed that there were so many non-Italians on the trip, but it's not like it mattered: he was totally incompetent, barking out instructions in grammatically incorrect Italian that made Marco wince and sent the boat careening into rocks and spinning wildly in a whirlpool. When the brother of the sibling duo mentioned he'd been a lifeguard, I felt slightly better about our chances of survival, but my relief didn't last long.

Marco and I were sitting in the very front of the raft, and towards the end of the trip, when Marco was ready to strangle the guide and I was eagerly anticipating dry land, we got caught in a current and pushed straight over the wall of a dam with absolutely no warning. The German couple began screaming and the brother grabbed his sister and held on to her as the nose of the raft, with me and Marco in it, plunged directly into the water below.

It felt like hitting concrete. Marco flew backward over the side of the raft. His paddle went airborne and missed knocking out my teeth by a fraction of an inch. I dropped my own paddle and grabbed Marco's legs and held on for dear life until he was able to contort himself back into the raft, the top half of him soaking wet and all of him cursing furiously. When we got far enough downstream to meet up with his paddle, Marco refused to lean out and pick it up, telling the guide that if he wanted the fucking paddle, he could get it himself—and shove it up his ass while he was at it.

After the rafting trip, when we'd dried off and put on warm clothes, Marco and I drove into the town of Norcia, which had been totally decimated by back-to-back earthquakes in 2016. Rebuilding was a slow process, and there hadn't been much to see in the town center except for the altar cross of the beautiful medieval cathedral of St. Benedict, which was the only thing left standing after the 6.2 and 6.6 quakes.

After deciding we needed to eat before we argued any more about what it meant that the cross was spared—Marco insisted it was a fluke, which I said was a ridiculously cynical stance for someone from the same town as Saint Francis—we found a little taverna and sat down for lunch and a bottle of wine.

When we finished eating, the waitress, who'd been a frequent visitor to our table since the minute she clapped eyes on Marco, delivered a bottle of *amaro francescano*—a type of herbal after-dinner drink I absolutely loved—with a smile she directed only at him.

Marco chatted with her for a minute, and when she left the table, he asked me, "Did you understand her? We drink this for free."

"Oh, that's nice."

"Is because she want me badly," he said, shrugging. "She make me drunk and kill you, then she have me. This is her plan."

"Well, in that case," I said, shoving the tray that held the bottle of amaro and two small glasses toward him, "let me go out with a bang." I was exhausted from the raft ride and already pleasantly buzzed from the wine, but amaro was a treat I wasn't going to pass up.

"I tell her we almost die on this raft," Marco said, filling the little tulip-shaped glasses to the rim. "She say is terrible, this guide, and bring this as a gift." He pushed one of the glasses across the table towards me, leaving a trail of spilled liquor, and lifted the other glass, sending a stream of amaro down his hand. "*Salute, mia cara*!"

We both tilted our heads back, downed the amaro, and set the glasses back on the table.

"Amaro is medicine, you know," Marco said, wiping his mouth. "Is made from the bush of Saint Francis."

"You mean it's herbal," I said, starting to laugh. "It's not made from his bush."

"You are wrong," Marco said, shaking his head. "Amaro come from the bush of Saint Francis. He grow a big bush and say to other monks, 'Look at my bush! I make a drink from it for you, is something very special!'"

"No, no," I said, gripping the edge of the table to stay upright as tears of laughter ran down my face. "A bush is something different."

"Why you say this? Bush is where we go to see the nature and smell the nature smells," Marco said. "Next to Basilica of Saint Francis is his bush."

I was practically hysterical at that point, laughing so hard I was wheezing. "Do you mean the *Bosco di San Francesco*?" I managed.

Marco nodded. "*Sì*. The bush of Saint Francis."

"The forest! It's the forest of Saint Francis!" I wiped my eyes with the hem of my shirt. "Oh my God, I think I'm going to be sick. My ribs hurt."

"Drink the bush drink. It make you healthy. Then explain me why you laugh."

I leaned across the table and whispered, "A bush is the hair above your *cazzo*. Australians call rural areas the bush, but for us it's something totally different."

After a minute, Marco started to laugh. "I understand now. I do not want to drink from the bush of Saint Francis."

"No," I said, dabbing the tears out of my eyes. "Me either."

Once I'd pulled myself together, Marco leaned across the table and whispered, "Do not look, but this girl watch you very hard. She try to kill you when I go make *pipi*."

"That seems to be a common theme today, people trying to kill me."

"She is very . . . *civettuola*. How you say this? Like when a woman talk to you and think you are beautiful?"

"Flirtatious?"

"*Sì*. She tell me would be terrible if I die and is very shocking for her, this story. She say I should kill this guide."

"Maybe she's just being nice?"

"No." Marco shook his head. "She want me bad."

"I want to murder this fucking guy that day," Marco said, leaning back against the stone wall of the hut and exhaling a plume of cigarette smoke into the air. "I think he never guide a boat before in his life."

"I've never seen you that angry. You were scary."

"Is because he almost hurt you badly." Marco shook his head. "We go tonight and murder him. Did you bring your *lupara*, Apollonia?"

I smiled at him and took the cigarette he extended. "Nobody's called me that in a long time."

"Was first thing I tell you when we meet. I am Michael Corleone for you and you are Apollonia for me."

"I remember," I said, exhaling a stream of smoke. "But no, sorry, I forgot to bring my *lupara*. I didn't bring any gun at all."

Marco snorted. "You never have gun with you. I start to think you are not really American."

Marco was digging in his backpack as we laughed about the rafting adventure and the drunken lunch afterwards. He pulled a sweatshirt out of the bag and handed it to me, then extracted a second bottle of wine, which he held up triumphantly.

"The waitress in Norcia, was necessary I tell her a lie to protect you," he said. "You remember? I defend you like a soldier in all situations."

"Except for almost taking my face off with a paddle," I said, shucking off my jacket. I pulled the sweatshirt over my head then put my jacket back on and repositioned myself against the wall of the hut, shaking my head at the cigarette Marco offered.

"Was a surprise, this dam," Marco said. "Not a good surprise like when you kiss me." He stood up. "Wait here. I get a light."

I'd surprised myself too, by kissing Marco that day in Norcia.

Most of the time, his claims about being the object of female lust were just to make me laugh. He was relentless about it, declaring that every woman we saw, even the nuns, were dying to go to bed with him. But the waitress at the taverna in Norcia really had been flirting with him. By the time we were finished eating, she had come to our table so many times that we'd both grown annoyed with her. She hovered nearby the whole time we were drinking the amaro, then came back to the table to chat with Marco as soon as I got up to use the bathroom.

When I teetered back to the table, she didn't budge, so I tried to tune into their conversation. I didn't catch much of what she was saying, but I did understand when she asked Marco who I was and Marco told her I was his cousin from America. Then he widened his eyes and gave me an SOS look.

I wobbled to my feet, leaned over the table, and put my hands on either side of Marco's face. "It's so good to see you again, cousin," I said in Italian, then planted a long kiss on his lips.

The look of confusion on the waitress's face before she turned away had been well worth it, but Marco's face was even better. His expression transformed several times in the span of a few seconds, reminding me of the language learning worksheets I'd done where you had to match different facial expressions to the corresponding emotions.

How does Marco feel? *Come si sente Marco?*
Marco is shocked. *Marco è scioccato.*
Marco is delighted. *Marco è incantato.*
Marco is laughing. *Marco sta ridendo.*

My ploy seemed to work because the waitress backed off. We paid the bill and left the restaurant soon afterward and walked back through the center of Norcia arm in arm. As we crossed the main piazza, Marco grabbed my hand and pulled me into an alleyway and kissed me, hard. Then he caressed my cheek, said, "*Terrò sempre nel mio cuore il ricordo di oggi.*" I spent the rest of the day trying to ignore the electric shock that had buzzed through me with both kisses, and then, in an unspoken agreement, Marco and I both acted as though none of it had ever happened and never spoke of it again. Until now, anyway.

"You surprise me with this kiss," Marco said, showing me the candle he'd retrieved from inside the hut. He resettled himself next to me on the blanket and lit the candle, dripping wax onto the small plate and setting the candle upright in the melted wax. When the candle was secure, he leaned back against the wall of the hut and took a swig from the bottle of wine. "This is when I know you love me too."

"It was totally worth it to see the waitress's reaction," I said, pulling the sleeves of his sweatshirt down over my hands. It wasn't cold, exactly, but there was a definite chill in the air now that it was dark. I could smell a woodfire burning somewhere nearby. "That's what I remember—the look on her face."

"I remember everything about that day," he said. "Is why I tell you I will keep the memory in my heart always. Remember I say this to you?"

I nodded and leaned against his arm. "You said that in the alley. That was a crazy day. Everything about it is burned in my memory."

"Is because we almost die. When you almost die, it make you know what is important to you."

By the time we reached the bottom of the second bottle of wine, laughing about all of the crazy adventures we'd had together, I was desperate to pee. Marco's hut didn't have a bathroom and I couldn't put it off any longer, so I told Marco, thinking we would have to drive into town and find a bar that was open somewhere—which would have the added benefit of a cup of coffee. But instead, Marco popped up, went inside the hut, and returned with a packet of tissues.

"Come," he said, extending his hand to help me up. "We make water for the trees."

The faint glow of the moon offered a bit of light in the clearing, but as soon as we stepped into the olive trees, it was pitch black. I tripped over a tree root immediately and started laughing.

Marco grabbed my elbow. "Why you are laughing? I think you are a little crazy tonight," he said, guiding me deeper into the trees. Finally he stopped in a small patch of moonlight and handed me the tissues. "I make *pipi* here too, to protect you."

"What are you protecting me from?"

"Angry Japanese. Wolves."

I don't know if it was the absurdity of being in an olive grove with Marco in the middle of the night, the two bottles of wine, the memories we'd unearthed, the way Marco said "wolves"—*woofs*—or the fact that he sounded like a Clydesdale peeing, but I started laughing again and couldn't stop, not even when I began tipping over.

"No, no! Here is not Pisa," Marco yelled. "You cannot lean!"

He took a few steps towards me, his jeans hanging open, and reached for my arms. I was laughing so hard that I didn't have the strength to right myself or form words, and simply pointed to Marco's open zipper.

"I know," he said, letting go of me with one hand to tug his T-shirt over his privates. "He is like a snake. *Un pitone.* I don't know how you call this in English. But he don't bite."

"A python," I said, howling with laughter. Then I toppled onto the ground.

Marco managed to find the packet of tissues I'd dropped. He held onto my hands to steady me, then hauled me to my feet and held my elbow as I pulled my underwear and jeans back up. Then Marco zipped up, shoved his T-shirt into his jeans, and guided me back to the blanket.

At some point I must have fallen asleep, because my phone buzzing in the pocket of my jeans woke me up. I blinked, momentarily wondering where I was, then lifted my hips to pull the phone out of my back pocket. I read the email that had just come in through blurry eyes.

Beth,

It's 3:00 in the morning and I would love to know where you are.

Nicolette was asking me about the property—they want to buy a place. Trust me, I did everything I could to dissuade her. Then she asked me what kind of workouts I do—fitness is part of her lifestyle bullshit—and I said just working around the house. She said she didn't believe me, that I was too muscular. That's what you saw. Nothing more.

When we were walking this afternoon, you said there was something about the sperm donation story that didn't sit right with you, about my needing money. You were right.

First, I want to tell you that I have never, not one time, thought about being with someone else since you came back to Italy. And when we were together in college, I never cheated. But when you left for grad school and things started to get really fucked up on my end, I couldn't stand going home to an empty house. I stayed at the bar after work, went out with the kitchen crew, drank and smoked weed and acted like a moron. I've told you all that. And after we broke up, I went to a party and Kick was there.

We hooked up a few times. It was a distraction, that's all. But she wanted a relationship. I didn't and told her so. I thought that was it until I came out of work about a month later and found her leaning against my Jeep. She told me she was pregnant.

I asked her what she planned to do. She asked if I cared about her or was still hung up on you. I had the distinct feeling that if I said I still loved you, she would have kept that baby out of spite. She was always so fucking competitive with you. So I said you and I were done, which was true. I told her I liked her a lot, which was a lie, but I didn't want kids. Which I didn't—not with her, anyway. She told me she would need $480 to take care of it.

I didn't have $48, much less $480, thanks to booze and pot. Plus I'd locked myself out of the house a few days before and smashed the window to get in, which cost several hundred dollars to fix. I asked a couple guys at the restaurant for a loan, but they were just as broke as I was. One of them made a joke about selling plasma and I thought, there's my solution—I'll donate sperm. I didn't drink or smoke for the next couple days, and then I went in and did it. Two days later, I did it again. And twice the following week.

That's why I needed money. To get rid of Kick. It may have all been a lie, her saying she was pregnant. I didn't even care. I just wanted her gone. And now here we are in this clusterfuck.

All this shit with Sloan . . .I can't stand it. I don't know what the fuck I'm supposed to do about her. You keep saying we'll figure it out, but all we do is fight.
Porter

"Who send you a message so late in the night?" Marco asked, yawning. "Is a man?"

I shook my head and put the phone back in my pocket. "It doesn't matter."

"Okay. You don't have to say." He used his free hand to scratch his leg. "I am happy you like my *rifugio*. Was nice to find you here."

After reading Porter's email, I was wide awake. I did not want to think about what he had written because even though it had happened decades ago, the idea of Porter and Kick in bed together made me nauseous, not to mention furious. I felt like I had been dropped into a soap opera I did not want to watch, much less participate in. So when Marco suggested we take a little trip and extended his hand to me, I was more than happy to let him pull me up off the blanket.

We took the empty wine bottles and the blanket inside, packed the olive oil and leftover food into his backpack, and then went out to the motorcycle. He picked up the helmet and started to hand it to me, then said, "Maybe we take your car. What do you think?"

I shook my head. "No way. That's boring."

Marco popped the helmet onto my head and leaned forward to fasten the strap under my chin.

"So, where are we going?" I asked.

"Is someplace you know. Get on. I hold for you."

Once we were both on the bike, I wrapped my arms around Marco's body and leaned my head against his back. He patted my hands and started the engine.

We went fairly slowly down the narrow dirt path, but once

we turned onto the deserted paved road, Marco sped up. Soon we were headed up the mountain and circling the roundabout near the *Tigré* where I used to buy my groceries. But rather than passing through the stone arch to enter the historic center of Assisi, we took the road that arced to the right, then swerved to the left and headed uphill. We passed the Nun Spa, where I'd spent my fiftieth birthday alone in a swimming pool that used to be a Roman bath, then we went through the wall that marked the outer boundary of the historical center and joined the winding road that snaked up the side of Mount Subasio.

Suddenly, I knew exactly where we were going.

Once we were high up, Marco turned onto a one-lane dirt track and began cutting across the face of the mountain. We rode as far as we could, but the bike kept wobbling and threatening to dump us in the dirt, so we parked the motorcycle in the trees, left the helmet on the seat, and started to walk.

I squinted at my watch as I followed behind Marco, holding onto the back of his shirt. It was almost four thirty in the morning. There was no light as the path passed under a thicket of trees, but once we entered the meadow, the landscape was illuminated by moon and starlight.

The path widened and Marco reached behind him, grabbed my hand, and pulled me up to walk alongside him. With his hand firmly wrapped around mine, we crossed the meadow in silence and trudged up the steep incline on the other side. Both of us were breathing heavily as we stepped into an expanse of rocky terrain.

Marco squeezed my hand and looked at me. "*Ti ricordi?*" he asked.

"Of course I remember."

Marco had brought me here, to the enormous cross that looms over Assisi on the edge of Mount Subasio, when I was working on the tourism project and trying to figure out how my life had fallen apart so completely in such a short time. I'd sat on a rock that day and opened the book in the box at the base of the cross and read the entries that pilgrims walking The Way of Saint Francis had left behind, all of their prayers and hopes for peace, and I'd wondered whether that peace would ever be available to me. In the years since, I'd come back to this place a million times in my mind.

We picked our way carefully across the rocky terrain to a boulder at the base of the cross and settled ourselves on top of it. Marco put his arm around my shoulders and I leaned my head against his chest.

"Tell me something you want, *cara*," he said after a few minutes.

"To be happy and have a calm life."

He kissed the top of my head. "Yes, I understand. But something more small. One thing you want to do."

"More specific? Hmm." I thought for a minute. "I really love being awake in a city when everyone else is asleep. The first time I ever saw Vienna, it was about three in the morning. There was no one else around and it was just magical. That's something that makes me very happy—being out in a new place in the middle of the night."

"I understand."

"When I travel, I always try to go out before the city wakes up. I've done it all over the world but never here in Italy; I don't know why."

"And where you want to do this? Milano? Roma?"

"Rome. I want to ride on the back of a motorcycle through Rome while everyone else is asleep."

Marco nodded. "Would be very nice to do this together." He checked his watch. "Soon the sun will be born behind us, in Nocera Umbra. Watch how the whole valley become light."

We sat quietly as the sun rose and light crept across the mountain as if a blanket were being pulled back. The rock-strewn landscape behind us was illuminated first, then the cross and the cliff edge in front of us, then the tower of Saint Clare below us, the Basilica of Saint Francis at the far end of Assisi, and finally Saint Mary of the Angels and the valley beyond.

"It's so beautiful." I sighed. "Thank you for hanging out with me all night and bringing me here."

"Was a wonderful night," Marco said. "Now we get a coffee, then is time for real life again." He looked down at me. "I am sorry about this. I would like to stay with you all day but is not possible."

We had coffee down by the highway, where Marco was less likely to be spotted by someone he knew, then went back to the hut to pick up Marco's backpack and my car. When I was getting ready to leave, I wrapped my arms around Marco.

"I never do this before I meet you," he said. "I never hug nobody in all my life."

"Well, you're getting pretty good at it. But put your arms around me tighter. Otherwise it's not a real hug."

"We see each other again soon," he said, squeezing me.

"Take care of yourself, okay? And thank you for keeping me company last night."

I let Marco go ahead of me down the lane. Just before he turned onto the paved road, he waved, and then hit the throttle and took off. I took my time easing the Panda onto the road and stopped in Saint Mary for another coffee before getting on the autostrada.

As I was passing the first exit for Perugia, my phone rang.

"What are you doing up, Jen?" I asked when the call connected. "It's the middle of the night for you."

"I don't sleep anymore. Is this an okay time to talk?"

"Yeah, of course. I'm in the car but if you can hear me, we're good. What's going on? Are you okay?"

"I went on a date."

"Seriously? How was it?"

"Hideous. I mean, I didn't expect much. Scott's the only guy I've dated in thirty-three years. But I felt like if he was going to shack up with Amber, I needed to at least go on a date."

"He's living with Amber?"

Jenny sniffled. "Yep."

I was quiet for a minute, then said, "I'm sorry. I hadn't realized things were so . . .final. I guess I thought he'd get it out of his system and come home."

"Me too. But he definitely wants a divorce."

"Oh fuck, Jenny. I'm so sorry. Hang on, let me pull over."

"No, no, it's okay. I'm okay. I mean, I'm not okay, but I will be. Keep driving. Where are you going, anyway?"

"Home."

"At seven o'clock in the morning? Is Porter with you?"

"Uh, no. I'll fill you in on all that another time. I want to talk about you. Who did you go on a date with?"

"Hang on, Bits. What are you up to?"

I sighed. "I don't even know. There's this couple staying next door and the wife keeps hitting on Porter, and he talked to her about Sloan and it just made me furious. I had to leave so I drove to Assisi and hung out with Marco in an olive grove all night."

"What the fuck?"

"I know. I was just—I was desperate to get away. Nothing happened with Marco, but Porter will be pissed."

"I would be too."

"I know. Me too. I've got to get over this shit with Sloan and figure out how to help Porter, Jen. I've been acting like it's all about me, but obviously it's not." I turned to look over my shoulder before changing lanes and downshifting. "There's more, though. Remember how I said Porter was being weird about why he donated sperm in the first place?"

"He said he needed money, right?"

"Uh huh. Want to guess why?"

"Rehab? New soccer cleats?"

"To pay for an abortion for Kick. Remember her?"

There was a long silence, then Jenny said, "What?"

"I know. I'll call you when I get home and fill you in. I haven't even digested that news yet," I said, exhaling audibly. "Can we talk about you? Who was your date with?"

"A guy from the neighborhood who's recently divorced."

"And it was awful?"

"Well, awful may be too harsh. But it was weird. I just kept looking at him and wondering why I was sitting in a booth across from a stranger."

"I get it."

"That's not why I called, though. Were you serious about my coming over?"

"One hundred percent! Yes, please come over."

"I'm glad you said that, because I just bought a ticket."

"Yay! For when?"

"Thursday."

"Like two days from now Thursday?"

"Yep. Off-season special on Air Canada. Syracuse to Toronto to Rome."

I started laughing. "This is the best news ever. I'm kind of delirious at the moment, but send me your flight details and I will pick you up at the airport, okay? I can't wait to see you!"

"Thank God you're fine with it. I don't know what I was thinking, buying a ticket without talking to you. If you've got work to do, don't worry—I'll entertain myself."

"Don't even worry about it. And you can wear my stuff, so don't bother packing a lot. I'll see you Thursday!"

Fifteen

"How are things going?" David asked on a video call that afternoon. He was wearing his clerical collar, which I hadn't seen on him in a while. "Any improvement?"

I shrugged. "I haven't talked to him yet today. I think he's just really confused about what to do about the Sloan situation. He actually talked to this horrible Instagram influencer from Australia about it—while she was aggressively hitting on him, mind you," I said, waving my hand. "It's a whole story, but it just felt like such a betrayal, him talking to this random stranger instead of me. And wait until I tell you why he donated sperm in the first place."

I filled David in on the contents of Porter's email. He groaned when I finished telling him that Porter had needed the money to terminate Kick's pregnancy.

"Do you remember how competitive she was with me, David? I mean, I always knew that our friendship was based on Kick feeling superior, and when I started dating Porter, she only ever had bad things to say about him. But whatever, you know? She was someone to go to the bars with and beyond that, I didn't really care."

David nodded. "I remember her. Not the healthiest friendship, but I get it."

"When Porter and I got engaged, she asked me if I really thought he was going to stay with me."

"Yikes."

"And Porter knew all this, and he still slept with her! And not just once, either," I said. "God, just saying the words makes me feel sick. Kick must have felt so . . . *victorious*, thinking she was seducing Porter behind my back."

"I'm sorry," David said. "I can imagine this comes as a real blow. But, as you said, it was a long time ago. And I do wonder if part of Porter's reluctance to deal with the situation with Sloan is that he's intensely afraid of losing you again? I'm not excusing anything, but it must have been hard for him to tell you about Kick, even all these years later."

I shrugged and went back to cleaning the countertop. "We're just not on the same page anymore and it feels kind of . . . I don't know. Unnerving, I guess." I sighed. "I can't go through this again, David."

"Through what, exactly?"

"Finding out I've been a fool. That I've put my trust in someone who doesn't deserve it."

"Is that what you think is happening?"

I shrugged. "Maybe. I mean, the problem isn't even that he had sex with Kick, although hello? Wear a condom, dumbass," I said. "But it's the fact that he's kept it a secret for so long. And he never would have told me if this whole thing with Sloan hadn't come up. I *knew* he was keeping something from me," I said, shaking my head. "So now I'm just wondering what else he's hiding."

"Have you asked? The answer may be nothing, you know."

"No," I said, rubbing my eyes. "I got his email in the middle of the night when I was in Assisi. I went to this little cabin-type place Marco has and we hung out." I stifled a yawn. "Sorry. I haven't been to bed yet."

"Is there a story there?"

"With Marco? No," I said, shaking my head. "When we're together, it's really fun. He makes me laugh and we have the same interests. But that's it."

"Nothing more?"

"Nope. Even if he was available, I'm not interested. He's a player, and I don't want to worry every day that some man is lying to my face or making plans to leave me while I'm trying to figure out why I'm so unlovable. Been there, done that. I won't do it with Porter, and I certainly won't do it with Marco."

David was quiet for several moments.

"Do you think that's part of the reason you reacted so strongly to this woman—what was her name? The one who was hitting on Porter?"

"Nicolette."

"It stirred up some feelings, huh?"

"Of course it did. She was hitting on him right in front of my face and Porter seemed not to care. It brought back all kinds of feelings from when I finally realized what Crawford had been up to right under my nose." I ran my hand through my hair and dropped the strands that came out in the sink. "I just want things to be calm, and I don't want to be anyone's fool. Is that too much to ask?"

"No," he said. "Hang on, kiddo. Someone's knocking."

I grabbed a knife from the drawer and jabbed the point in the corner of the countertop. The little bit of coffee grounds I spilled each day between the canister and the Bialetti gathered there and did not want to leave, no matter how many times I cleaned the counter.

"I'm back. Sorry about that," David said, reappearing on the screen. "Let me ask you something. Do you remember the paisley comforter?"

"The one on my bed at your house?"

He nodded. "The one you didn't admit to hating until years later."

"I didn't want to hurt your feelings! I've just never been a big fan of paisley."

"Right, well, the point is, we all keep things from the people we love in an effort to spare them pain. I know a comforter isn't comparable to getting a girl pregnant, but my point stands," he said. "And the second thing I want to say is that I had no idea what I was doing bringing my traumatized seventeen-year-old niece to live with me after your mom died. Jenny's family wanted you to stay with them for the summer, but my gut told me to bring you down to Chapel Hill right away. I was a nervous wreck about it, though."

"I couldn't wait to get out of Syracuse."

"Sure, I know. But I had serious trepidations. What do I know about orphaned teenagers? It was Margaret who told me to make it happen and then get out of my own way."

"Well, thank God you did," I said. "Or thank Margaret. I don't know what would have become of me if you hadn't taken me in." I put the knife down and gave up on the coffee grounds. "What made you think of that comforter?"

"I was thinking about how scared I was to make room for you in my life when I went out and got that comforter, and what a blessing you turned out to be," David said. "You've been a tremendous light in my life, kiddo. A tremendous light. And if I hadn't taken that leap of faith, we might just be polite strangers at this point."

"I can't even imagine that. But I know what you mean. We definitely wouldn't have the same relationship we do now."

"Are you getting my point?"

"Yes," I said, rolling my eyes. "You're telling me I need to take a chance on Sloan."

David smiled. "Precisely."

"You're so subtle, David."

"Like a hammer."

"Well, I get it," I said. "Obviously I still need to talk to Porter about everything, which I'm not looking forward to, but I get what you're saying about Sloan."

"All right. Keep me posted." He looked at his watch. "Right now I'm off to Neil's funeral. Love you, kid."

After I hung up with David, I wiped the counter clean one last time and went over to Porter's to borrow some bed linens for my guest bed.

Two of the boxes we'd never finished unpacking were still sitting in the hallway upstairs, blocking the door to the linen closet. I intended to simply drag the boxes back to the closet, but when I peered into the first one, I saw a ton of stuff from Porter's restaurant that I'd never seen before. I lowered myself to the floor and sat cross-legged to go through the contents of the box, sifting through menus and recipes and press clippings and notes from customers and staff.

One of the clippings, which had been pulled directly out of a magazine, was a rave review about the biscuits with pimento cheese Porter's restaurant served as an appetizer. He'd told me all about them one night during the pandemic after he'd tried—and failed—to duplicate the recipe. Both the biscuits and the pimento cheese had been Delia's recipes, he'd said, same as the tomato pie, oyster stew, and peach cobbler he rotated on and off the menu.

I'd just finished reading the review and was digging into the box again when I heard the kitchen door open and shut. A moment later, Oliver appeared in the hallway, followed by Porter.

"Hey. Whatcha doing?"

"I came over to get some sheets for Jenny's bed. I was going to pull this box into the closet," I explained, handing him the clipping, "but then I saw all this cool stuff from your restaurant."

Porter took the clipping and skimmed it while I petted Oliver, who was trying to make himself fit on my lap.

"I wish I could replicate those biscuits," Porter said, handing the clipping back to me. "Delia made them for us every Friday night. It was the reward for sitting through dinner with my grandparents." He shook his head. "God, those dinners were torture. As soon as we were excused, Ford and I made a beeline for the kitchen."

He bent down and extracted a handful of papers from the box and flipped through them.

"People went ape shit for those biscuits," he said. "I printed out the first couple of reviews and sent them to Delia in the mail. She was so proud."

Delia, his grandparents' housekeeper, had been the brothers' rock, Porter had always said. All during his childhood, Porter's father was hellbent on converting every penny of his trust fund into bar tabs, and the brothers had been left to fend for themselves. Ford would wake Porter up for school every morning and the two of them would get dressed and tiptoe into the kitchen, wary about who they might encounter there. Usually it was a woman they vaguely recognized from the country club or the neighborhood, but on one memorable occasion, they'd walked in to find Ford's English teacher pouring herself a cup of coffee. She'd taken one look at the brothers in their Forten Hall blazers, dropped her coffee cup in the sink, and fled.

"Delia used to take us back-to-school shopping every year," Porter said, handing me the clipping and picking up a menu. "She'd pick us up in her brown Vista Cruiser and we'd get all our school stuff and then go have lunch in Jackson Ward." He shook his head. "My grandmother would have shit a chicken if she'd known Delia was taking us over there, but we loved it. It was like a foreign country."

He lowered himself to the floor next to me and dug in the box again.

"Delia would give us a little lecture on the way to the lunch place," he said, scanning a receipt before setting it to the side. "'These are my people,' she'd say, and we'd be on our best behavior. And oh, man, the food."

"What did you have?" I asked.

"Fried catfish, stewed collard greens, fried okra, corn casserole. Hush puppies. Banana pudding. Stuff Grandmother Claire would never have allowed on her table."

"You're making me hungry."

"I'm sure it was all cooked in Crisco and fatback, but man, it was excellent. We were sworn to secrecy, though. If anyone asked, we were supposed to say we had lunch at the S & W Cafeteria." Porter glanced up at me. "I'm sure Delia was risking her job, taking us there."

"Why do you think she did it?"

Porter shrugged and got to his feet. "I never really thought about why." He dropped the papers he was holding next to the open box. "Most of this is probably trash. I'll go through it at some point. Right now, I've got to get back outside."

He clicked his tongue for Oliver, who lumbered to his feet and followed Porter down the stairs.

I returned the menus and other restaurant paraphernalia to the box and slid it across the floor, then opened the second box. There were reams of paper in this one, too—receipts for restaurant equipment, hospital discharge information, IRA statements, tax returns. I was about to close the top and push the box into the closet when my name in the top right corner of a piece of paper caught my eye. I tugged the paper out. It was a printout of a story I'd written years earlier. It had been published in an online journal and then disappeared into the ether, and I'd forgotten about all about it.

I sat on the floor with my back to the wall and started reading.

Sixteen

Magical Thinking
by
Beth Steeler

Peter Miller made a mental note to tell Heather to punch up his introduction and include something more interesting than his board memberships and degrees. Like the fact that he'd been a highly ranked varsity tennis player when he was only in seventh grade, or that he still had a PGA-worthy handicap. Or—as he'd proven on a recent fishing trip with some of his former fraternity brothers—that he could still shotgun a beer in under seven seconds.

The auditorium was packed. Peter's appearance on *Squawk Box* three months earlier had caused a stir. A clip of his interview had been widely circulated, and suddenly he was being booked for speaking engagements every time he turned around. Peter wanted to believe this was due to his business acumen and subject matter expertise, but the demographic of his audiences made him think Heather was right: his popularity was due to his salt-and-pepper hair, incredible bone structure, dazzling smile, impeccably tailored suits, and lack of a wedding ring. Heather took great pleasure in naming the subsets that now augmented his core following of pension fund managers and bankers: *wanton widows, desirous divorcees, amorous amateurs.*

"Did you see this?" she'd asked him that morning on the way to the venue. She held up the business section of the newspaper. "Sizzling CEO is Wall Street's Hottest Commodity," she read. "That's the headline." Heather shook her head. "No offense, boss, but your audiences these days are looking kind of . . . hungry."

The woman from the law firm underwriting the event finished Peter's intro, and Heather gave him the signal to flip the switch on the receiver attached to his belt and bring his mic to life. He stepped to the podium amid enthusiastic applause and a few catcalls, flipped open his notebook, and cleared his throat. As many times as he'd done this, some part of him still held onto his junior high fears every time he stepped up to a podium—losing his place, garbling the text, launching an ill-timed erection—but as soon as he got a paragraph or two into the speech, the fears faded and he found his rhythm.

As we enter yet another year of depressed market conditions, Peter began, *smart investors should beware. The recent optimism surrounding the real estate market is based far more on hope than fact. The unwarranted enthusiasm has many market watchers anticipating a resurgence, believing that capital—which has been sitting on the sidelines for the last few years—will now be propelled into action as investors see their opportunities narrowing and record low prices beginning to climb.*

This was his fourteenth time delivering this particular speech. Heather tweaked it for each engagement to include location-specific statistics and information, but the majority of the text remained the same. Three years into the recession, Peter felt it was his calling as an expert in distressed real estate investments to disabuse the public of the notion that things were going to improve anytime soon. While everyone else was peddling some variation of a prosperity gospel—*Follow me and you shall have endless riches!*—Peter was laying down hard truths. Wise investors would have to learn to profit from the current mess; that was his message. The irony, of course, was that he was now pulling in ridiculous fees for delivering this bleak news. The economy might be a steaming pile of shit, but he was getting richer as a result.

According to the Federal Reserve's latest Beige Book, new commercial construction is characterized as "subdued or slow" overall, indicating a continued lack of demand, as well as slow absorption of existing vacant space. And while there has been speculation that the potential for as much as $30 to $40 billion in new commercial mortgage-backed security activity exists for 2011, the truth is that underwriting has tightened up significantly, and the vast majority of developers will continue to search—in vain—for financing.

Peter scanned the audience as he spoke. The tech guys with their dorky lanyards were up in the back, huddled over their equipment, and the reporter from *The Commercial Real Estate Journal*, who had put Peter on the October cover, was sitting on the center aisle, six rows up. Peter had signed Heather's copy of the magazine right across his face: *Heather, Get back to work. Pete.*

His eyes snagged on a woman sitting four chairs in from the aisle on the second row and he stumbled over the words *CMBS delinquency* and lost his place momentarily. He swallowed hard and forced himself to deliver another page of his speech before allowing himself to look in her direction again.

It was her. Jean Pearson. The last time he'd seen her, she was pulling on her clothes in the grimy summer sublet he shared with three of his fraternity brothers. He vividly remembered watching her back as she hooked her bra, knowing that she was crying but clueless as to why or what he should do about it.

Pete and Jean were high school friends. More than friends, based on the hours they'd spent groping on the plaid couch in his parents' den, but never officially boyfriend and girlfriend. There was always someone else: a girlfriend Pete couldn't seem to cut loose, a foreign guy who took Jean to listen to bands Pete had never heard of. Yet they kept spiraling back toward one another, over and over again.

In the company of their peers, Pete and Jean maintained a charade of platonic disinterest, but in their own universe, they operated as a happy unit. Pete picked Jean up for school every morning, and took her to breakfast every Wednesday, the two of them racking up demerits for skipping morning chapel. Jean packed him a special lunch on important match days, stuffing a small blue cooler with two turkey, apple, and brie sandwiches, two bananas, two cookies, and two orange Gatorades. *Tibi bonam fortunam!* she wrote on the napkins, a nod to the Latin class where they'd met in seventh grade. Pete kept those napkins in the pocket of his tennis bag and wiped his hands on his shorts.

By the time they were seniors, it was Jean's reaction Pete anticipated when he had something funny to say, Jean's presence that gave him renewed energy when a match point was at hand, and Jean's applause that he heard afterwards, as if she were the lone spectator in the stands. Occasionally they argued about meaningless things, but they never once addressed the question simmering just below the surface: *What are we doing?*

Pete went a few hours north after graduation, and Jean went out of state. He didn't even have her phone number the first year they were apart and only saw her once, at a party back home where they spent the entire evening ignoring the cold on a bench in the host's backyard. Eventually, whatever place Jean had occupied in his precollege life was blurred by the girls who lounged around his fraternity house like life-sized candy, free for the sampling. When Peter thought of his future, though, it was always Jean he saw in stark relief, Jean he pictured by his side. They would reunite when the time was right. It was inevitable.

> *The American entrepreneurial spirit is a wonderful thing. But it's also responsible for why we witness a wave of optimism across the country each January—a bold confidence that borders on mania and has very little to do with facts. The wise investor will resist being swept up in a tide of emotion that cannot be borne out by market analysis.*

Jean called out of the blue one night the summer before their senior year of college. Her voice on the phone had made him ridiculously happy.

"I'm here in town," she said. "I rode down with friends. They're going out, but I'd rather see you."

Pete picked her up just before 10:00 p.m. They sat on the front porch of his sublet in crappy aluminum lawn chairs, lighting cigarettes and setting them on the porch railing to keep the mosquitoes away, talking over the call and response of the cicadas. After his second beer, Pete jogged to his car and dug out the Elton John CD that had lived under his seat since 1986. He snaked an extension cord through the window, popped the CD into a portable player, and pushed play on "Little Jeannie," the song he'd sung to her a hundred times. As the opening notes sounded, Pete dropped into his chair and reached over to grab Jean's hand. She squeezed his fingers and didn't pull away.

The next time Pete returned from the kitchen, he stood in front of her and held out a fresh beer, grinning. As Jean leaned forward to take it from his hands, Pete snatched the bottle away and leaned down and kissed her. The taste of her lips was like coming home to a favorite meal. Pete set the beer bottles on the porch railing, pulled her up out of the chair, and pressed her against the wall of the house while Elton John sang *Oh oh Jeannie, I'm so in love with you.*

He heard later that she'd moved to Amsterdam, then Zurich, and then London. He found her byline in various business journals and looked for her at LaGuardia and O'Hare, Schiphol, Kennedy and Heathrow.

2010 facts did not provide a basis for optimism unless you owned and sold an institution grade property in Washington DC or New York City, or an "A" or "B" multifamily property in a 24/7 city, which is where foreclosed homeowners and jobseekers are moving. And while it's true that transaction activity in 2010 for properties over $5 million increased 109 percent, this must be kept in perspective: we were climbing out of a pit.

Jean kept her head down and took notes. When she'd received the assignment from her editor, she'd promised herself that Pete—the benchmark against whom every other man in her life had paled, failed, and disappointed—would be just another story.

The last time she'd seen him, Pete was sitting on his bed, sheets gathered around his midsection, worrying about a paper he had to turn in that afternoon.

The night before, she'd been stupidly nervous to call him. It was just Pete, she told herself. Pete, whose face and voice and hands were as familiar as her own, whose sweaty tennis socks and racket strings had cluttered the backseat of her car, whose other relationships had tormented her when they were apart, but who—when they were sitting on his dock or sailing on the lake or chatting on the phone every night—was so obvious in his affection for her that she could never bring herself to risk it all by saying what she wanted to say, which was: *Make a fucking decision, Pete. Choose me.*

On the entire ride down, Jean had debated whether to call him. But finally—with the encouragement of her friends and a shot of Jägermeister—she'd dialed Pete's childhood home, made small talk with his mother, and asked for the number at his sublet. Then she took a deep breath and called him. When he arrived to pick her up—a wish made flesh materializing in front of her—Jean couldn't stop smiling.

"You still haven't cleaned this thing," she said, climbing into the passenger seat of his car and tossing a roll of grip tape and a sweat-salted tennis hat into the back seat.

As Pete pushed play on the goofy song he'd always claimed was written just for her, Jean thought she might levitate off the porch with happiness. When he pulled her out of her chair, the webbing sticking to the back of her thighs and causing the chair to drop with a clatter, the entire universe collapsed to a pinpoint on the tip of Pete's tongue as he inscribed a love song down her neck and across her collarbone.

And then, as had happened so many times before, they reached the Rubicon and hesitated to cross. Jean excused herself to the bathroom, and when she came out, Pete suggested a movie. They sat together on the couch and were soon asleep, Jean curled against Pete's body and the DVD player silently pulsing its question: Would they like to restart the movie or select scenes to view?

Early the next morning, Jean eased herself off the couch. She was bent over the sink washing her face when Pete pressed in behind her and reached over her shoulder to pluck his toothbrush from its holder. He offered the toothbrush to her when he was done, waited for her to finish, then took the toothbrush from her hand, placed it on the edge of the sink, turned her around, and kissed her.

Jean's fear of being embarrassingly inexperienced had been laid to rest over the past three years with insignificant college guys, all of whom she regarded as nothing more than useful stepping stones on the way back to Pete. The early morning sun was shining through the window of his bedroom and every nerve ending in her body was zinging as they moved together. She felt more awake, more confident, more alive than she'd ever felt. The phrase *making love,* which had always struck her as archaic and banal, was exactly what it felt like with Pete: their bodies creating love and releasing it into the universe. When Pete finally collapsed on top of her, Jean inhaled the familiar scent of his skin, then screwed up her courage and said what she'd wanted to say for as long as she could remember: "Pete, I'm in love with you."

Our states and municipalities are struggling to make the strategic cuts necessitated by the decline in the real estate market. To make matters worse, the FDIC reports that one hundred and fifty-seven banks failed in 2010—seventeen more than in 2009.

Pete's response to her declaration was to begin talking about the paper he hadn't started, the one he was stressing over, due that afternoon. He hadn't changed since high school, he said, still leaving things to the last minute. Someday he'd have an assistant or a secretary to keep him on track, but until then . . . well, he could probably get an extension; summer school was laid-back like that.

Jean was stunned. She'd imagined this reunion, this moment, a million times, and it had never once ended with Pete simply ignoring what she said. Unable to staunch the tears that began rolling down her face, she pulled on her clothes and fled, telling Pete she was late to meet her friends and running down the road to a convenience store, where she used the pay phone to call for a ride. Her last glimpse of Pete—the one she wanted to erase—was his face as he untangled himself from the sheets and told her to wait a second, he'd drive her if she'd just let him get dressed. She still burned with embarrassment all these years later.

> *2011 will see a small improvement in real estate markets, both residential and commercial, up from steep declines in previous years. However, headlines with words like "soar," "blockbuster," and "turnaround year" must be understood to reflect the need for good news and the general spirit of entrepreneurship, not the reality of the marketplace.*

Peter stared at the top of Jean's head as she scribbled notes, willing her to look up. How many times had he thought of that night in Gainesville? A hundred? A thousand? He saw flashes of her on the street, in the subway, running to catch a flight, and his heart never failed to drop when he realized it wasn't Jean after all. In every relationship he'd been in since, he'd never found the same ease, the same level of comfort, the same feeling that he was truly seen and *known,* as he'd had with Jean.

It was a childhood thing, Pete reminded himself often. He was a grown man, and a wildly successful one at that, with no time for sentimental bullshit. But that didn't stop him from thinking of her.

Pete remembered the smallest details of that morning. The freckle on the underside of her breast, the way she gasped and then laughed when he ran his hand over her ribs. The way she said his name as he moved inside her—the most intoxicating sound he'd ever heard, somewhere between a sigh and a plea—as if his name, so upright and rigid and unimaginative, was a sacred song or ancient prayer. Pete had wanted to stop time and savor the surprise of getting, at long last, what he'd wanted since the moment he could put a name to the peculiar tug in the pit of his stomach every time he saw Jean's face or heard her voice.

Afterwards, she'd turned and put her head on his chest. Pete wrapped his arms around her and pulled her close, lost in the lyrics that played on repeat in his head. *Oh, oh Jeannie, I will always be your fool.*

When he saw Jean looking at him, obviously expecting a reply to something that hadn't pierced his reverie, he assumed she'd said she had to go. So Pete began talking about the paper he had to write, knowing she would offer to help, the way she always had in high school. They would spend the day together and he'd convince her to stay another night, and somehow he'd find the courage to tell her that he was in love with her and had been for years. First, though, he'd take her to lunch, to the place down the street with the Cuban sandwiches, her favorite.

But he didn't have time to suggest any of that. Jean sat up and began pulling on her clothes. She was obviously crying, and Pete scrambled to figure out why. He ran through a variety of scenarios before settling on the one he had some experience with: she hadn't meant to go that far and regretted having sex. Pete knew he needed her to understand that it had been something special, something incredible; she wasn't just another conquest, another notch on his bedpost.

> *While optimism has its place in your portfolio, magical thinking does not. The wise investor will double down on due diligence and avoid being swept up in hopeful—but baseless—hyperbole.*

Peter continued to stare at Jean as he came to the end of his speech, but she didn't look up. When the applause died down, he waited for the photographers to signal that they had what they needed before stepping back from the podium, his eyes fixed on her as she shifted from foot to foot, waiting for the people on her right to move into the aisle. Peter hurried towards Heather, unclipping the microphone and telling her to gather their stuff.

"The reporter from the Co-Reg is waiting," Heather said. "You promised them five minutes."

Peter answered questions, shook hands, and gave out his business card, all the while tracking Jean's progress through the auditorium. But while he was answering questions from a trio of eager, fresh-faced young brokers, she slipped out. When he looked around again, the only person remaining in the rows of chairs was an employee of the venue. He nodded at Heather, who lifted her bag to her shoulder and told the brokers they had another engagement.

"We're going to have to start booking bigger auditoriums," Heather said, sliding across the seat of the Town Car and pulling her bag behind her.

"I need you to punch up the intro," he said, taking the bottle of water she handed him. "Don't make me sound so fucking boring."

"Sure thing." She looked at Peter. "You okay, boss?"

He nodded. "What do I always say, Heather?"

"Make the best of the shit you're in. Magical thinking is for fairytales."

Peter pushed against the black leather seat, stretching his long legs out in front of him. "Where are we tomorrow?" he asked.

"Toronto. Canadian governmental pension funds." She peered into her bag and extracted a piece of paper. "Depart LaGuardia just after 8:00 a.m. and get into Toronto at 9:40. We'll be back in the city by seven tomorrow night."

Pete nodded.

Two more airports. Two more departure lounges. Two more gates. Two more chances to spot her at the airport bar, two more opportunities to walk onto the plane and see her smile up at him from across the aisle.

It could happen, Pete thought, closing his eyes.

That was reasonable optimism.

Not magical thinking at all.

Seventeen

I sat in the hallway for a long time when I finished reading the story, wondering how Porter had gotten hold of it and why he'd kept it. The rest of his souvenirs made sense—concert stubs and trophies and stuff from his restaurant that reminded him of important moments in his life. But this short story?

I tucked the story underneath the other papers, then folded the cardboard flaps of the box and dragged it into the hall closet. It took me a while to find the right size bed linens, and then I went downstairs to grab some kitchen shears and head home.

Porter was standing in the middle of the driveway.

"You look like you're thinking big thoughts."

He glanced at me and shook his head. "Nah. Just thinking about what I want to do out here. I want to soften it up and plant something colorful by the kitchen door. What are you up to?"

"I found the sheets," I said, lifting them up to show him. "I was going to cut some flowers for Jenny's room."

"There are three purple blooms on the other side of the barn. I saw them this morning. The color is still really good."

"I'll get them, thanks."

"You excited?"

"I'm really looking forward to hanging out with her. And hopefully distracting her from what's going on at home. Did I tell you Scott moved in with his girlfriend?"

"Good luck to them. I don't think the statistics on affairs working out are too good."

"How could they be? You're starting the relationship with a lie."

"Right," Porter said, then sighed. "On that note, do you want to talk about the whole Kick thing? I just want—"

"Not really," I interrupted, shaking my head. "I don't even know what I think about that, Porter. I mean, it was ages ago, but I can't pretend it doesn't hurt. Why her, of all people?"

"I know. I'm sorry. All I can say is, she was there and she was obviously very willing," he said. "No excuses, though. It was stupid."

"It almost feels like you were putting the last nail in the coffin of us. I mean, if I'd known about you two back then . . . Well, you and I would not be having this conversation now. I would never have spoken to you again."

Porter nodded. "I know."

"But the thing that really gets me is the irony of it all. I mean, we loved each other, didn't we?"

"I loved you more than anyone."

"But we went to such great lengths to keep me from getting pregnant, and then you went and knocked up Kick, of all people—someone you didn't even like! And now you have a daughter because you needed money to pay for Kick to *not* be pregnant." I shook my head. "Irony doesn't even begin to cover it."

"I know. I'm sorry."

"And what if there are more?"

"More what?"

"More children. What if you have more children?"

"Jesus," Porter said, running his hand through his hair. "I hadn't thought of that."

"Did one donation just go to one mother, or did one donation provide sperm for multiple mothers?"

"I have no idea."

"And you donated more than once, right? Chances are there's someone else."

Porter sighed loudly and shook his head. "I'm so over thinking about this."

"You and me both. But that doesn't help anything. She's not going away."

"Are you going away, though? That's the question. Where did you run off to last night?"

"I don't want to do this right now. I've got to get ready for Jenny."

Jenny was waiting outside the terminal when I arrived twenty minutes later than I'd intended, having come to a screeching halt in a traffic jam that I thought would never let up. I honked the horn when I saw her and pulled up next to the curb, then turned the car off and hopped out.

"Hi!" I said, wrapping her in a hug. "Oh, it's so good to see you! I'm sorry I didn't park and come in. Traffic was awful."

A cop behind us blew his whistle. I let go of Jenny and put her suitcase in the trunk and we made our way out of the airport.

"God, Bits, I don't know how you drive here," Jenny said as an Audi with French plates flew out of the roundabout and nearly took off our front bumper. "These people are nuts."

"You get used to it. It's kind of like a dance," I said, peering over my shoulder and easing the Panda towards the on-ramp for the autostrada. "No one gets too bothered as long as the traffic keeps moving."

"Does everyone tailgate, or just the people behind us?"

I laughed. "Everyone. It's not a problem unless you get hit. And luckily road rage here is just yelling. You don't have to worry about getting shot."

Jenny reached into her purse, which was sitting on the floorboard between her feet. "Gum?" she said, holding out a pack of Big Red.

"Oh wow. I haven't had Big Red since high school."

"I'm regressing. Trying to recapture my lost youth," Jenny said, unwrapping a stick of gum and shoving it into my open mouth as I shifted into fourth and picked up speed.

"Are you hungry or thirsty? Need a bathroom? It's about two and a half hours home. We can stop anytime."

"I'm fine for now. I can't wait to see your place. Is Porter home?"

"Yeah. He was going to come to the airport, but I wanted you to myself."

"I can't believe I'm finally going to meet him."

I glanced at her. "He's excited. I'll fill you in on the latest, but I want to hear what's happening with you first."

Jenny dropped the empty gum wrappers into her purse. "Well, Scott got his ear pierced."

I laughed out loud. "Seriously?"

"I know. I could barely keep a straight face. He's working out like crazy and is letting his hair grow out too. Oh, and his teeth could blind people in space."

"He must get free treatments from her."

Jenny nodded. "I guess so. Would you believe that when he found out I was coming here, he had the nerve to ask me to get him some stupid Ferrari jacket he wants?"

"Why'd you tell him you were coming?"

"In case I drop dead," she said, shrugging. "So he knows he

has to fly my corpse home to my children."

"Good plan. How are the kids?"

She looked out the window. "What's that big castle-looking thing?"

"I don't know," I said, peering out the windshield. "Something Mussolini built, that's what Marco always says."

Jenny nodded. "Brent seems kind of nonplussed by the whole thing. He's on the road for his job a ton, so I don't see him much."

"And my namesake?"

"Betsy just got moved to teaching third grade, so she's all wrapped up in that. She doesn't want to talk about it with me, which I understand." Jenny reached in her purse again and extracted a small hairbrush. "Amber's only five years older than Betsy, which I think makes it hard for the kids to take this relationship seriously."

"I have the same problem. I don't take it seriously, either."

Jenny pulled the brush through her hair. "It's hard for me to take seriously too. But I guess I should, since he's blowing up our family to be with her," she said, pulling her hair into a ponytail.

"Are you sure you don't want to stop for coffee?" I asked, pointing to the Autogrill spanning the highway ahead of us. "They have coffee and sandwiches."

"Yeah, let's stop," she said, dropping the brush back into her purse.

I maneuvered the car into the right lane and narrowly avoided being clipped by a Volkswagen. Jenny and I went inside and waited in line for the restrooms, then I ordered two coffees from the counter and we stood at a small, sticky table to drink them.

"I can't believe I'm finally here," Jenny said, looking around. "This is exactly how I pictured Italy. Just like the Autogrill."

I laughed. "It gets better, trust me. I have a whole list of places I want to take you, but I also don't want to wear you out, so you have to promise to tell me if it's too much."

"I will," Jenny said, lifting her coffee cup to her lips. "Fill me in on what's happening with Porter."

I pressed my torso against the table to let a group of guys in tracksuits squeeze by. After giving Jenny an overview of all that had happened, I said, "Porter told me last night that Sloan is actually in London for a conference and wants to meet him. As in, soon."

"Oh boy. This is going to be an interesting vacation."

When we got back in the car, Jenny waited until we'd rejoined the traffic on the highway before asking, "How do you feel about all of this stuff with Sloan?"

I made a face. "I don't know. Dismayed, I guess. I mean, I can't blame Porter for donating and I can't blame Sloan for wanting to meet him and I can't even blame Kick—I knew what kind of person she was, and I also knew she was insanely jealous of me and Porter."

"That was obvious just from what you told me back then. I always had the impression she wanted Porter for herself. Not because she liked him, but just to have him, ya know?"

"Yeah, I mean, I think she would have preferred a basketball player, but—"

"She'd settle for a soccer player."

I smiled. "That's a good band name. 'Settled for soccer.' I'm gonna add it to my list."

"So okay, you don't blame anyone, but still, Bits . . ."

"He has a daughter now and I don't. That's the main problem."

Jenny reached over and patted my arm. "I know."

"All I want is for things to be normal, Jen. Quiet and drama-free. It took so much to get over losing Mia . . . " I looked away from her, then said, "That's not what I mean. I'll never get over losing Mia. I just meant it took forever to get functioning again. To enjoy any part of my life again. For such a long time, I couldn't find any reason to get out of bed in the morning."

"I know, Bits."

"And then all the bullshit with Crawford, and the fucking pandemic! I just want peace in my life. But apparently that's not in the cards."

"Does Porter want to have a relationship with her? With Sloan, I mean."

I shrugged. "I don't know. We can't talk about it. We can't talk about anything right now."

"Oh dear."

"No, don't worry. I promise, we're completely friendly. It's just that things are weird below the surface. And that makes me feel even worse because I know he's trying to figure out how to handle this, and I'm only compounding his problems."

Jenny was quiet, looking at the scenery.

"You know what I always think of when I think of Porter?" she asked after a few minutes.

"What?"

"Remember when you drove from DC to Chapel Hill in a blizzard? It must have been for Christmas."

"Yeah. The windshield wipers on my rental car barely worked and I'd had no idea it was going to snow like that."

Jenny nodded. "You said you couldn't see at all."

"It was a total white-out. I had to stay behind a semi to follow his taillights, and when he pulled off the highway, I had to pull off too. God, that was a nightmare. I had a death grip on the steering wheel the whole time."

"What I remember is that you stopped at some crappy hotel and called Porter."

I nodded. "And he showed up three hours later."

"Yep. He drove through that horrible storm to be with you, and then the next morning, he drove behind you all the way to Chapel Hill to make sure you got there safely. That's what I think of when I think of Porter."

"He was a great guy. He still is. I just . . . Sometimes I

think there's been too much water under the bridge for us to be together. Maybe we should just carry on with our lives, you know? Maybe we'd be better off with other people."

Jenny looked over at me. "Is that what you want?"

"No. I don't know. Maybe."

"Well, maybe a bit of sightseeing with your best friend will help you figure it out."

As we drove into the valley, the early morning fog had burned off and the whole landscape was glowing in the pale golden light.

"Wow," Jenny said, inhaling sharply. She leaned forward to look through the windshield. "Holy cow. This is incredible."

I pointed to the turn-off to the village. "That's where we go to get a coffee or run errands. There's a little area with some shops, but not much. There's a bigger town about twenty minutes away with a decent-sized grocery store."

"What do people do out here?"

"For work? It's a mix," I said. "Some are farmers, some people drive to Umbertide to work in factories, and I know there's at least one couple who teach at the university in Perugia. Oh, and there's a family of falconers." I pointed out the window at a cluster of buildings set far back from the road. "That's their place."

"Falconers, like bird trainers?"

I nodded. "They use falcons to get rid of pigeons here. Porter and I were having lunch in Orvieto one time when this guy walked in with a falcon on his arm. Massive, fierce-looking thing. He said they bring the falcons to the restaurant every day for a couple weeks and that scares off the pigeons."

"That would totally freak me out, to be eating lunch with a falcon at the next table."

"It was crazy. Anyway, here we are," I said, turning into the long driveway that led to my house and Porter's.

"What kind of trees are those? I love how they line the road."

"Cypress trees."

"Who owns all this? The fields and all the trees back there?"

"Porter," I said. "Speak of the devil."

Porter was standing on the side of the driveway near the turn to my house. He had Oliver by the collar and was looking down, talking to him. As we got closer, Oliver started to bark and pull away from Porter, who waved and smiled at us.

"Wow. The man, the myth. I can't believe it," Jenny said. "He's even more beautiful in person than he is on video."

Oliver wriggled free and launched himself at my door as soon as I stopped the car, then ran around to the passenger side and stood on his back legs to bark at Jenny through the glass. Porter jogged over and pulled Oliver away so Jenny could get out of the car.

"Sorry about that," he said as Oliver ran in circles between me and Jenny, his tail wagging at top speed. Porter reached for Jenny and hugged her. "At long last, the famous Jenny Fife."

"And it only took thirty-five years to make it happen," Jen said.

"Can I get your stuff?"

"Thanks. There's only one bag, in the trunk."

Oliver pushed in front of us to go in first and Porter followed with Jenny's suitcase in his hand.

"Oh, Bits," Jenny said, stopping just inside the door and clapping her hand over her mouth. "It's beautiful! It's like a jewel box."

"You like it?"

She nodded. "The colors are fantastic. And the artwork!" She stepped toward a group of framed paintings. "What are these? I love the flying monks."

"That's the Four Seasons from Norberto, an artist in Assisi."

"I love them." Jenny turned in a circle. "Aw! Look at us!" she said, spotting a framed photo on the bookshelf. It was a picture of me and Jenny and my dad on the stoop of our house in Syracuse. My dad was in his police uniform and Jenny and I were wearing roller skates and had yarn ribbons in our hair. All of our mouths were stained by the popsicles we were eating.

"I had a place in London restore it for me. It turned out great, didn't it?"

Jenny nodded and reached down to pet Oliver, who was sitting on her feet.

Porter deposited Jenny's suitcase in the guest room. When he came out, he said, "I'd like to invite you ladies to lunch on the terrace. I figured you'd be hungry so I already put it together. We can eat whenever you want. If it's too chilly, we can eat inside."

"I have a jacket," Jenny said. "I just need a shower and then I'll definitely be ready to eat."

"Need me to do anything?" I asked Porter.

"Nope," he said, shaking his head. "I'll see you guys whenever you're ready." He clapped his hands. "Come on, Oliver. They don't need your help."

I took Jenny into the kitchen and showed her where the basics were. She glanced out the window at Porter, who was walking across the field with Oliver on his heels.

"He's a prince," she said, turning to look at me. "Sorry. I know it's complicated right now, but you gotta admit, the guy's a gem."

I gave her a half smile. "Let me show you how the shower works and then we'll go have lunch."

Porter was sitting on his terrace flipping through a seed catalog and Oliver was stretched out under his chair, his head resting on his paws, when we walked over. They both got to their feet as we approached.

"Here you go," Porter said, gesturing to the chair he'd been sitting in. "Take this one for the view, Jenny. I'll just run in and get everything."

"You sure you don't need help?" I asked.

"Not at all. Relax."

Jenny sank into the seat and looked from side to side. "This is about as different from Syracuse as you can get."

"Probably why it appealed to me."

She laughed. "Come on. Syracuse isn't that bad! Don't you miss scraping ten feet of snow off your car every morning?" She pointed to Villa Rosmarino across the fields. "Is that where the new neighbors live?"

Porter reappeared as I was telling Jenny about the boozy night we first met Dean and Darren. He was pulling the wagon and started unloading its contents onto the table.

"My liver hurts just thinking about that night," he said.

"We've made a resolution to stop drinking so much," I told Jenny. "The pandemic turned us both into lushes."

"Can you wait until I'm gone, though?" Jenny asked.

"Yeh, I think that would be okay. Porter?"

He nodded. "I'll do my best." He set a glass bottle with two stems in it on the table. "Those are the last sunflowers of the season," he told Jenny. "They waited for you."

"They're beautiful."

He pulled two bottles of Acqua Panna out of the wagon and set them on the table, and then unloaded a bottle of Sangiovese and three wine glasses.

"A lot of people drink white wine with what we're having, but your buddy here," he said, jerking his chin toward me, "likes red with everything. This is a dry red that's not too aggressive."

"Oh, good," Jenny said. "I don't like aggressive wines. I got jumped in a back alley by a Pinot Noir once and I still haven't recovered." She picked up the wine bottle. "What's the story on this wine?"

"What did you say about this wine the other night, Porter?"

"It's smooth and doesn't insist upon itself."

"That's right. It just sits back and waits to be noticed. Looks pretty but doesn't flirt."

"Just like us," Jenny said. "It's the middle school dance all over again."

Porter went back to the kitchen after pouring the wine and returned with a plate.

"Some crostini to tide you over," he said with a little bow, setting the plate between us.

Jenny leaned forward to look at the toasted bread. "Is that topping made of beans?"

Porter nodded. "Cannellini, with thyme, garlic, and a little balsamic on top. Beth said you're not a big meat eater."

She smiled up at him. "I'm not. This looks amazing."

"Enjoy. I'll be back in a few minutes."

Jenny picked up a crostino and sat back in her chair. "I think I'm in love," she said. "Is he always like this? I can't remember the last time Scott cooked."

"He's a great cook," I said, licking the bean mixture off my finger. "We definitely eat well."

"He's so . . . kind, I guess, is what I mean. He just seems genuinely kind."

I nodded.

"And this place . . . Wow." She pushed a bite of bread into her mouth and reached for her wine glass. "I'm going to need a nap later, but I don't want to be inside in this glorious weather. It was gray and in the forties when I left Syracuse."

"You can use Porter's hammock. It's tucked in the trees back there," I said, pointing beyond the house. "I like to take a blanket and nap there sometimes."

"What's up with your star-crossed lovers in the barn?" Jenny asked.

I'd kept her up to date on the animal population ever since the pandemic, when we'd needed something else to think about besides the virus that was reshaping the world.

"Brutus is still devoted to Clara," I said, "but Clara is aloof. It's torment for him."

"Hmm," Jenny said. "Reminds me of two people I know . . ."

I threw a piece of bread at her.

"Hey!" she said, laughing. Oliver jumped to his feet and ate the bread off her lap. "Good boy," Jenny said, petting Ollie's ears. "Much better than a vacuum."

"I'm not aloof."

"No," she said. "But you're a tough nut to crack. And he is devoted to you, that's obvious." When I didn't answer, Jenny said, "So why are there two houses on this property? Did it used to be two separate places, or what?"

I shook my head. "This was all one big farm, called a *cascina*. Porter's house was the main house where the owners lived, and my house was probably for the farm overseer. See how there's a sort of a triangle between the barn and the two houses?"

Jenny swiveled in her seat to look and nodded.

"There was a fourth place over there," I said, pointing to the area across from my house. "The buildings would have enclosed a square courtyard. Porter wants to try to uncover the foundation and maybe build something there. Bring it back to what it originally was."

"Did one family own the whole place?" Jenny asked, turning back to the table and picking up another crostino.

"Originally, yeah. The old guys I bought my place from grew up here, in Porter's house. It was their family farm. But during World War II, German officers moved into the big house and the family had to move into my house," I told her. "I guess they moved back into the big house at some point after the war, but when they were old, they sold the big house to Porter and lived in my house again. Then they moved in with their sister after her husband died, and that's how I got my place."

"How old is this property?"

"It's from the 1600s, so pretty new."

Jenny laughed. "The Syracuse historical society would lose their minds." She nodded in the direction of Porter's house. "Here comes the chef."

Porter set a stack of three flat-bottomed bowls on the table, then took the cover off a serving bowl and picked up a large fork and spoon.

"Where did you get the mushrooms?" I asked, leaning forward to inhale the steam coming off the pasta. Porter had made linguine with fresh porcini mushrooms and chopped parsley, one of my all-time favorite meals.

"Bought them this morning in town."

"The old men I was telling you about hunted mushrooms every fall," I told Jenny. "I got a whole lecture from Alberto once about the proper care and treatment of mushrooms. He was horrified that I'd rinsed them instead of using a dry brush."

"Mushrooms were his religion," Porter said.

"I'm considering converting myself," Jenny told him. "It would be much easier to be a divorced Mushroomist than a divorced Catholic."

"I'm really sorry about all that's been going on," Porter said, dishing pasta into the bowls. "Scott's an idiot."

Jenny dabbed the corners of her eyes with a napkin and smiled up at Porter. "Thanks. I appreciate that." She leaned back so Porter could set a bowl of pasta in front of her. "This looks so good. I haven't had pasta in ages."

"Pasta in the US is crap," Porter said. "The flour is so processed. That's why it makes you tired—your body has to work too hard to digest all the chemicals. This will be totally different." He walked over to the wagon and lifted a bowl of salad out of it. "I almost forgot this," he said, adding the salad to the table. "Okay, we're ready. *Buon appetito.*"

After a leisurely lunch, Porter refused to let us help and stacked the plates in the wagon, hauled them to the kitchen, and then came back to the table and topped off our wine glasses. Jenny stifled a yawn and slumped in her chair.

"This is heaven," she said, twirling a strand of hair around her finger. "I can't thank you guys enough for letting me crash here."

"I'm so happy you're here," I said.

She reached down to pet Oliver, who was resting his head on her knee. "So tell me about your life, Porter."

He glanced at me. "Has Beth not filled you in?"

"She's never mentioned you at all," Jenny said. "This morning was the first time I ever heard your name."

I laughed out loud. "Way to keep him humble, Jen."

Porter smiled. "You want the official version? Okay, I was born in Richmond, Virginia, in 1969. I'm pretty sure I was born on a Monday."

"Wait—what is Monday's child?" Jenny asked me.

"Fair of face," I said.

"Figures."

"Right? Of course he would be a Monday."

"You guys have totally lost me," Porter said.

"It's an old poem," Jenny explained. "We had to learn it when we were little kids. *Monday's child is fair of face, Tuesday's child is full of grace.*" She looked at me. "What day are you, Bits?"

"Thursday."

"*Thursday's child has far to go*. That fits—you're not one to stay put," Jenny said. "I'm Friday."

"*Friday's child is loving and giving*. That suits you perfectly."

"I don't have a clue what you're talking about," Porter said. "I've never heard that poem in my life."

"I guess it wasn't a thing where you're from," Jenny said. "Must never have made it below the Mason-Dixon Line."

"That poem is why Wednesday Addams is called Wednesday," I told Porter. "*Wednesday's child is full of woe.*"

He looked at Jenny. "The bizarre shit she knows . . ."

"Don't get me started," Jenny said. "Anyway, we've established that you are fittingly fair of face, Porter, and now you may continue with your life story."

"Band name!" Porter and I said in unison.

"'Fittingly fair of face' would be a great one. Imagine the merch," I said to Porter. "We'd kill it on T-shirts alone."

Porter clinked his wine glass against mine, then turned back to Jenny. He gave her a brief overview of his life prior to college, then said, "And then when I was a senior at Carolina, I met Beth. I'm guessing you pretty much know the rest."

"She already said I've never mentioned you," I teased. "God, Porter. Check your ego."

"Sorry, I forgot."

"Tell me something random about yourself," Jenny said. "One fact that no one else would know."

He thought for a second, then said, "I was terrified of the Oompa Loompas as a kid."

"Me too!" Jenny shrieked. "They're so evil!"

"They're supposed to be scary, you dingdongs," I said, laughing. "It's a cautionary tale about gluttony and greed and being a demanding little bitch like Veruca Salt."

"Yeah, but the Oompa Loompas go way too far. Think about how they dance and sing while they cart the kids off." Porter shuddered dramatically. "They obviously enjoy it."

"That chocolate river was probably loaded with dead bodies," Jenny said.

"I came across somebody's thesis in the library once that said Roald Dahl based the Oompa Loompas on the Vietcong," I said, pushing my glass across the table towards Porter.

"Of course you did," Jenny said. "And not only that, but you sat there and read it."

"It's a nice theory, but the book came out in the early sixties," I said. "Dien Bien Phu fell in 1954, so okay, Vietnam might have been on Dahl's radar screen, but the British were never formally involved there, and I don't think a whole lot was known about the Vietcong until later. So that theory seems a little flimsy."

"Ladies and gentlemen, my best friend," Jenny said, and clinked her glass against Porter's. "Do you ever get tired of hearing the contents of her brain?"

"Nope," Porter said, pushing my refilled wine glass back to me. "Somebody should do a remake and have the Oompa Loompas actually be Vietcong. It could be like *Willy Wonka* meets *Apocalypse Now*. Marlon Brando could rise out of the chocolate river, and Beth's boy Robert Duvall could surf through that freaky red tunnel," he said.

I raised my wine glass to Porter. "*Apocawonkalypse*. That's brilliant. We should shop this around Hollywood."

Jenny shook her head. "If I ever doubted you two belong together," she said, looking pointedly at me, "this conversation would erase those doubts entirely."

After lunch, Porter showed Jenny where the hammock was and got her a blanket from inside while I scraped the plates and loaded them into his enormous ceramic sink.

"Oliver tried to get in the hammock with her," Porter told me as he came through the kitchen door.

"She probably didn't mind," I said, turning on the hot water and adding soap to the dishes. "The Fifes had a Lab named Roscoe when we were kids. He slept on Jenny's bed."

Porter walked over and wrapped his arms around me from behind. "I miss you," he said into my shoulder.

I nodded. "Things have been crazy lately."

"I'm really glad to be meeting Jenny. It's nice to know something about your childhood."

"You know lots about my childhood," I said, rinsing a wine glass.

Porter let go of me.

"Thank you for lunch," I said. "It was delicious and really thoughtful of you."

He nodded and tugged on the handle of his ancient refrigerator. "Want anything to drink?"

I shook my head. "Nah. I thought later maybe we'd go for a walk and then we could take Jenny to the pizzeria in the village?"

"Do you want me to come or would you rather have girl time?"

I set the plate I was rinsing in the drying rack and looked over my shoulder at him. "Of course I want you to come, Porter. I'm not mad at you, you know. I'm just working through this Sloan stuff. I need some time to process it, and I know you do too."

He finished pouring a glass of Acqua Panna and twisted the cap back on the bottle. "I've been meaning to ask where you stayed the other night," he said, putting the bottle of water back in the refrigerator.

"You already asked."

"Remind me of the answer?"

I dried my hands on a dish towel and turned to face him. "Assisi."

He laughed, a short bark of sound. "How'd I know that?"

"Come on, Porter. Marco's in a relationship, first of all, and—"

"So's Nicolette, yet you seem to think we're fucking in the bushes."

I stared at him for a minute, then shook my head, dropped the towel on the counter, and said, "Maybe don't come for pizza."

Eighteen

When Jenny got up from her nap, we took Oliver for a long walk through the valley, then cleaned ourselves up and drove over to the village pizza place.

As soon as we had our drinks, Jenny looked at me across the table and said, "Out with it."

"With what?"

"With what's really going on with you."

"About what?"

"Look, I know I'm parachuting into this situation without all the context, but you've got this guy who obviously adores you, yet you seem totally oblivious to that fact," Jenny said. "Actually, not oblivious. You seem annoyed by it."

I was inspecting a hangnail and didn't answer.

"I know you've been through hell, Bits, but you've gotta ease up on him. Are you really going to ruin the life you've built with Porter over a girl you might see once or twice a year?" she asked. "And who knows? You might even really like her."

"You sound like David."

"Well, David's a smart guy." Jenny reached across the table and squeezed my hand. "What's this really about, though, this irritation with Porter? The whole Kick thing is way in the past, so I don't think that's it."

I shook my head.

"Is it just about Sloan?"

I looked around the restaurant before answering. "I don't even know, Jen. I'm still just so angry about what happened to Mia that I want to scream. I don't want to have to get to know Sloan," I said. "Why should I? Porter's surprise sperm donor kid isn't my circus."

"No, it's not," she agreed. "But it is your life and I feel like you're about to destroy something great." She sighed. "Look, I get it. You've been served a whole platter of shit sandwiches, Bits. You've had to pick up the pieces again and again and again."

"And I'm tired of it. Absolutely exhausted."

"I know." Jenny leaned back in her chair. "You know, I always admired how you kept it together after your dad died."

"I was nine years old," I said, shrugging.

"Yeah, I know. But you stayed on track. You did your homework and went to ballet and didn't turn into some kind of 'oh poor me' insufferable piece of shit. And when your mom died, you—"

"I went off the rails, remember?"

"You think every other high school senior wasn't drinking and having sex? That wasn't off the rails."

"You weren't."

"I was a late bloomer," Jenny said, then laughed. "In fact, I think I'm long overdue for some casual sex and drunkenness. Scott shouldn't have all the fun."

"That's for sure."

"My point is, you haven't had an easy time of it. And I think after Mia's accident and the whole Crawford fiasco, you're trying to control everything because you think that will keep you from being hurt again. But you're never going to be able to control everything, Bits. No one can."

"Oh, thank God," I said as the waiter arrived with our pizzas. "Saved by food."

After the waiter left, Jenny said, "I'm sorry. I'm not trying to harp on you, I promise. I just don't want to see you make a huge mistake."

We didn't talk much as we ate. I was thinking about what Jenny said. I knew she was right. I was still grieving my daughter. I'd always be grieving my daughter. But I couldn't let that grief ruin my relationship with Porter. Running him off wasn't going to bring Mia back. And if I wanted to stay together with Porter, then I had to accept the situation with Sloan and make the best of it.

"I know you're right," I said, laying my knife and fork on top of the remnants of my pizza and pushing my plate away. "I've been keeping Porter at arm's length ever since he found out about Sloan. The truth is, I'm terrified to meet her. What if I actually like her?"

"Would that be so terrible?"

"It feels incredibly disloyal to Mia," I said, using my napkin to fight against the tears that were threatening to spill. "She had her whole life in front of her! If that dumbass hadn't tried to beat the traffic light, my daughter would still be alive."

Jenny nodded.

"But she's not, and it feels like if I let Sloan in my life, I'm . . . I don't know. Replacing Mia somehow."

"Oh," Jenny said, dropping her fork and putting her hand over her heart. "Oh no. That's what this is about?" She reached across the table and grabbed my wrist. "Okay, don't cry. It's okay. Let's get the check and go."

I nodded and dried my face, then asked for the check, rebuffing the waiter's questions about coffee and dessert.

I left cash on the table, and we got up and went outside. Jenny stopped me before we got in the car.

"Come here," she said, opening her arms.

I walked into her hug and started bawling.

"I understand why you feel that way," she said, "but no one will ever replace Mia. That's just not possible, Bits. You've got to let that idea go."

We stood like that for a minute, Jenny rubbing my back in soft circles. Finally, I pulled away and used the cuff of my sweater to wipe my eyes.

"I'm sorry. This isn't what you came to Italy for."

Jenny patted my shoulder. "I'm pretty sure my husband is getting regular blow jobs from a perky-titted twinkie. I came to Italy to think about anything but that."

I nodded and walked around to the driver's side door. "Okay, well, I'm glad I could help, then."

Jenny laughed. "By the way," she said, getting into the passenger seat, "you can use that if you want. 'Perky-titted twinkie' would be a great band name."

When I came out of my room the next morning, Jenny was already sitting at the kitchen table drinking coffee.

"I hope I didn't wake you up?" she said. "Jet lag's a bitch."

"Not at all. Is the coffee okay?"

Jenny nodded. "I followed your instructions. I like that little coffee maker. I think I need one."

"There's a Bialetti store in Florence with all the models," I said, unscrewing the top of the moka. I took the metal basket to the trash can and banged it against the side to get rid of the coffee grounds. "They have them in all colors and sizes. We'll get you one."

"Cool."

"Can I make you breakfast? Or do you want to go somewhere? I was thinking we could go to Orvieto today. We can always stop for coffee and a pastry on the way."

"Yeah, let's do that," Jenny said. "I just need to brush my teeth again."

"No hurry. I need coffee before I can drive."

When the water was boiling, I turned the heat down and let the coffee finish brewing, then brought the Bialetti and a coffee cup to the table.

"Tell me about Marco," Jenny said. "How's he doing?'

"What made you think of him?"

"I was looking at those flying monk pictures this morning."

"He's fine. Survived the pandemic and is back to work as a tour guide."

"Still with the psycho wife?"

"Hard to say. He said she's staying with her sister, but I don't really know what that means." I shrugged. "Who knows? But he seems all right. I worried about him a lot during the pandemic, being trapped in the house with her. I had nightmares about finding out she'd killed him."

"Why do you think he stays with her?"

"Social pressure. It's a small town, plus he feels responsible for her. And he'd probably be way too embarrassed to admit how abusive she is. I think he's just resigned to living this way."

"Sad."

"I think so too. But we don't really talk about her."

I told Jenny about the night I'd spent hanging out with Marco at his hut, and how much fun we'd had. "I haven't laughed like that in ages."

"But is there an attraction there?" she asked. "Is that part of the problem with you and Porter?"

"Porter's pissed that I stayed over there, but you know what? I can do what I want. We're not married. We're not even engaged."

"Do you want to be?"

I almost said no, then stopped myself. "I don't even let myself go there. The idea of tethering my life to someone else's again is really—"

"Terrifying," Jenny said, then laughed. "Sorry, I'm projecting. But that's how I feel. I'm so shocked by what Scott is doing that it's hard to imagine ever trusting anyone again."

I nodded. "That's how I felt, too. The Crawford I thought I knew would never have treated me with so much disrespect."

"It's not like we're stupid, either," Jenny said. She sighed. "I guess we all see what we want to see."

"Just for the record, I do realize that I'm imposing a real double standard here. I was furious with Porter about Nicolette, and yet I went and hung out with Marco all night."

"Well, I think the sting with Porter is that Nicolette's a stranger and he talked to her about something really personal and painful to you," she said. "That's the betrayal, not that she felt him up."

I laughed out loud. "She totally did! Over the bra, but still."

Jenny got up and put her coffee cup in the sink. "Well, if we're making statements on the record, then I will just say that Porter seems like a really good guy."

"So did Crawford. So did Scott."

"Touché," Jenny said. "I'm gonna go brush my teeth."

After stopping for coffee and a pastry, I parked at the train station in Orvieto, then we crossed the street to the funicular that takes passengers up the mountain to the historic center.

"There's a parking lot at the top," I told Jenny after I'd purchased the tickets, "but I love riding this thing."

The little cable car pulled by a chain deposited us in the station at the top of the mountain, and we walked outside to take in the view from the castle ruins next door.

"In terms of views, this isn't great," I said as we stood looking down at the valley. "Pretty industrial looking from here. Let's cut across the parking lot and walk up Corso Cavour."

"Why do I keep seeing that name?" Jenny asked as we crossed the street and skirted the parked cars.

"Cavour?"

"Yeah. I think we've passed at least twenty streets with that name already."

"He was the count who unified Italy under the Savoys in the 1800s," I said. "There's a Corso Cavour in every Italian town I've ever been in. Stop me if you see any place you want to go into."

We took our time making our way up the street, ducking in and out of stores and window shopping. When we got to the intersection in the center of town, we turned left toward the cathedral.

"Oooh, look at all the pottery!" Jenny said, pointing to a colorful window display of dishes and ornaments. "Is this where yours came from?"

"I pick it up all over. There's a town near Assisi called Deruta that's famous for ceramics and I've gotten some things there, but the real treasure trove is in a place called Vietri sul Mare near Sorrento. That's where all my dishes came from," I told her. "I can't go back there, though. I was like a drug addict in a pharmacy."

Jenny stopped in front of a jewelry store and inspected the window display. She lifted her left hand and showed me her wedding ring. "I haven't been able to bring myself to take it off," she said. "Actually, I don't even know if I can get it off anymore. I may need the Jaws of Life."

"I know a trick. If you want to, we can do it when we get home."

"It's time," she said, nodding. "That's going to be my quest while I'm here, then. To buy something to replace my meaningless wedding ring."

We continued to the cathedral. I left Jenny to take photos of the massive bronze doors and intricately carved facade and went next door to the ticket office. Without the crowds of summer it wasn't necessary to wait for the timed entrance to the cathedral, so once I had our tickets, we handed them to the sleepy old man in the booth and went right in.

"Oh, wow," Jenny said, looking up at the cathedral's vaulted ceiling as we stepped inside. "This is incredible."

"It's layers of two different types of marble. That's how they make the stripes in the stone."

She grabbed the back of a pew and looked up again. "Wow."

"Wait until you see the chapel." I pointed to the front of the church. "That's where I'll be, down there on the right. Unless you want me to walk around with you?"

Jenny shook her head. "I'm just going to do a couple of laps and take it all in. I'll come find you."

I left Jenny to wander and went to the Brizio Chapel in the cathedral's south transept.

Luca Signorelli, a Renaissance painter from Cortona, had covered every inch of the chapel's walls and ceiling with scenes from the Last Judgment. It's overwhelming to try to take it all in, and I was always tempted to lie on the floor so I could look without feeling like I was going to fall over. I'd never had the nerve to do it, though.

I turned in circles until I found the scene I was looking for. It's called "Sermons and Deeds of the Antichrist," and the devil—complete with a pointed chin and horns—is standing behind Jesus and whispering in his ear. The way Signorelli positioned the figures of Jesus and the devil, it's impossible to tell exactly whose left arm is extending from the robe of Jesus. It's almost like the devil is pressed up against Jesus with his hand around his waist, which gives the whole pose a very disturbing sexual air.

In other scenes on the chapel walls, people are being judged, burned, cast down into hell, killed, tortured, and devoured by demons, including demons who look uncannily like Luca

Signorelli himself. But it's not all bleak. There are also scenes of paradise, and people being guided to heaven by cherubs and angels. A lot of the scenes follow Dante's *Divine Comedy*, and Dante himself is painted into the frescoes, along with other literary greats like Ovid and Homer and Virgil.

The first time I visited Orvieto, on an outing with Marco, I'd picked up a book about the cathedral's artwork and learned that Luca Signorelli was the third painter hired to do the chapel. He followed on the heels of Beato Angelico and Benzolo Bozzoli, and supposedly was chosen because he worked fast and came in with the lowest bid.

"Benzolo Bozzoli must have been a hard act to follow," I'd said to Marco, holding on to his jacket so I didn't tip over while I tried to figure out the arm situation between Jesus and the devil.

"I don't know what this mean," Marco said. "Bozzoli was painter, not actor."

"I just meant that Benzolo Bozzoli was probably really good at what he did, so coming onto the job after Benzolo Bozzoli would be hard."

"No." Marco shook his head. "Is not true. Fra Angelico was better. Very famous."

"Better than Benzolo Bozzoli?"

"*Sì.*"

"Really? I find it hard to believe that anyone was better than Benzolo Bozzoli. Benzolo Bozzoli was just a beast when it came to frescoes. To my mind, Benzolo Bozzoli can't be beat."

Marco realized what I was doing and looked down at me, shaking his head. "Why you are like this?" He peeled my fingers off his arm and pushed me away. "I go to the chapel on the other side."

"Do you mean the chapel where the miracle of Bolsena is? I wonder if Benzolo Bozzoli ever went to Bolsena?"

Marco walked away, pretending to call to the guard. "Help, *signore*! I am followed from this crazy American who talk in continuous about Benzolo Bozzoli!"

I smiled at the memory and tore myself away from the Brizio Chapel to cross over to the north transept. Jenny was still looking at the paintings and statues that lined the perimeter of the nave, so I went to the Cappella del Corporale, the Corporal Chapel, on the other side of the church.

The chapel is home to a reliquary containing a piece of cloth—a corporal—that used to sit under the chalice and host during the Eucharist in Bolsena, a town in the province of Viterbo that I'd visited briefly with Marco. There is a volcanic lake ringed by umbrella-shaped maritime cypress trees there, and a small historic center with a castle and a couple of ancient stone buildings, but Bolsena's real claim to fame is the miracle that occurred there in 1263.

According to legend, a German priest named Peter of Prague was celebrating Mass in Bolsena when the host began to bleed onto the corporal. The drops of blood formed the face of Jesus on the cloth. This was seen as undeniable proof that the host does, in fact, transform into the actual body of Christ during the Eucharist—a process known as transubstantiation. My favorite thing about the story is that Peter of Prague had been very vocal about his doubts concerning transubstantiation, making the whole episode something of a giant middle finger, like Jesus saying, "Oh, you don't believe I can be anywhere and do anything? Watch me bleed, asshole."

I took a seat on one of the pews in the chapel and thought about what Jenny had said at the pizza place, about my trying to control everything. I'd always been a Type-A sort of person who made plans and liked to be prepared, but Jenny was right. I now had an obsessive need to eliminate any surprises from my life. After the horrible one-two punch of Mia's death and my divorce, I'd spent way too many hours worrying about things that would never come to fruition, making myself crazy trying to eliminate the possibility of being dealt a shock like that again.

"You've always been independent, Bits," Jenny had said, picking at the crust of her pizza, "and that's a good thing. But sometimes you have to let someone else in. Let someone else help pull you through. You won't ever be able to predict what's coming down the pike."

"I know. David calls it 'the chaos' and says nobody escapes it. I think I've just had more than my share of chaos."

"Which is why it makes total sense that you're scared."

I was quiet for a minute, thinking. "I *am* scared, Jen. I was in such a dark place, and it took so long to climb out of it, that the thought of going through something like that again terrifies me."

She nodded. "That's totally understandable."

"It makes me physically nauseous to rely on other people. You get comfortable doing that and then poof! They're gone, and you're worse off. If I count on Porter, if we make things official, am I not just setting myself up for heartache? He could decide he wants to be a real father to Sloan and pack up his shit and move back to the US! I mean, who knows?"

"I get why you feel that way," Jenny said, "but I really don't see that happening. Sloan's not a child. It's not like she needs a dad. And you can't just cut yourself off from life to avoid pain, Bits. You're not an island."

I immediately thought of a Carly Simon song called "Island" I'd always liked and asked Jenny if she knew it. She shook her head.

"The chorus is '*I would rather fall from grace completely than let you change my mind; I would rather bet my life against the rising of the sun.*'"

"Well, that's quite a statement."

I laughed. "Yeah, well, she meant it. She was isolating herself from other people's bullshit."

"That's a nice idea, but it doesn't work," Jenny said. "You have to rely on other people, Bits. That's how we're wired. Sometimes things don't work out, but that doesn't mean you can cut yourself off from everyone and go it alone. People need other people."

"You sound just like David. Should we do a round of 'Kumbaya?'"

"It couldn't hurt," Jenny said, making a circle of olive oil on her plate. "Why do we all know that song, anyway? And 'Michael, Row the Boat Ashore?'"

"I actually know the answer to this."

"Shut the front door."

I stuck my tongue out at her. "The *New York Times* did a story on the origin of 'Kumbaya.' It came from the Gullah people in the lowcountry of South Carolina and it's literally someone saying, 'Come by here.' They're asking God to stop by and notice what's going on, but the accent makes it sound like they're saying 'kumbaya.'"

"Seriously? I thought it was an African word," Jenny said, dragging a piece of pizza crust through olive oil. "I'm kind of disappointed, no lie."

"Me, too. Anyway, the song got picked up by folk artists like Joan Baez and Pete Seeger and that's why everyone knows it."

"And 'Michael Row the Boat Ashore?'"

"Also from South Carolina. Also recorded by Pete Seeger. Also a slave song. Michael's the archangel, I think, ferrying people to heaven."

"Fascinating." She finished her drink and set the glass on the table. "If I sing it with you on the way home, will you promise to ease up on Porter?"

"Depends on how well you sing."

She laughed. "I'm serious, Bits. Don't wreck a good thing out of fear."

I was still mulling over what Jenny had said when she slid in next to me in the pew of the Corporal Chapel.

"I am blown away by this place," she whispered.

"Amazing, huh?"

She nodded. "Kind of puts my church to shame."

"Wait until you see the basilica in Assisi." I pointed to the reliquary and gave Jenny the bullet point version of the miracle of Bolsena story. "Where do you stand on transubstantiation, Jen?"

"Nowhere. I'm content to not know." She shrugged. "I figure I'll find out when I get to heaven."

"Do you think there will be a Q and A with Jesus when you get there?"

"Sure, why not? An orientation cocktail party. Or maybe they'll just hand out brochures of frequently asked questions."

We got up and began making our way out of the church, stopping to look at the marble statues that lined the sides of the nave and the carved wooden baptismal font in the back.

Outside, I asked Jenny if she was ready for lunch. There was a trattoria just across the small piazza from the church. Ordinarily I wouldn't suggest such a touristy place, but it was such a beautiful day that I didn't want to eat inside.

We found a table near a heater and sat so Jenny had a view of the cathedral. I ordered a bottle of Orvieto Classico and when the waiter brought it and put it in a terracotta wine cooler on the table, Jenny lifted the bottle and looked at the label.

"That's another thing I keep seeing here, these letters," she said, pointing at the DOC label. "What does that mean?"

"It's an authenticity standard. DOC means the wine is from a specific Orvieto Classico region with a specific blend of grapes." I laughed. "I used to call Marco the *DOC Umbrian* because his family has been in Assisi for like a thousand years. Plus, he's certifiable."

Jenny smiled. "Am I going to meet him?"

"Oh, for sure," I said. "When we decide which day we're going to Assisi, I'll let him know, I promise."

Jenny nodded. She picked up her wine glass and looked around at the other tables. "I was kind of hoping there would be a falcon here today."

Nineteen

Over the next few days, we didn't see much of Porter. I texted every night to let him know the plan for the next day and invite him to come along, but he always said he had stuff to do around the house. Jenny and I left early each morning and drove to wherever we were going—Arezzo, Montepulciano, Todi, Cortona, Siena—and came back late at night. I was always exhausted after driving and sightseeing all day and fell into bed while Jenny curled up on the couch with Oliver to read.

On Tuesday, as we sat in the Mercato Centrale in Florence devouring a plate of desserts, we decided we would go to Assisi the following day. I set the *cannolo* I was eating on my plate, licked the ricotta off my fingers, and dug my phone out of my purse to tap out a message to Marco on WhatsApp. He responded with an emoji of a blond man waving.

"What the hell?" I asked, turning the screen toward Jenny. "Does he think that looks like him? He's got black hair and brown eyes."

"Maybe he doesn't know there are different looks. Does that mean he agrees with what you wrote?"

"Who knows? Anyway, when we're there tomorrow, I want to stop in and make appointments for us at the Nun Spa. We can go back at the end of the week and spend the whole day getting massages and swimming."

"A spa for nuns?"

"That would be something, but no. It was a convent at one point—St. Catherine's, I think—so maybe they just went with the English word. Anyway, it's heaven."

"I can't wait. I'm dying to see this place you love so much."

I checked my watch. "Do you want me to try to get tickets to the Uffizi, or have you had enough art?"

"Is it terrible of me to want to just shop and walk?"

I shook my head. "Nope. You're on vacation."

"Then let's do that. We might also have to check me into the hospital, though, because I'm pretty sure I'm going into sugar shock."

We spent the entire afternoon strolling and shopping through Florence, checking out the Porcellino market and the stalls in front of the church of Santa Croce. I could tell Jenny wasn't interested in any more religious art, so I just ducked into Santa Croce for a few minutes, then rejoined her for more shopping. We'd managed to get Jenny's wedding ring off using dental floss and olive oil the night before, so we spent a long time looking for something to replace it at the jewelry shops on the Ponte Vecchio. After perusing all the stalls, though, Jenny said she'd know the ring when she saw it and it wasn't there, so we gave up and went to the Rinascente department store. Jenny bought a pink cashmere sweater, and then we went to the Bialetti store, where she bought one of the new red Dolce and Gabbana mokas.

"Okay," she said as the sales associate bagged her purchase. "I think I'm done. My feet are killing me."

I was tired too, and glad to navigate us back to the train station at Santa Maria Novella. We caught the tram just outside the station and rode it to the big public lot on the outskirts of town where I'd parked the car. We didn't talk much on the way there, but once we were in the car and I'd managed to get us pointed in the right direction on the autostrada, I told Jenny about helping Porter sort through the boxes he'd shipped over.

"There was all this crap in the boxes—soccer stuff and ticket stubs and menus and that teddy bear head that's on the mantel—and then I found this story I wrote years ago. I have no clue where he found it."

"What's the story about?" she asked.

"High school sweethearts. Well, kind of. They were never officially together and never admitted they loved each other, but they did. The girl goes to visit the guy in their last year of college and they finally have sex and she tells him she's in love with him, but he literally doesn't hear what she says."

"Then what?"

"She's devastated and takes off and he's confused and they never talk again. She becomes a business reporter and he becomes a finance bro and years later, she's assigned to cover a speech he's giving."

"And they finally get together?"

I shook my head. "Nope. The point is, he lectures people about not engaging in magical thinking in business, but that's exactly what he does in his personal life. He thinks he can just sit back and wait and they'll eventually reunite, when what he should be doing is tracking her down and being honest about how he feels."

"That's kind of sad."

"I was just playing around with the idea of the future turning on something very small like not hearing what someone said to you. If he'd heard what she said, things might have worked out really well for them. But that single moment changed the course of their lives."

"When did you write it?"

"I don't even remember. 2012, maybe? It was in an online journal at some point, but I have no idea how Porter would have seen it."

"But you said the other boxes were full of your stuff too, right?"

"Not my stuff. Stuff from when we were dating. Ticket stubs, things like that. I had no idea he'd saved it all."

Jenny was quiet for a few minutes, looking out the window, then said, "Can I say something to you, as your best friend?"

I glanced at her. "Sure."

"Don't take offense, Bits, but seriously? Pull your head out of your ass."

"Wow," I said. "Okay."

"I mean it," Jenny said.

I expected her to make a joke and lighten the mood, but instead she reached over and snapped off the radio.

"You have all the evidence in the world that Porter loves you, and that he's loved you for years," Jenny said. "Okay, sure, he's messed up here and there. Who hasn't? But this is the guy who pulled you back from the brink after Mia was killed. This is the guy who drove through a blizzard to come get you, and who saved every scrap of paper you ever touched and read your stories and opened his home to you and cared for you when you were down and out."

She looked out the window for a second, then turned back to me.

"And did I mention that Porter is *kind*? And attentive? And smart? And funny? But you won't work with him to get through this situation with Sloan, even though a blind man could see that it's killing him not to be able to talk to you about it. I don't get it." Jenny folded her arms over her chest and shook her head. "Porter was also shit on by the people he was supposed to be able to trust, you know—the drunk dad and the mom who abandoned him and God knows who else. I'm no psychologist, but I would guess he's just as reluctant to trust people as you are," she said. "But Beth, he obviously trusts you. He obviously loves you. But you just don't seem to be able to reciprocate."

She looked out the window again and I thought—I hoped—she was finished, but after a few seconds, Jenny turned back to me and said, "You know what? I don't even care if you're mad at me. I have to say this. Pull your fucking head out of your ass and give the guy some credit. He deserves better than to be cut off at the knees and he's obviously trying to figure out how to handle the situation without losing you."

My hands tightened around the steering wheel and I stared straight ahead at the car in front of us.

Jenny's tone softened. "Mia was my goddaughter, and I loved her. It breaks my heart every time I think about her," she said, reaching over and putting her hand on my arm. "And I want to kill Crawford for what he did to you. Not because he's gay—I don't care about that—but because you were a good wife and you deserved so much more than years of lies." She squeezed my forearm. "I know your heart was broken, Bits. I know it was. But don't shit on this gift you've been given because you're scared. Don't ruin things with Porter. Mia would hate to be the reason you ran away."

I turned the radio back on and we rode the rest of the way home without speaking.

Twenty

The next morning when I got up, Jenny was outside throwing a stick for Oliver. I watched them through the kitchen window as I put coffee on the stove. When the water started boiling, I knocked on the window and held up a coffee cup. Jenny smiled and waved and came inside, followed by Oliver.

"Hey. Sleep okay?"

"I can't remember the last time I slept well, to be honest," Jenny said. "But it gave me quality time with Ollie. And the sunrise was incredible." She reached down and scratched behind Oliver's ears. He craned his head backward to look at her.

"I think he's in love," I said.

"It's mutual. We're going to tell our parents soon." She leaned down to pull a twig of rosemary out of the curls at the base of his ear. "So do you hate me and want me to go home?" she asked, straightening up.

I held out my hand and Jenny dropped the twig into it. I put it in the trash can under the sink, then sat down across from her at the kitchen table.

"No, I don't want you to go home. And I could never hate you, Jen. That would be like hating part of myself."

"Which part? Your spleen? Appendix?"

I laughed. "No. I think you can live without both of those, and I could never live without you."

"Well, that's good," Jenny said, stroking Oliver's head. "I don't think I could bear to leave my new boyfriend."

"Do you want breakfast here or should we eat something on the way? Nothing gets going until ten or so, so we've got lots of time."

Jenny checked her watch. "I'm happy to get on the road if you are." She looked up at me. "Promise you're not mad?"

"I promise," I said, nodding. "I needed to hear all of that. Now I've just got to figure out what to do about it."

We plugged Jenny's phone into the Panda and listened to her '80s music playlist at top volume all the way to Assisi, which lifted my spirits enormously. I detoured off the highway to show her a little bit of Lake Trasimeno, but soon we were zooming down the road again with Adam Ant blasting.

"Remember my mom freaking out about us watching MTV? And oh my God, when she found my Prince tape," Jenny said as Adam Ant faded away and the opening notes of "Purple Rain" came on. "It's so PG compared to what's out now."

"I remember the older girls at ballet saw the *Purple Rain* movie, but we weren't allowed to see it."

"And they made fun of us," Jenny said, nodding. "We were pretty sheltered. I'm grateful for that now."

"Life before the Internet." I pointed to a sign next to the highway. "We're getting close."

As we took the Assisi exit off the highway, I told Jenny I was going to do a quick drive-by of the Basilica of Saint Mary of the Angels.

"I know you've been in a thousand churches already," I said, "so we won't go in, but I just want you to see it. There's this really cool chapel called Porziuncola inside that's from the 300s. Hermits from Josaphat came here with relics of Mary and they built a chapel in the woods."

"Sister Mary Michael would be so disappointed in me for asking this, but where's Josaphat?"

"I'm not sure exactly. I know it's a valley and I know it has to do with the Last Judgment because 'Josaphat' means 'Yahweh judges.' It's mentioned in the book of Joel, I think."

"I skipped that book."

I laughed.

"And they brought a piece of Mary?"

"I guess so. Something special, anyway. But then the chapel fell into ruin for almost nine hundred years," I said. "Hang on, I'm going to make a very illegal turn."

I whipped the Panda to the left and did a U-turn, then pulled the car next to the curb. Jenny peered up through the windshield.

"Look at that gold Mary," she said, pointing to the statue on the top of the basilica. "I love that."

"It's absolutely blinding in the sun."

"I can imagine. So go on with the story—there's a chapel that's falling down?"

"Yeah, and Francis repaired it and moved in with some of his followers. So the chapel is doubly important because it's connected to both Mary and Francis."

"And the chapel is inside the basilica?"

I nodded. "Right in front of the altar. They brought it out of the woods. And there's a garden on the side of the basilica where Francis grew roses without thorns." I glanced in the rearview mirror. A white police car was approaching from behind. "Shit. I gotta move."

Jenny sat back in her seat as I pulled away from the curb.

"That's the first McDonald's I've seen here," she said as we rejoined the two-lane road that went up the mountain to Assisi.

"I've never seen anyone actually go in it. There's one in Viterbo that's always packed, but I think that's because there are lots of students there. Assisi's not exactly hopping with teenagers." I pointed to the left as the Basilica of Saint Francis came into view. "Look, Jen. There it is."

She leaned forward and craned her neck to look out the windshield. "It looks just like the postcards."

"Right? You could have saved yourself the airfare."

We wound our way up to Piazza Matteotti, where I squeezed the Panda in between a camper van with Dutch plates and another Fiat. I looked around the parking lot but didn't see Marco.

"Do you want to go to the basilica first and then shop and eat?" I said, checking my watch. "By the time we get over there and see the church, everything else should be open."

We grabbed our sweaters off the back seat and locked up, then I grabbed a parking ticket from the machine and stuffed it in my purse. As we walked toward the center of town, I pointed out the two castles above us—the Rocca Maggiore and the Rocca Minore—and the Church of San Rufino where Saint Francis and Saint Clare were baptized. We stopped to look in a jewelry store, then peered in the window of a shop full of pen and ink drawings.

"What's the word for castle again?" Jenny asked, looking at a print of the larger of the two stone castles.

"*Rocca*. They weren't very creative with the names. Big castle and little castle."

Jenny laughed. "That's so logical it's almost German."

"I dare you to say that to Marco. He'll have an infarction."

We continued down to the main square and I pointed up at my favorite restaurant, Taverna dei Consoli, with its terrace over the Piazza del Comune.

"We can go there for lunch if you want," I said. "Or there's a really good pizza place owned by a family from Naples. It's called I Monaci, the monks. It's legit."

"I'd love to sit outside on that balcony," Jenny said. "Ooh, let's go in that purse store on the way back, too."

We continued walking across the Piazza del Comune. I told Jenny a little bit about the history of Santa Maria sopra Minerva as we passed, then pointed to a shop where I'd bought my table linens and the apron embroidered with sunflowers I'd practically worn out.

We kept walking, passing the store where priests could buy vestments and chalices and traveling Eucharist kits and the pottery store with the window full of hanging ceramic Christmas ornaments. Jenny took a few photos of the valley from an overlook near the Convent of the Swedish Sisters, and then we continued around the corner to the left and headed downhill.

As the basilica came into view, Jenny gasped. "Whoa. It's massive. And the rose window is so beautiful."

Inside the basilica, we slid into a pew so Jenny could take in the frescoes covering the interior walls and the vaulted ceilings. There were only a few people inside and the guards at the back—who spent the entire summer yelling *Silenzio!* and *Niente foto!* at chattering tourists with cameras—were talking with the priest behind the desk who will pray for you for a small sum. His little prayer-for-hire booth always reminded me of Lucy van Pelt dispensing psychiatric advice for a nickel in Charlie Brown cartoons. I pointed him out to Jenny and offered to buy her a prayer, but she said she preferred to get her prayers for free, thanks.

As Jenny scooted out of the pew to walk around, I leaned back and closed my eyes. I'd sat inside this church so many times, feeling utterly lost and despondent in the aftermath of Mia's death and my divorce. Jenny was right. Porter had pulled me back from the brink, and in return, I'd basically done a runner on him when he found out about Sloan. I'd been so wrapped up in my own grief that I hadn't made any allowance for the upheaval Porter was experiencing. No wonder we'd argued more in the past few weeks than we ever had before.

"Should we walk to the front?" Jenny whispered as she came back.

I nodded and followed her to the front of the nave to admire the intricately carved woodwork of the *sedilia*, the seats where the clergy and monks sit behind the altar. Then we turned around and looked back at the expanse of the church.

"This just makes me feel so small," Jenny whispered. "When you stand in this incredible place and think about all the people who've been here and everything this church has witnessed, it kind of makes my drama with Scott seem stupid. Actually, it makes all of our dramas seem stupid."

"I suppose that's the point," I said. "They make the churches grand to glorify God, but also to remind us that we're merely mortal."

"Just useless bits of ash and dust."

"Insignificant pox marks on the face of the universe."

"Meaningless fragments of worthless flesh."

"Tiny little specks of shit."

We laughed out loud. A passing monk looked over at us and hissed *Silenzio!* and we turned and scurried down the narrow staircase to the lower basilica.

"How did they do this?" Jenny asked at the bottom of the stairs. "It looks like the ceiling shouldn't stay up."

"Marco has told me how barrel vaulting works at least ten times and I still don't get it," I said. "And how did they build a whole second church right on top of this one? What's holding this place up?"

"Faith," Jenny said, and snickered.

I laughed. "I hope it's more than that or we're toast."

"*Silenzio*!"

I nodded at the monk and pulled Jenny into one of the side chapels. "We've been here half an hour and already gotten in trouble upstairs and downstairs," I whispered.

"We are nothing if not quick and thorough."

When the monk had turned the corner, I said to Jenny, "Before we get thrown out, I'm going to go to the other side, to the tomb of Saint Francis. You'll see a couple of steps down into a small room. I'll meet you over there, okay?"

Jenny nodded and I crossed the nave and went down the stairs to the tomb. She caught up with me several minutes later and we stood quietly, taking in the stone altar and the sarcophagus of Saint Francis.

"There's a whole saga around the body of Francis," I whispered to Jenny. "He was declared a saint really quickly, within two years after he died, I think. They took his body and hid it to keep it away from grave robbers who might want to sell pieces of him to other churches. But they hid him too well, because no one found him for six hundred years."

"Oops," Jenny said. "So where did he finally turn up?"

"Here in the lower church. He was hidden with some coins and a ring and some other stuff."

Jenny nodded and we stood there a few minutes longer, then she crossed herself and nodded at me that she was ready to go.

We made our way out of the basilica's lower entrance and peered through the gates of the monastery, then walked up the steep ramp on the side of the church and rejoined the pedestrian traffic towards the main piazza. We stopped at a bar nearby for another coffee, then spent a long time looking at the window display of a jewelry store.

"Do you want to go in?" I asked.

"Maybe," Jenny said. "It seems somehow appropriate to replace my wedding ring with something religious, doesn't it?"

"Because you're married to Jesus now, like your father always wanted?"

"Ha ha. He wishes. No, because it would help me remember that things are going to be okay. That this is just a moment in time. That there are much bigger forces at play in the universe than my petty problems."

"Makes sense to me." I pointed at a ring in the back of the window. "I like that one. It's got something written on it," I said, squinting. "A prayer, I think. Should we go in?"

"Let's come back later. I need to think about it. I don't know why it feels like such a big deal, but it does."

I showed Jenny the art gallery where I'd purchased the flying monk paintings, then we stopped to check out a stack of scarves. Marco texted while we were deciding which blue scarf Jenny should buy and said he would meet us after lunch with his three-wheeled *Ape* cart.

After the scarf shop, we stopped in the pharmacy for a box of Spididol to counteract the persistent headache I'd had for a week and then went to the taverna for lunch. The waiter and I chatted as he showed us to a table on the balcony overlooking the piazza and rolled the upright heater from the corner to our table.

"Well, the hot waiter certainly knows you," Jenny said after he'd gone back inside.

"He's the owner's son," I said, tugging off my jacket. "I asked him to go heavy on the vegetables and bring us whatever's fresh today. I hope that's okay."

"Of course. I'm starving."

Jenny grabbed a piece of bread out of the basket and stuck a corner of it in her mouth.

"Oh," she said, putting the bread down and reaching for her water glass. "I think this is the first thing I've had here that I didn't like."

"They don't use salt in their bread in Umbria. I have no idea why not but honestly, it's the most tasteless thing ever."

Luckily, the rest of the meal—*strangozzi* pasta with truffles, a platter of grilled vegetables drizzled with olive oil, a plate of fruit and cheese—was delicious. At the end of the meal, we were both absolutely stuffed and had to wave off the bottle of *amaro* the owner brought to our table. We thanked him, said goodbye to the hot waiter, and walked down the stairs to the edge of the piazza to meet Marco. About two minutes after I texted him that we were finished with lunch, he zoomed around the fountain on the edge of the piazza and kept the engine idling while Jenny and I jumped into the back seat.

"Ciao, *cara*," he said, looking over his shoulder. "Ciao, friend. I must go fast before we get a ticket."

Marco rolled the throttle forward and the three-wheeled cart lurched and took off. I pointed to Via Sermei as we zoomed past and told Jenny that's where I'd lived for a few months.

She nodded, her eyes wide. "Is this thing safe?"

I laughed. "Yeah, pretty much. Don't worry—we've only had one accident together, and it was in a car. We'll be fine."

Marco took a right at the end of the road and headed downhill, away from the historic area. I thought he was going down to St. Mary of the Angels, but as I leaned forward to tell him we'd already stopped at the basilica there, he took a sharp left into the woods.

"Jesus!" Jenny shrieked, grabbing the side bar of the cart's canopy.

"Ah, we're going to San Damiano," I said. "I wasn't sure where he was taking us. San Damiano is the convent of Saint Clare, where the Poor Clares started."

Marco pulled over on the side of the road near the entrance to the convent and shut off the engine. He turned around and looked at Jenny.

"Welcome to Assisi," he said. "Is first time?"

Jenny nodded.

"And you enjoy so far?"

"I was enjoying it until I got in this death trap."

"Good," Marco said. He got out and opened the door to let us out, then took my hand and leaned forward to kiss both of my cheeks. "*Ciao, cara. Sono felice di rivederti.*"

"I'm happy to see you again too. And this is Jenny, my best friend in the whole world."

Marco took Jenny's hand and gave her a little bow. They chatted while I walked to the little booth and bought two tickets to go in the convent, guessing Marco would prefer to stay outside.

"Are you sure you don't want to come in?" I asked when I rejoined them. "I can get another ticket."

Marco shook his head. "I have a smoke and enjoy the sun."

Jenny and I walked into the convent and showed our tickets to the nun by the door.

"Just think, Jen," I said as I followed her up the narrow staircase inside. "If you'd done what your dad wanted, you, too, could have lived in a convent."

"Everything is so small. Do you think people from the Middle Ages would be terrified of us?" she asked, poking her head into the sparsely furnished room where the nuns used to eat. "I like that table, though."

"They'd be amazed at our lack of lice."

"And our indoor plumbing."

I followed Jenny into the convent's chapel, and then we went to the courtyard to look at the medieval well. We took a quick walk around the grounds, admiring the flowers, then went back to rejoin Marco, who was sitting on a low rock wall looking at his phone.

"*Tutto a posto*?" I asked.

He looked up. "Yes. All is fine. Have a seat, darlings," he said, scooting down the wall to make room for us. "What do you want to see, friend? She is crazy for church and art," he said, jerking his chin in my direction, "and together we have seen everything. Today we do only what you like."

Jenny glanced at me before she answered. "I feel stupid saying this, but I'd really like to just take it easy a bit. We've been going full speed. Could we just ride around and sightsee for a while?"

Marco nodded. "Is not possible with your friend, but with me, is possible to relax. Come. I show you Saint Mary of the Angels and then we go for a drive. Is a beautiful day."

"Oooh, do you want ice cream, Jen? There's a good place in Saint Mary."

"Do I want ice cream? Was that a serious question?"

Marco stood up and clapped his hands. "So, we have the ice cream, we see some beautiful things, we enjoy life. Let's go. *Andiamo.*"

Jenny and I piled into the back seat of the three-wheeled cart again and Marco made sure our door was latched. Then we took off, barreling down the mountain with Marco looking over his shoulder to talk to Jenny as he drove. I wasn't really listening and just kept inhaling deeply. Every autumn, as soon as people started lighting fires, Assisi took on a very particular smell that I loved. It was like a mix of campfire and church incense, and I wished I could bottle it and take it home.

Marco came to an abrupt halt on a side road and announced that we had arrived.

"What's the difference between gelato and ice cream?" Jenny asked as she ducked under Marco's arm and stepped inside the ice cream parlor.

"Gelato has less milk fat and sugar," I told her. "Fewer calories too, and more intense flavors."

"Oh, goody. I can get a big one."

"I eat ice cream when I have been in America," Marco told her, shaking his head sadly. "Was shit. Also pizza was shit. Pasta also shit."

"Okay, great," Jenny said. "Did you like anything about America?"

"I like one thing from America very much, but we are meeting here in Italy," Marco said after pausing to think. "Also food from Asia. I never have this before in all my life."

We walked up to the counter. Marco was very solicitous with Jenny, translating the flavors and ordering for her.

She turned around to look at me as the girl behind the counter scooped her gelato. "Do you know what you want?"

I shook my head. "Not yet. I like to decide under pressure."

Marco looked down at Jenny. "I do not order for her," he said, nodding toward me. "When I first meet her, yes, because she do not speak Italian. But now she do everything herself." He reached out and placed his hand on my cheek. "And she love me, but she pretend is not true."

"Oh, here we go," I said, grabbing his hand and squeezing it before letting go.

"She's very independent," Jenny told him. "We were just talking about that."

"Is good, to be independent. But sometimes is nice also to allow love." He shrugged and took the cup of gelato from the girl and handed it to Jenny, then stepped aside so I could order.

"Aren't you having any?" Jenny asked Marco.

"I wait to see what she have. Is better this way."

When I had my gelato, we sat outside at a small iron table on the narrow sidewalk. I took a bite and passed the cup to Marco.

"The Nutella is so good," Jenny said, licking her spoon. "What did you get, Bits?"

"Lemon."

"What a surprise."

Marco laughed. "I say this too! She eat all with lemon. Old shoe, piece of wood." He picked up the spoon and dug into my ice cream. "Tell me where you have been?"

"Let's see if I can remember . . . Florence, Orvieto, Cortona, Arezzo. Siena. What's the wine town, Bits?"

"Montepulciano. We went to Montalcino too, but we didn't

stay long. And Todi. Tomorrow we're going to Pienza, I think, or Civita di Bagnoregio. Although I'm not sure I have the energy to walk across the bridge to Civita."

Marco nodded. "We have been together all these places," he told Jenny. "We go everywhere together. In all my life I never see so many things."

"I told Jenny all about working with you," I said. "And how much fun we had."

"First when I meet her," Marco said to Jenny as though I hadn't spoken, "I am thinking she is serious and also very sad. I think this will be terrible, to stay with her so many days. But then we are becoming friends and laughing in continuous. Is like a festival to be with her." He stuffed another spoonful of my gelato into his mouth, then slid the paper cup back across the table to me. "I start to love her very much," he told Jenny. "She feel this too, but she hide it."

"Bravo," I said. "You said that perfectly, Marco. If I hide my love for you, then my love for you is . . .?"

"Hidden," he said and beamed at me. "See? I am learning."

When we were finished, I collected the cups and tossed them in the trash can and went back to the counter to buy two bottles of water. Then we piled back into the cart. Marco drove us around for nearly three hours, stopping at everything interesting and giving Jenny a comprehensive tour of the valley. Jenny laughed at all of Marco's jokes and I could tell she found him charming.

When we finally returned to the top of the mountain, Jenny suggested we grab a drink. We went to a wine bar on the main road in the historic center and Marco went inside to choose a bottle while Jenny and I settled into one of the four tiny tables in the enclosed courtyard. Marco returned with a platter of snacks, two glasses, and a large bottle of water, which he plunked down in front of me. I poured a glass of water and slid it toward Jenny. She started to push it over to Marco, but I stopped her.

"He doesn't drink water."

"What?"

"He says it makes his insides rust."

Marco nodded. "Is true. Why I need water? What I am, a tree?"

"You wouldn't survive a day in the States," Jenny said. "It's now mandatory to have a giant water bottle with you at all times. Hydration has become our national sport."

"Well, that and mass shootings," I said.

The waiter arrived with a bottle of wine and three glasses. He and Marco chatted while he uncorked and poured the wine, and then he left.

"I hear that in America is normal to shoot the gun from the car," Marco said. "For practice."

"What do you mean?" Jenny asked. "Like a drive-by shooting range?"

"I don't understand what you say."

"Never mind," I told Marco. "It was a joke. We're not quite that bad yet."

"Give it a few years," Jenny said, picking up her wine glass.

Marco told us he was leaving the next day to go see his uncle in Bologna. "I stay only two days. Together with my uncle I go to Modena. He have business there."

"Oh, super. Can you pick up a Ferrari jacket for Jenny's idiot husband while you're there?" I asked, laughing.

"Honestly, the nerve of him," Jenny said, rolling her eyes.

"Why he is idiot?" Marco asked. "Is not nice, this word."

"Because he has a girlfriend who's about twelve years old and he lies like a rug," Jenny said. "Never mind all that. What's in Modena, anyway?"

"Besides the cars, vinegar. Remember the DOC stamp on the wine? Balsamic vinegar, the real stuff, comes from Modena. I think it might be called DOP, not DOC, for vinegar, but it's the same meaning. Balsamic vinegar is a regional specialty, like ham or cheese from Parma." I looked at Marco. "Remember when we did the vinegar tasting in Modena?"

He nodded. "Was a good day."

"Is the vinegar special just because it's from there or what?" Jenny asked.

"No," Marco said, shaking his head. "Is something very particular. I explain you. They make the juice of the grapes and cook it. Then this juice go into a special wood *botte*. What means *botte* in English?" he asked me.

"Cask."

"Cask," he repeated. "Each *botte* is from a different kind of wood," he told Jenny. "They are keeped in the top of the house."

"Kept."

Marco turned to me. "*Eh?*"

"Kept, not keeped."

"Is what I say."

Jenny's brow furrowed. "Kept on a shelf, or what?"

I shook my head. "The casks are made of different kinds of wood, like juniper and ash and cherry. They put the grape juice in the casks, and then put the casks in the attic. It stays warm up there, so the juice evaporates over time."

"Explain her how the juice go from big to little *botte*," Marco prompted.

"The casks are all different sizes, and as the juice evaporates, it gets moved from the bigger casks to the smaller ones. Once you get to the smallest cask, the liquid is really thick and has absorbed the flavor from each of the different types of wood. That's real balsamic vinegar. And to get the DOP certification, it has to be at least twelve years old."

"And is only the juice of grapes," Marco added. "This is important."

"Oh, right. The stuff that's not from Modena has other vinegar added, but real balsamic vinegar is just pure aged grape juice."

"And it takes twelve years to make?" Jenny said. "No wonder it's expensive."

"At least twelve years. Oh, wait, you'll love this! There are families that have been doing this for a zillion years, and when a baby is born, the family sets up a new battery of casks for them. By the time the kid hits puberty, they've got their own batch of real balsamic going."

"That's so much more useful than a savings bond," Jenny said. She looked at Marco. "You won't be here when we come back?"

Marco looked confused so I explained that Jenny and I were planning to come back to the Nun Spa for massages.

He shook his head. "Maybe I will not be here. Is too bad," he said, looking at me. "I like to see you always."

"I'm sure I'll be back soon," I said, then checked my watch. "Are you about ready to get rolling, Jen?"

She nodded and Marco took my wallet and went inside to pay the bill. When he reemerged, we left the cart in front of the tourism office so we could walk back uphill to where I'd parked. Marco looped Jenny's arm through his and kept up a steady stream of information about the places we passed. I walked behind them, happy to be lost in my own thoughts.

When we got to the car park, I fed the ticket into the machine and paid, then we said goodbye to Marco.

"Have a safe trip to Bologna," I said. "Call me soon?"

He nodded. Before I slid into the driver's seat, he put his hand on my arm and stopped me from getting in the car.

"What is it?" I asked, turning back to him.

Marco took my chin in his hand. "*Ti fidi di me*?" he asked.

"Yes, I trust you. Why?"

"*Qualunque cosa ti stia disturbando andrà tutto bene, mia cara. Non preoccuparti.*"

I nodded. "Okay, thank you. I'll see you soon, okay?"

"Ciao," Marco said, then walked away.

"What did he say?" Jenny asked as I got behind the wheel.

"He said that whatever is bothering me will be fine and not to worry."

She was quiet for a minute, then said, "Huh. It's almost like he knows you."

Twenty-One

Two days later, Jenny and I were sitting in my kitchen, trying to decide between a trip to Bologna or Sorrento and Pompeii.

"I feel like you'll have seen more of Italy if we go south," I said, setting a cup of coffee on the table in front of her. "It's a different landscape, a different accent, different food. Bologna is great, but my vote is for Sorrento and Pompei."

"I'm happy to do that," Jenny said. "And then I'm afraid I've got to get home."

"Why?"

She shrugged. "I don't know. To get started on the next phase of my life, I guess. Find a job. Figure out what to do about Scott and the house."

"There's no hope he's coming back?" I asked, putting the sugar bowl on the table in front of Jenny and going to the drawer for a spoon.

Jenny shook her head. "Even if he did, I don't want him back. I've been thinking about it a lot. I don't think people have affairs because of sex, you know? It's something else."

"I interviewed a psychologist once who said people have affairs because they prefer who they are with the other person. An affair lets them escape the confines and habits of the relationship they're in and see new possibilities for themselves. It lets them be the person they wish they were every day."

"It would be better to just become that person without the affair."

I nodded. "Of course. But inertia is powerful." I unscrewed the bottom of the moka, dumped the grounds in the trash, and refilled the bottom with water. "I think most people have a hard time taking the first step toward the future they want. They feel trapped. I definitely did. I knew something was wrong but I had no idea what or how to fix it."

"I wish I'd known, Bits," Jenny said, wrapping her hands around her coffee cup. "We never talked about it."

I nodded and finished spooning coffee grounds into the metal basket and screwed the pieces of the moka back together. "I know. I felt like I couldn't complain, since so many other parts of my life were really nice."

Jenny stared into her coffee cup for a few minutes. "Yeah," she said finally, looking up. "I understand that."

"But I was so lonely, Jen." I set the moka on the stovetop and leaned against the counter with my arms folded over my chest. "Not at first, when Mia was little, but when she grew up and got her own life and didn't need me so much. . . " I sighed. "It's amazing how lonely you can be in the company of the person you're married to."

"I get it," Jenny said, nodding. "I'm sure Scott feels great with Amber. He's got a whole new life now, and it's probably the exact life he wanted before I got pregnant and we got married. Plus, she's twelve, so he probably feels really smart . . ."

I laughed. "Chock full of wisdom and experience."

"Is it crazy that I think I'm going to like myself better without him?"

I shook my head. "Nope. It's going to be hard at first, but then things will come together. You'll have a life that belongs only to you. You can be exactly who you want to be and write your own story, and you'll be the main character for once."

"I just want my kids to love and respect me," she said. "That's all that really matters to me."

"I know." I lifted the moka off the stove, turned the flame off, and slid into the chair opposite Jenny. "They do. And they will support you. I'm sure they want to see you happy."

There was a rap on the kitchen door, then the door opened a crack and Oliver pushed his way in. He did two laps around the kitchen table, his tail beating a rhythm against the backs of the chairs, then sat next to Jenny and put his paw on her knee.

"Ollie, my love. Come home with me," Jenny said, bending to kiss the top of his head. She looked up and smiled. "Hey, Porter."

I wrapped my arm around Porter's leg as he came to stand next to me. He put his hand on my back and leaned down to kiss my hair.

"Can I get you a cup of coffee?" I asked. "I just made some."

Porter shook his head. "No, thanks. Listen, I, uh, just wanted to let you know that Sloan is coming. And not just Sloan, but her parents too."

"Oh. Wow. When?"

"Tomorrow. She called last night and said her conference has wrapped up. I guess her parents have been traveling or something, but now they're all in London and want to come over." Porter looked down at me. "I know this is weird and if you don't want to be here, I understand. But I hope you will be." He looked at Jenny. "You too."

I glanced at Jenny. "We were going to Sorrento and Pompeii," I told Porter, "but nothing's set in stone. We can go the day after."

Jenny nodded. She looked up at Porter. "I'd be happy to meet her. Meet them, I mean."

"Are they staying here?" I asked.

Porter shook his head. "No, they've rented a place in Perugia for two nights. I think they're going to travel around for a couple of days." He cleared his throat. "I said I'd pick them up from the train station in Cortona and we could have a late lunch."

"Okay," I said. "Let me know what you want me to make."

Porter exhaled loudly. "Thank you. I wasn't sure you—well, thank you. I'll let you know about the food, okay?"

He left to run to the hardware store in the village, whistling for Oliver to ride shotgun. Jenny looked across the table at me. "You okay?"

I nodded and picked up my coffee cup. "I'm fine. I'm glad you're here, though. And I'm actually glad we didn't have much advance notice. Less time for me to stew."

We put on music and spent the rest of the morning getting caught up on all of the tasks I'd been ignoring for months. Jenny pulled the drawers out of my desk and started going through them, trying to help me impose order on the endless stacks of notes and research for articles. She sat on the floor and read snippets of each piece so I could say what story the notes pertained to, then she made folders.

"Okay, here's some stuff that looks like it's about riding bikes," she said, skimming a coffee-stained sheet torn from a yellow legal pad. "Let's see . . . The average weight of a bike in the Tour de France is sixteen pounds."

"Oh, that's about Gino Bartali. There should be more notes there somewhere."

"I'll start a new folder. Who's Gino Bartali?"

"A cyclist from Assisi who transported documents for the Jews."

I continued emptying and cleaning my bookshelves while I told Jenny what I remembered about Bartali. He'd won both the Giro d'Italia and the Tour de France in the 1930s, and when Italy declared war on France and the UK in 1940, his irregular heartbeat kept him from being a soldier. Instead of serving in the military, he was allowed to be a bike messenger for the Italian army.

"Wait—he was a champion cyclist with a faulty ticker?"

"Yep. Ironic, huh?" I said, moving a pile of books to the floor. "David said he thinks Bartali's heart defect was God sparing him for something much more important than dying on a battlefield."

"Hmm. I wish I had David's mindset. It must be nice to see God everywhere you look."

"Me too. I think it gives him confidence that even when things are crazy, there's an order to the universe. A point to it all."

"I could use some of that confidence. I've got to work on having more faith."

"Me too."

"So what happened to Bartali?"

"When Germany moved into Italy in 1943, life for Italian Jews became very tricky," I said. "A cardinal named Della Costa was helping Jewish people get fake identity cards, and he got in touch with Bartali. Assisi was a hospital city, meaning it was supposed to be off-limits to German bombs, so it was a safe home base for Bartali. He hid the documents in the frame of his bike, and whenever he was stopped and questioned by German guards, he claimed to be on a training ride."

"And that worked?"

"Apparently he would get really huffy if the guards asked to inspect his bike. He'd tell them the bike was specially calibrated for him and if they touched it, they'd ruin the bike."

Jenny laughed. "Clever."

"I was buying water in the piazza one day when I was doing research on Bartali in Assisi," I told Jenny, "and this group of cyclists rode up and swarmed the store. I happened to strike up a conversation with one of them—an American guy who lives in the south of France with his wife. He rides all over the Mediterranean."

"Nice life."

"I asked him how he gets up the mountains. Like when he looks up and sees this huge climb in front of him, does he look at the scenery to distract himself from how exhausted he is, or does he count the rotations of his wheels, or give himself a pep talk, or what?"

"I would never try to ride up a mountain in the first place, but if I did, I'd need some very motivational music," Jenny said, writing BARTALI on a folder. "Or someone screaming in my ear. Or chasing me with a machete." She laughed. "What did he say?"

"He said that whenever he approaches a climb, he forces his mind to focus on the small details—the placement of his feet in the pedals, the position of his body over the bike, where his fingers are on the handlebars."

"And that gets him up a mountain?"

I nodded. "Well, that and being incredibly fit. He said that when he focuses on the small things, the big task takes care of itself."

Jenny was quiet for a few minutes, scanning the cyclist notes. Then she flipped the folder closed.

"You know what? I think that's exactly what I need to do. Starting over on my own feels totally overwhelming. It's like an emotional and financial and logistical Mount Everest. But maybe if I focus on the little things, it will all come together," she said. "Or I'll become an incredible cyclist. Either way, I win."

"You would have loved this guy," I said, spraying cleaner onto the bookshelves. "He told me the bikes these guys ride cost tens of thousands of dollars and he's got dozens of them. He has a recurring nightmare that he's dead and watching his wife sell his bikes for what he told her he paid for them."

"That's hilarious," Jenny said. "Imagine the torment!"

"Dante should have made that one of the circles of hell—watching your loved ones sell your things at discount prices." I finished cleaning the shelf and bent down to grab a stack of books. "But I think he's right. We both need to focus on the details, and let the big things come together on their own."

Jenny shrugged. "Can't hurt."

It was getting decidedly cooler out, so when we'd imposed order on my notes and finished purging my little office space of pencil nubs, paper scraps, and dried-up pens, we walked over to Porter's house to raid his linen closet for duvets. While we were there, I opened the window to let fresh air in while I changed the sheets on Porter's bed, dusted his nightstands, and put a fluffy duvet on the bed for him.

Jenny went downstairs and grabbed Head Teddy from the mantel. "I'm not gonna lie," she said, rejoining me in Porter's bedroom. "I love that he carried this head around instead of getting a new teddy bear." She placed Head Teddy in the center of Porter's pillow. "It says a lot about who he is. And bodes well for you too."

"Because if my head comes off, he'll carry it around?"

"I was thinking more along the lines of Porter being a loyal, stand-up kind of guy who's not going to trade you for a dental hygienist who didn't breastfeed his nine-pound babies," she said. "But you've made a good point. It's very useful to have someone who's willing to tote your head if it falls off."

Porter came home while we were carrying the duvets back to my house. He stopped in the drive and waved, let Oliver out, and then parked his car and went into the barn. Jenny and I put duvets on the beds at my house, then gathered up a couple of shopping bags and called for Oliver to climb in the backseat of my car.

"Oliver, I'm in love with you," Jenny said, twisting in her seat to look at him as I cranked up the car. "I don't want to be the guy in that story, never telling you how I really feel and just hoping to run into you at an airport."

Oliver sighed, stretched out across the seat, and put his head on his paws.

"Exactly," Jenny said. "It won't be easy. We're from two different worlds. But I love who I am with you and I don't want our affair to end."

I drove us to a nearby farm to buy vegetables, eggs, and fresh flowers. Oliver got too excited about the farmer's chickens that were roaming freely and had to be wrestled back into the car. When we came home, I parked in front of Porter's house and we unloaded everything into his kitchen.

"What do you need me to do?" Jenny asked.

"Just keep me company while I put together the soup. Peeling the squash is the hard part, and then it's just a matter of putting the ingredients together."

Jenny asked for a piece of paper and a pen, then pulled out a chair and sat down at the kitchen table while I tried to find a peeler that would work on the thick-skinned squash. When I got the squash peeled and cubed and on a tray in the oven, I chopped some onion and garlic and put it on low heat.

"Huh," Jenny said suddenly.

I looked up from the herbs I was rinsing. "What is it?"

"I'm making a list of all the stuff I need to do when I get back, and I just realized I can move." She looked up at me. "I can leave Syracuse if I want to."

"It's true. You can look for a job anywhere."

She chewed on the end of the pen. "I could go somewhere totally different. New Mexico or Wyoming or Florida. The kids are fine, right? They have their own lives and I can visit them. And my brothers will be around to look after my parents."

I nodded. "Yep. You'll be totally free."

"I've never been free before," Jenny said. "That's what happens when you get knocked up in college." She laughed. "That smells great, by the way."

"Thanks. It's really easy—just squash and apples and chicken broth, really. Porter loves it and I figure it will take some of the pressure off him about cooking for Sloan and her parents."

"I wonder what her parents are like," Jenny said. "And why they needed a sperm donor? Maybe the dad has faulty plumbing."

"No clue," I said, shrugging. "I haven't heard a word about them."

Twenty-Two

The answer to the sperm donor question became obvious as soon as Porter arrived home from the Cortona train station the following day. Jenny and I were waiting on the terrace, braving the chill in sweatshirts and jeans, when Oliver suddenly perked his ears, stood up, and started barking furiously. I looked down the driveway and could just make out Porter's car turning in.

"You ready?" Jenny asked.

"Yep," I said, then exhaled audibly. "David messaged me this morning, telling me to give Porter my support and give myself the freedom to like Sloan. He reminded me that he took a gamble on me and it turned out great, and he said I need to do the same. So that's the voice in my head right now."

Jenny grabbed Oliver's collar and held him in place as Porter pulled up to the house. When the car came to a stop, Jenny and

I both said, "Oh!" There was a young woman sitting in the passenger seat, and in the back were two middle-aged women.

I took a deep breath and walked toward the car. Porter got out and reached for my hand and gently pulled me next to him.

"This is Beth," he said. "Beth, this is Sloan, and these are her parents, Dale and Libby."

I shook hands all around, then introduced Jenny, and then Oliver, who was straining against Jenny's grip. When she let go of him to shake hands with Sloan, Oliver lunged for Sloan and stood on his back legs, putting his paws on her shoulders.

"Oh, wow," Sloan said. "I think he likes me."

While Porter tugged Oliver off Sloan, I asked Libby and Dale about their trip from London, then Porter suggested we all go inside. Jenny and I had already set the table for lunch, and we'd also made snacks and put them on the coffee table in the living room, where I'd built a roaring fire. I could tell Porter was nervous by the way he fussed around, pouring everyone a glass of wine and moving the snacks around on the table.

"This all looks amazing," Dale said. "We had breakfast, but it's been a while."

"I sense several spirits here," Libby said, looking around the room. "When was this house built?"

"In the 1600s," I said.

Libby nodded. "Yes. That makes sense. There has been a lot of turmoil here."

I glanced at Porter. He was looking at Libby with his head cocked to the side like Oliver when he hears the word "walk."

"I'm sure you're all hungry," Jenny said.

"I was going to buy something in the train station, but I couldn't understand the announcements and was afraid I'd miss the train," Sloan said.

"Well, never mind. We've got loads of food. Please, have a seat." I gestured to the oversized leather couches in front of the fireplace. When everyone was settled in, including Oliver, who smashed himself in between Sloan and Jenny, I asked Sloan about her conference in London.

"Oh," she said. "Are you sure you want to hear about this? It's pretty esoteric."

Jenny laughed. "Esoteric is Beth's middle name."

Sloan smiled at her before turning back to me. "Well, I went back to school for my PhD two years ago. I've been researching the beneficial effects of repetitive music on patients with complex trauma," she explained.

"Sloan has always been a stellar student," Dale said. "Always in the gifted classes."

"Do you mean the same song played over and over again?" Jenny asked.

Sloan nodded. "My research is focused on the part of the brain called the amygdala," she said. "That's where we process sensory input and regulate decision making and various endocrine functions. Music activates the amygdala, and certain types of repetitive music have a calming effect, so we're looking at how music can be used to treat complex traumas like child abuse or chronic neglect."

"But what kind of music? I get that it's repetitive," Jenny said, "but are we talking about any song on repeat, or what?"

"I'm looking at sung chants. Right now my focus is a song called 'Ubi Caritas.' A specific version from the Taizé community in France," Sloan said.

"Hmm. I can't say it's on any of my playlists," Jenny said.

"I know it."

Sloan's face lit up and she turned back to me. "You do?"

I nodded. "My uncle David is an Episcopal priest and he loves Taizé music. He even went there once, to the community in France. We always sang 'Ubi Caritas' on Maundy Thursday during the foot-washing service."

"Aligning the foot chakras is very important to spiritual balance," Libby murmured.

Jenny glanced at her, then said, "Back up, Bits. You lost me. What's Taizé?"

"It's a monastic community. Founded in the 1940s, I think," I said, looking at Sloan for confirmation. "'Ubi Caritas' definitely makes me feel peaceful," I told Sloan. "It sort of lulls me into a trance, honestly."

"Exactly," Sloan said. "And that trance-like state can be coupled with various therapies to help survivors process complex trauma."

"I'm quite interested in the therapeutic use of psychedelics," Libby said. "Not only for overcoming trauma, but for opening the third eye and accessing the wisdom of the universe."

"Wasn't the founder of Taizé murdered?" I asked Sloan. "I seem to remember David telling me that back when it happened."

Dale picked up the plate of cheese and offered it to Libby, who used her fingers like pincers to pick up a chunk of pecorino.

"Mushrooms, for instance," Libby said. A small bit of cheese fell out of her mouth as she talked. "Native Americans have used psychedelics for ages to connect to the wisdom of the ancestors."

"He was murdered," Sloan said, nodding. "Brother Roger. And during a prayer service, no less. He was stabbed by a woman who was mentally ill."

"Horrible," I said.

"We were just discussing mushrooms last week," Jenny told Libby. She turned to Sloan. "What do the words mean? The name of the song, I mean."

"Where there is charity and love, there is God," Sloan said. "That's the gist, anyway."

"Wasn't it originally a Gregorian chant?" I asked Sloan. "But maybe that wouldn't have the same effect?"

"Personally, I don't think so. A colleague of mine is studying Gregorian chants, but I'm focused solely on the Taizé version."

"Sloanie, sing a verse for us," Libby said, reaching for another piece of cheese.

"No thanks, Mom."

"Come on," Dale said. She was systematically making her way through the snacks, sampling everything on the table. "You have a fabulous voice." She looked at me and Jenny. "Sloan was first soprano in the choir and always the lead in her school plays."

"Beth and I were trees in fourth grade," Jenny said. "We rocked. Several encores."

Sloan sighed and looked at me. "Help me, please?"

We sang two rounds of the chorus, then stopped.

"Wow," Dale said. She finished making a sandwich of slices of cheese and *sopressato* and shoved it in her mouth. "You guys sound good together."

Porter, who'd been sitting silently on the other couch the whole time, suddenly spoke. "So, Dale, Libby, what kind of work do you guys do?"

"I'm a financial consultant," Dale said, "and Libby's a poet." She reached for Libby's hand and squeezed it. "Kind of a yin and yang in our household."

"Any other kids?" Porter asked.

Dale shook her head. "Just one perfect one. Which I guess is thanks to you, in part. She got great genes," Dale said. "Beautiful and smart."

"I can definitely see the resemblance," Jenny said.

It was true. Sloan had Porter's green eyes and light brown hair, and she was long and lean like him, with legs that took up half her body. Both Dale and Libby were shorter. Dale's dark hair was sprinkled with white and closely cropped, while Libby wore her long gray hair twisted into a clip.

"When we went to the sperm bank, we actually chose your profile," Dale said to Porter. "Did you know that?"

Porter shook his head. "I had no idea how it worked. Maybe they told me, but I don't remember."

"We read through dozens of profiles and let the universe guide us to yours," Libby said.

"Huh," Porter said. "I guess I'm flattered? Anyway, I'm curious about why you went that route, instead of adoption or whatever."

"At the time," Dale said, "not only was gay marriage illegal, but gay parents basically couldn't adopt. The only avenue was to find a mother willing to place her child with a same-sex couple in a private adoption. It's only since 2016 that the last state ban on gay adoption was overturned."

"Did you always know where you came from?" Jenny asked Sloan.

"Well, once I got old enough to notice that my friends had dads, I knew something was different in our house," she said, laughing lightly. "Luckily, my moms were really open with me and when I was old enough to understand, they explained about the sperm donor."

"Did you always want to find your father?" Jenny asked.

Sloan shook her head. "Not really. I mean, I have plenty of parents, and who knows what you're going to find, right?" She looked at Porter. "I don't know you yet, but I get the feeling a lot of my fears were unfounded. Thankfully."

"Oh, well, yeah, I hope so," Porter stammered.

"What were you afraid you might find out?" I asked Sloan.

"Well, I knew that the donor was a college athlete and in a fraternity, so I kind of imagined—"

"He'd be a cocky asshole," Jenny interjected, then laughed. "Sorry. I had the same thought when he and Beth first met. But I can assure you he's one of the nicest guys on the planet."

"What else?" I prompted Sloan. "What else were you afraid of?"

"Well, I have two moms, right? And they're everything to me. I worried that he might be a homophobe or something."

I shook my head. "He's not that, either. Not an asshole and not a homophobe."

"And my fiancé is black, did I mention that?" Sloan said,

then laughed. "I mean, I come with a whole bucket of reasons to reject me."

"None of which are problems for him," I said. I looked over at Porter. "Sorry to talk about you like you're not here."

"No, I don't mind," he said. "I just—I understand. I mean, it could have gone really wrong."

"Did you guys think this was a good idea?" I asked Dale and Libby. "For Sloan to find Porter, I mean?"

Dale shook her head. "Nope. I was dead set against it. Those things she just mentioned were reason enough, but for us"—she looked at Libby, who nodded in agreement—"the primary concern was Sloan getting her heart broken. It seems foolhardy to open yourself up to a stranger. Libby and I have dealt with our share of rejection and prejudice, and obviously we didn't want that for Sloan."

Libby looked at Porter. "And we didn't know if you had other children who might not be happy about this."

Porter shook his head. "No other kids."

"Or a wife who might object."

He glanced at me. Dale noticed and turned toward me.

"I can imagine you had your own concerns about what this was going to do to your marriage," she said.

"We're not married," I said.

"Oh, sorry. I just assumed you were," Dale said.

"Not for lack of Porter trying," Jenny said, reaching for the wine bottle and refilling her glass.

"I think it's good that we are talking about all of these things," Libby said. She reached up and took the clip out of her hair, causing her stack of silver and turquoise bangles to jingle, then re-twisted her hair into a loose chignon. "Porter, Beth, I'd love to hear from both of you what your concerns were," she said. "We should begin this journey from a place of honesty and vulnerability and hold space for our individual doubts and fears."

"Libby's studying to be a therapist," Dale said, patting Libby's leg. "She keeps us all grounded."

Libby gave Dale an adoring look, then turned toward Porter. "We place a lot of emphasis in our household on maintaining an open *visuddha chakra*. That's the chakra of communication, where healing speech and intuition reside," she said.

"Is that so?" Porter asked.

Libby nodded. "I'm very intuitive."

"She can read auras too," Dale said.

"What's that exactly?" Porter asked.

"Your spiritual energy field," Libby told him. "It's all around you." She squinted at Porter. "Yours is very dark, I'm afraid."

"What does that mean?" Jenny asked.

"That there is a blockage in the flow of energy. He has feelings that are not being expressed." She reached over and patted Porter's knee. "It can be very difficult for men to open up and express their emotions." She looked at Jenny. "Your aura is a beautiful pink, the color of love and empathy."

"What's Beth's?" Jenny asked.

"Oh, that's okay," I said, flapping my hand. "Let's go back to what you were saying about open communication, Libby. I think it would be great to hear more about what everyone's concerns were going into this . . . unusual situation."

Sloan looked at Porter. "What were your concerns?"

He shrugged. "Not liking you, I guess," he blurted, causing the rest of us to laugh out loud.

"That's an honest answer," Libby said, leaning forward to put her hand on his knee again. "I want to thank you for that, and express how much I appreciate your willingness to be vulnerable, particularly surrounded by feminine energy, which can be uncomfortably fluid for someone rooted in the traditional constructs of the masculine."

Porter shot me a pleading look.

"Porter was very surprised to get your call," I told Sloan.

"Obviously when he donated, his understanding was that it would be anonymous."

Sloan nodded. "I get it. When Joseph—that's my boyfriend—gave me the DNA test for Christmas, I wasn't even going to do it," she said. "But then I heard this story on NPR about genetic diseases and I decided I should take the test." She looked over at Porter. "I was surprised when your niece showed up as a relative. Everyone else was related to Mom's side."

"Wait—which one of you is mom?" Jenny asked.

"I am," Dale said. "The gestational carrier, anyway. I had health insurance."

"I don't have any genetic diseases," Porter said. "Not that I know of, anyway."

"Do you have a big family?" Libby asked him.

Porter shook his head. "Just one brother, Ford. That's Lauren's father. Ford and Courtney have two daughters. My father is"—he hesitated—"dead, and I didn't grow up with my mother."

I was impressed. Porter hated talking about his family and I'd never heard him volunteer so much information. He was on his second glass of wine, which probably helped.

"My grandparents were a big part of my life," he continued. "My father's parents. But they're gone now too."

"Sorry to hear it," Dale said. "And you never had kids?"

Porter shook his head. "Nope. Never married, either."

"Really?" Libby said. "I would think you were quite popular with women."

"He was too busy pining for Beth," Jenny said, then slapped her free hand over her mouth. "Sorry." She set her wine glass on the table and picked up a cracker. "Have you guys tried these crackers?" she asked. "What are they called, Bits?"

"*Taralli*," I said. "I make them with rosemary, but there are other flavors."

"The cheese is delicious too," Dale said. She leaned forward to grab a few more crackers and crunched loudly.

"Thank you for sharing your life with us," Libby said, reaching over to pat Porter's arm. He nodded at her and shifted just out of her reach. Libby turned her attention to me. "What were your concerns, Beth?"

"Same as Porter's, I guess," I said. "What kind of person Sloan would turn out to be." I looked at Sloan. "And what you might want from Porter."

"Fair question," Sloan said, setting the cheese she'd been nibbling on her plate. "The answer is nothing, really. I'm in good shape, financially and emotionally. I think I was just curious about my origins and whether we shared any traits or interests or whatever. Plus I wanted to know about any genetic diseases, like I said."

"I can understand your reticence, Beth," Dale said. "For someone without children, the idea of suddenly having a child in your life must seem very daunting—even a child who is already grown."

"I always wonder what people who don't have kids do with all the time and energy parents devote to their children," Libby said. "When Sloan was a baby and Dale went back to work, I remember having plenty of days when I didn't shower until dinner time." She smiled at Sloan. "Of course, I wouldn't trade a minute of it. But being a parent is a full-time job, even when your child is grown up and successful like ours. You never stop worrying."

I kept my eyes on Libby, but I could feel both Porter and Jenny looking at me.

"It's definitely a challenge to raise an emotionally healthy, intelligent child," Dale said. "But please don't worry, Beth. Sloan is far beyond needing to be raised and—"

"Beth had a daughter," Jenny said. "Her name was Mia and she was beautiful and smart and full of life. She was killed by a bike courier in London when she was only eighteen."

A deafening silence settled over the room.

"I'm sorry," Jenny said, looking at me. "I just . . . You were a great mom. I thought they should know that."

I took a deep breath, then turned towards Libby and Dale. "I did have a daughter. She was killed about five years ago and I miss her every day." I turned to Sloan. "That was actually my biggest concern. The idea of Porter suddenly having a daughter came as a shock, to say the least, and I was afraid of the emotional toll it might take on me." I glanced at Porter before turning back to Sloan. "I didn't react very well to the news, I'm sorry to say, but I think Porter would agree that meeting you has put a lot of our concerns to rest."

Jenny reached over and squeezed my hand.

Libby looked aghast. "I just can't imagine. Losing Sloan has always been my biggest fear."

Dale cleared her throat. "I'm so sorry," she said.

I met Porter's eyes and was surprised to see they were full of tears. *Thank you,* he mouthed. Then he pushed himself off the couch and clapped his hands together. "How about lunch?"

Twenty-Three

The rest of the afternoon went surprisingly well. The soup was delicious, as was the salad Jenny had put together and the focaccia I'd bought in the village. We normally didn't eat sweets at lunchtime, but I'd been inspired by the last of the pears to make a tart, which I served with vanilla bean gelato.

As we were finishing dessert and having coffee, Sloan asked how long Porter and I had known each other.

"We met in college," Porter said. "We were going to get married when Beth finished grad school, but I messed that up. Luckily, we got a second chance."

"What was he like in college?" Sloan asked me. "I'm dying to hear."

"No, no," Porter said. "Let's keep the mystery alive."

"Well," I told Sloan, "he lived with a couple of other soccer players in a really nice old house, and they used to put on

Rollerblades and play hockey with beer cans. The house got very beat up because they were constantly slamming into each other and high-sticking the light fixtures."

"Which we wouldn't have done if I'd known I was going to end up buying that house," Porter said.

"I'm trying to remember how you described him to me back then, Bits," Jenny said. "Prep school something."

"Oh, yeah. 'Prep school feral.' He had perfect grammar and excellent manners, but let's just say there were some big parties at Porter's house. He liked to have a good time."

Porter shook his head and laughed. "I can't really argue with that. I was a bit feral."

"Tell them about the neighbor," Jenny said, laughing. "I love that story."

"Oh, that's not necessary," Porter said.

"Tell me," Sloan urged. "How bad can it be?"

"Their next-door neighbor was a real weirdo. He claimed to have been in the Marines and liked to act all tough," I told her.

"He told us he was in the CIA and had been a hired assassin in South America and killed dozens of men," Porter said, shaking his head. "I guarantee you the closest he ever came to the Marine Corps was a T-shirt."

"None of us could stand him," I continued. "The two houses shared a backyard—there was no fence—and he used to sit on the back porch in head-to-toe camo and clean his gun whenever we were outside."

"I can't imagine the darkness of his aura," Libby said, fingering the crystal hanging around her neck.

"We could never figure out if he was plotting to kill us or hoping to be invited over," Porter said.

"They used to do all sorts of pranks on him, like dragging his trash cans way down the street and stuff," I explained. "Nothing terrible. But then he called the cops on them for having a party."

"It was a very tame party too," Porter said. "He was just

doing it to be an ass. That's when we kicked into high gear."

"One of the guys saw him pack his car to go out of town one weekend," I said, "and Porter got hold of a roll of crime scene tape."

"Where'd you get that?" Dale asked.

Porter shrugged. "I have no idea."

"Porter and his housemates decided to stage a crime scene in the guy's backyard while he was away. They trashed the back porch like there had been a struggle, and dumped fake blood—"

"Which we made ourselves," Porter interjected. "Ketchup, syrup, and chocolate sauce."

"They even did a chalk outline of a body on the back porch and—"

"Gee," Jenny said, tapping her chin. "Who would have volunteered to be traced for her boyfriend's prank?"

I pretended not to hear her. "They topped off this artistic endeavor by leaving a very dog-eared copy of *Playboy* on the porch, like the criminal had enjoyed himself a bit before being shot."

"And teeth," Porter said. "Don't forget the teeth."

"Oh, yeah, and three teeth that had been knocked out during one of their hockey games."

"The teeth really added something special to the scene," Porter said, smiling.

"So what happened?" Libby asked.

"The neighbor came home and went berserk," I said.

Porter started laughing. "He came running over and asked us what was going on, but we'd seen him come home so we were all sitting in the living room, reading the Bible out loud—"

"Tate was sketching," I reminded him, "and I was painting his toenails, remember? He couldn't talk or else the guy would have seen his missing teeth."

"We told him the house had been swarmed by a SWAT team while he was gone," Porter said.

"Porter told him that a bunch of Spanish-speaking men had come looking for him, yelling about avenging their brother's death."

"And they'd threatened to kill us if we talked about it," Porter said, still laughing.

"That put the guy in a real conundrum, because of course he'd never killed anyone in South America, but he couldn't admit that after lying for so long," I said.

"Then what happened?" Dale asked.

"He moved out. Took off in the middle of the night," Porter said, wiping his eyes. "It worked out perfectly. Some of our friends took over the lease and then we had a really excellent yard for parties."

I lifted my wine glass in Sloan's direction. "That was your father. Occasionally he also studied or played soccer."

"He did nice stuff too," Jenny said, looking over at me. "You always said he was a very good boyfriend."

"He was. Very thoughtful and kind."

"Just like now," Jenny said.

I nodded. "Yep."

We sat around for a while longer making small talk, then Jenny, Dale, and Libby cleared the table while Porter and I took Sloan outside and showed her the animals. As Porter walked ahead of us into the barn, Sloan turned and touched my arm.

"I'm sorry about your daughter," she said. "I can only imagine how all of this has been for you. I just want you to know how grateful I am that you've been so welcoming. And I want to reassure you that I don't want anything from Porter. I don't want to cause any trouble."

"Watch out," I said, pointing to the step up into the barn.

"Thanks."

"I feel better after meeting you," I told her. "Porter and I were both unsure how to handle this."

"I get it," Sloan said. "I'm happy just to have met him. It's answered a question I've always had about where I came from, and that's enough for me. Anything more is just icing on the cake."

I nodded.

"I'd like to be friends," Sloan said. "If you want, I mean. Maybe we could email once in a while?"

"Yes, of course. I can't speak for Porter, but I'd like that. And I really am interested in your dissertation."

We joined Porter, who introduced Sloan to Brutus and Clara, our ovine lovers, along with the rest of the barn residents. Then the three of us walked outside. Sloan stood at the edge of the rows of lavender and rosemary and inhaled deeply.

"It smells amazing here. So fresh." She reached down and snapped a twig of lavender off a bush and put it in the pocket of her jeans. "Who lives over there?" she asked, pointing at Villa Rosmarino.

"That house was empty for a long time," Porter said. "Now we have neighbors—an American and an Australian. They've had company recently, but I'm delighted to report that the company has gone now."

"Have they?" I asked.

Porter nodded. "Couple days ago."

I was relieved. I'd been so busy with Jenny that I hadn't noticed any comings and goings next door, but I was glad to know I'd never have to see Nicolette, her phone, or her sycophant Naomi again.

Sloan chatted amiably with Porter as we walked around the property. I fell behind on purpose and watched the two of them together. I'm not sure I would have guessed they were father and daughter, but I was glad to see that Porter seemed comfortable with her, in the same way I imagined he was with his nieces and would have been with Mia.

When they got to the olive trees, Porter turned and waited for me to catch up. As I joined them, he checked his watch and told Sloan it was time to head back to Cortona if they wanted to catch the train.

"Or I can drive you guys to Perugia?" he offered.

Sloan shook her head. "No, but thank you. You guys have been amazing already and honestly, we enjoyed the train ride. Plus, I bought round-trip tickets."

"I hope you'll keep in touch," I said as we walked back to the house. "Porter's not a big fan of video calls, but Jenny and I do them all the time. And he's not a total Neanderthal," I teased, elbowing Porter in the ribs. "He can email."

"I use four fingers to type now."

Sloan laughed. "I would love to keep in touch. I know it's a weird situation, and trust me, I've got plenty of parental input from the banker and the poet, but I'd like to think I've made two new friends."

When we got back, we found Jenny deep in conversation with Libby at the kitchen table. Dale was standing by the sink eating a handful of crackers and Oliver was under the table, lying on Jenny's feet.

All four of them looked up as we came in.

"Time to roll, mamas," Sloan said. "We've got a train to catch."

After exchanging emails and hugs, Jenny and I stood on the driveway and watched them drive away in Porter's car.

"Somebody's over it," I said, pointing to Oliver, who was waiting to be let in the kitchen door.

"I may have promised him a belly rub," Jenny said. She looked over at me. "So? What did you think?"

"I actually like her," I said. "I like all of them, although Libby's a little woo-woo for my taste." I opened the kitchen door and let Oliver go in before us.

"I couldn't even look at Porter when she was talking about his third eye and feminine energy," Jenny said.

"Oh, me neither. Want a cup of tea?"

Jenny nodded. "Yes, please. I do think Sloan is sincere when she says she doesn't want anything from him."

"Me too."

"She said she was just curious about him. That's what Libby and Dale said too, that Sloan just wanted to meet him and that was really all. They said she had no expectations of any real relationship."

"Yeah." I turned on the faucet to fill the kettle with water, then set it on the stove. "I have to admit, I'm glad she doesn't look just like him or act like him or anything. That would have been too weird."

"You can definitely see the resemblance and some of their mannerisms are the same, but I know what you mean. It's not like you and Mia."

"What were you guys talking about in here?" I asked.

"My situation with Scott. Don't even ask me how that came up. Libby said she would send me a mantra and some crystals."

"Perfect. That should fix everything."

I pulled two mugs out of the cabinet and rifled through the drawer for teabags. When the kettle began to whistle, I started laughing, and told Jenny about the time Marco and I had come back from an excursion to San Gimignano and stopped in my apartment to go over our plan for the next week. I'd put the kettle on and then gone in to take a quick shower, assuming—wrongly, as it turned out—that making a cup of tea was a universal practice and Marco could take over.

"He started pounding on the bathroom door yelling, 'He cries, he cries!' I had to get out of the shower and take the kettle off the stove. He was frantic."

"How does a grown man not know how a tea kettle works?"

"Beats me," I said, shrugging.

When my own kettle started crying, I put two cups of tea on the table, grabbed my phone off the countertop where it had been plugged in since morning, and slid into the chair opposite Jenny.

"Speak of the devil," I said. "I got a message from Marco."

"What'd he say?"

"That his trip to Bologna got postponed and we should let him know when we're coming to the spa and he'll take us out for a drink afterward."

"Oh, that would be fun. Should we go tomorrow?"

"Instead of Sorrento?"

Jenny grimaced. "Does that make me a total wimp? I'm sorry. I'm just running out of energy for sightseeing and a spa sounds like heaven."

"I'm always happy to go to a spa. Remind me when we go home and I'll get on my computer and make the reservation. It's the off-season, so it won't be a problem."

"I have a better idea. Why don't I walk over and get your laptop and bring it back to you, and then I'll go back to your house for the night and you can stay here?"

I laughed. "Are you trying to get rid of me?"

She shook her head. "Not at all. But he needs you, Bits. You need some time together."

I nodded. "Okay. If you're sure."

"Can I take Oliver with me, though? And the focaccia?"

When Jenny went to get my laptop, I fed Oliver, wrapped the focaccia in foil, and poured some of the soup into a Thermos. When she came back, I made massage appointments for us online, and then gave Jenny a hug.

"Thank you for being so supportive during all this," I said. "I know you've got your own stuff going on and I really appreciate it."

"Oh, please. What haven't we been through together?" She picked up the bag of food. "But please remember how awesome I am when I steal your dog." She looked down at Oliver. "Your job tonight is to snuggle, Ollie."

"He's a champion snuggler. You're in good paws."

When they left, I washed the tea mugs and then made a little plate of pear slices and aged *pecorino stagionato* cheese and took it upstairs. I was pouring two glasses of wine when Porter pulled in the driveway.

"Hey," he said as he came in the door. "Where's Jenny?"

"She took Oliver to my house for the night."

"Ah." Porter hung his keys on the hook next to the door, took off his jacket and draped it over the back of a chair, then leaned against the counter.

"Did they get off okay?"

"Yeah. It was perfect timing. The train was pulling in as I left."

"Good. I was headed up to take a bath, if you care to join me."

Porter nodded. He picked up one of the wine glasses and followed me up the stairs. I'd left the water trickling and the tub was already two-thirds full. I added some of the lavender oil I'd bought in Assisi, put two fluffy towels on one of the wooden chairs next to the tub, set the plate of pears and cheese on top of the towels, and pulled off my clothes. Porter went into his bedroom and came back with the two thick Frette bathrobes we'd splurged on in Rome.

"I figure it's cool enough tonight that we can wear these," he said, draping them over the chair.

I slid into the tub while Porter dropped his clothes in a pile on the floor, then climbed in after me. I reached for the plate and offered it to Porter. He took a slice of pear and a slice of cheese and leaned against the back of the tub, sighing.

"Tired?" I asked, leaning over the edge of the tub to put the plate back on the chair.

"Relieved today went well. And glad it's over."

"Me too. I like her, though. Sloan, I mean. She's nice. Very calm, and obviously very intelligent."

He nodded.

"I like her moms too. Dale, anyway. Libby's nice, but she lives in a fourth dimension."

"You can say that again."

"I couldn't even look at you when she was talking about your chakras."

"I noticed." He took a bite out of the pear slice and then asked, "There's some of that pear tart left, right?"

"I saved you a slice." I picked up his foot and put it in my lap and massaged it.

Porter closed his eyes. "That feels great."

I didn't answer, just reached under the water and brought his other foot onto my lap.

After a few minutes of silence, Porter said, "I've missed you" without opening his eyes.

I squeezed his foot. "I've missed you too."

"I hate fighting with you."

"Me too."

"Can we agree to never fight again?"

"It's a deal."

Porter shifted his hips. "Sorry. I've got to take my feet back for a second," he said, stretching his legs out on either side of me. "My leg is cramping."

"I'm going to add some more hot water, okay?"

"Yeah, of course."

When I turned the taps off, Porter sighed and said, "Thank you for today. I know it wasn't easy, but it all went well, don't you think?"

"Better than I expected."

He nodded and was quiet for a minute. "Listen," he said finally, "I hope you know I would never have touched Kick if I'd thought I might get another chance with you."

I nodded. "I know."

"And I never would have donated if I'd known it wasn't going to stay anonymous."

"I know that too."

"I'm sorry you had to deal with the fallout from my decisions."

I was quiet for a minute, thinking. "I had an interesting conversation with David the other night. I couldn't sleep, so I FaceTimed him, and we started talking about unintended consequences."

"Mine?"

I smiled. "Not specifically, no. We were talking about the pilot who was flying the plane my dad and uncle were in. David said the pilot overloaded the plane with cargo, but the most he probably anticipated was that they might be a little slower getting to the fishing camp, not that they would crash and die."

"Definitely not."

"And then we talked about the drunk driver who killed my mom, and how the law distinguishes between intention and negligence. She should have known not to drive, of course, but she also didn't intend to kill my mom and nearly kill my aunt."

Porter nodded. "Right. Unintended consequences."

"As you would expect, David also had a biblical example."

"Hang on," Porter said. "If we're going to talk about Jesus in the bathtub, I need my wine." He leaned over the edge of the tub and retrieved his wine glass. "Okay, go," he said, resettling himself against the back of the tub.

"When Judas betrayed Jesus, he went to the Sanhedrin and asked what they would give him, right?"

"Remind me who the Sanhedrin were?"

"The high priests who upheld the law of Torah."

"Didn't he do it for money?" Porter asked, picking up the soap from the little dish attached to the side of the tub with his free hand. "I thought he got silver."

"Some people think so. Apparently he'd already stolen some of the disciples' traveling money."

Porter lathered his face with the bar of soap and I had a fleeting thought about how easy it was to be a guy. If I used a bar of soap on my face, my skin would let me know in a hot minute that it strenuously objected and needed to be soothed by an expensive concoction from the specialty drugstore.

"The other argument is that Judas wanted Jesus to kick off a rebellion against the Romans, and when Jesus didn't want to, Judas betrayed him in order to spur the rebellion." I leaned down and picked up my wine glass from the side of the tub. "Some people argue that it was the opposite—that Judas was afraid the Romans were going to destroy all the Jews, so he appeased them by handing over Jesus."

Porter returned the soap to its holder and rinsed his face, holding his wine glass in the air. When he was done, he looked at me. "Okay, so maybe not just for the money."

"There's one more theory. That Jesus asked Judas to betray him to bring the Kingdom of God into existence."

"Here's what I've never really understood," Porter said. "Didn't everyone know who Jesus was? There were crowds following him everywhere, so why did Judas have to identify him?"

"Jesus was claiming to be king of the Jews, but only to his inner circle. That's what mattered. The Romans were an occupying force, so a guy claiming to be the king was a real challenge to their authority," I said. "That's what Judas revealed. It wasn't just him saying, 'That's Jesus.' It was Judas saying, 'That's Jesus, and he claims to be king of the Jews.'"

"I get it," Porter said.

"The reason David brought it up is he wondered if Judas could have anticipated that Jesus would be crucified. Maybe Judas didn't even know about crucifixion. The rest of the disciples were from the north, but Judas was from a little town in the southern part of Judea."

"Judas was from the Alabama of Israel and the rest of the guys were from New York?"

I laughed. "Kind of, yeah. And if Judas was from a place where the Romans weren't active, would Judas have ever seen a crucifixion? Would he have even known about them? But he betrayed Jesus in Jerusalem, where crucifixion *was* a thing. Still, it begs the question of whether Judas could have anticipated things popping off the way they did."

"An unintended consequence," Porter said, nodding.

"David's other point was that Judas might not have anticipated the consequences, but without the crucifixion, there's no resurrection. There's no Christianity. So how do you weigh the consequences when some of them are terrible and some of them are good?"

"Hmm. That makes me feel better, I guess," Porter said. "Not the association with Judas, but that you know I didn't mean for any of this to happen."

I took a sip of wine. "David also reminded me that he took a real chance on me after my parents died. He said Margaret convinced him to invite me to move in with him."

"The church secretary?"

I nodded. "His *consiglieri* is more like it. He said I needed to take a chance on Sloan being a good addition to our lives."

"How do you feel about that now?"

"Like it's a real possibility."

Porter nodded. "Me too."

I let some of the water out of the tub and replaced it with more hot water. "I did something kind of crazy last night," I told Porter, swirling the water with my hand to distribute the heat. "I said a prayer to my daughter. I asked her to understand that she would never be replaced in any way, but that I needed to accept Sloan." I glanced up at Porter. "I asked her to give me a sign if she was okay with all of this."

"And?"

"This morning when I woke up, the first thing I did was turn on *Radio Subasio*," I said. "Would you like to guess what song was playing?"

Porter shook his head.

"What's the one song I've always said reminds me of you and only you? The song you used to sing to me?"

Porter met my eyes. "*Every time you touch me, I become a hero,*" he sang. "*I'll make you safe no matter where you are.*"

"Exactly. I haven't heard that song in years, but it was on when I turned on the radio."

"Wow," Porter said. "You know, I loved that song because that's how you made me feel, like I could do anything with you in my corner. I still feel that way. That's why this has been so hard." He ran his hand through his hair. "It has really scared me, how distant you've been. I thought you were going to leave."

I turned off the tap and leaned against the back of the tub. "I'm sure it's magical thinking, but that song made me feel like Mia was putting her blessing on all of this."

Porter was quiet for a few minutes. "I have that story, you know," he said finally. "The one about magical thinking."

"I saw it in one of the boxes. How did you find it? That journal went under about five minutes after it started."

"Oh, please. I used to search your name all the time," Porter said, splashing water towards me. "I totally cyber-stalked you."

I laughed. "Yeah? I wish I'd known. What did you think of the story?"

"That I was that guy. I was the dumbass who watched the girl he loved walk away and didn't do anything about it."

I reached for the tap and twisted it to add a little more hot water. The window wasn't completely closed and there was a stream of cold air coming in through the crack, making steam rise off the tub.

When I turned the water off, Porter reached out and grabbed my hand and pulled me toward him. He put his hands on the side of my face and sang, "*I'll bring you anything you ask for, nothing is above me, I'm shining like a candle in the dark when you tell me that you love me.*"

"Thank you for being so in touch with your feelings, Julio Iglesias, particularly in the feminine energy of the bathtub. Let's hold space for your emotions, shall we?"

"I'm going to hold you under water instead," Porter said, then leaned forward and kissed me. He put a hand on either side of the tub and pushed himself to his feet. "May I invite you to get out of the tub and join me in the bedroom?" he asked, holding out his hand.

I let him help me to my feet. We got out of the tub, careful not to step on the wine glasses, and dried off.

"Should I bother putting on this bathrobe?" I asked, picking it up off the back of the chair.

Porter shook his head. "Nah. I'm gonna have it off you in about ten seconds."

Twenty-Four

"I talked to Scott last night," Jenny said as we pulled out of the driveway the next morning.

"Oh yeah? How did that go?"

She reached into her purse for a tissue and blew her nose before answering. "Sorry. I think I have a cold."

"Maybe the spa will help. You can sweat it out in the sauna room."

"He said he was sorry. That he knows he hurt me and he's sorry, but his future is with Amber."

I glanced at her. "Are you okay?"

Jenny nodded. "I knew it already. It was actually a relief to hear him say it, in a weird way."

"Knowing something in your head and knowing it in your heart are two different things. But I think it's a relief when your head and your heart get on the same page, even if the truth is painful," I said. "I'm really sorry, Jen. I think when you get home, you need to get the ball rolling. Get a lawyer and settle things as soon as you can."

"I feel surprisingly peaceful about it all, to be honest. I mean, I'm not looking forward to the next few months, but I'll be okay. I can see now that things have been going downhill for a long time, and I don't want to grow old with someone I can't talk to. Or who doesn't want to be with me."

"Crawford always acted like he was doing me a favor by being with me. Like I was a burden he had to tolerate."

"That's it exactly," Jenny said. "And I have no interest in being married to a martyr who thinks he deserves a gold medal for staying with me."

"I think that means you're definitely doing the right thing," I said, pulling the car into the parking lot of the roadside bar I always went to on the way to Assisi. "Ready for coffee?"

"Yeah." Jenny reached down and got her purse off the floorboard. "I'm glad I talked to him before I fly home. It made me less anxious. And now I can use my airplane time to figure out the next steps."

After we'd ordered coffees and cream-filled croissants, we stood at a small round table to eat.

"It's going to suck going back to oatmeal," Jenny said, wiping her mouth with a waxy napkin. "I think I could live here pretty happily."

"I'm so glad you came. I'm sorry there's been so much drama."

"Your drama was interesting, at least," Jenny said, smiling. "Mine is so unimaginative. Is there anything more cliché than a middle-aged man bailing on his family for a fresh piece of ass?" she asked, licking pastry cream off her fingers. "Oh wait. Sorry. Scott and Amber have an intense emotional connection."

"He didn't really say that, did he?"

Jenny nodded. "I told him he misspoke, that the word was anatomical, not emotional. He didn't think that was funny."

"Ha! I do, though."

Jenny smiled. "I thought it was a pretty good line." She finished her coffee and set the cup down in the saucer. "I cannot wait to get to the spa and slip into a lovely pair of paper panties."

"Just be prepared. When I say paper panties, what I really mean is some dental floss and a postage stamp. But it's worth it."

Thankfully, we were the only customers at the spa because we were both a bit punch-drunk from all the tension of the past two weeks and started laughing hysterically about the ridiculous spa panties. We got heavenly massages, then toddled over to do the *percorso*, the circuit of four rooms with different temperatures.

"I love the names of these rooms," Jenny said as we made our way from the hellishly hot *sudatorium* to the freezing cold *frigidarium*. "It smells so good in here," she said, pulling the chain to release a batch of ice into the bin in the middle of the room.

"Eucalyptus," I said. "Hopefully, it will help clear your head." I held my breath and stepped under the ice-cold shower.

"Can we get in the pool again?" Jenny yelled over the roar of the ice hitting stainless steel. "I want to pretend I'm a wealthy Roman. Do you think we can get someone to feed us grapes?"

"Yeah, let's get back in the pool. I'm turning blue in here," I said, wrapping my arms around my torso and trying to stop my teeth from chattering.

The pool dates back to the first century after Christ, when Romans used to bathe in the healing waters that flowed down from Mount Subasio. It's a fairly shallow pool, with six large pillars holding up the low stone ceiling. Soft lights shine upward against the limestone walls, and candles light the perimeter. Sitting in the pool, you truly feel transported in time.

Jenny liked the section of the pool where you could push a button on the wall and activate enormous bubbles. That's where she headed as soon as we stepped into the water. I took a minute to stand under a stream pouring out of a spout in the wall, letting it beat down on the top of my head, then dog-paddled after her and took up my position on the ledge, bracing for the bubbles.

"*Double, double, toil and trouble; fire burn and cauldron bubble*," Jenny said as the water began to roil around us. Then she let out a hideous cackle that made me laugh out loud. "I don't remember anything beyond that."

"I think the witches just list all the things they're throwing in the pot. Eye of newt and slithering snake, that kind of stuff."

"I'm fresh out of both of those."

"Me too. We can make it a cathartic cauldron instead. Put all our problems in and boil them away."

Jenny nodded. "All right. I'm tossing in my fear about life after Scott."

"That's a good one. I'll add all my anxiety about Sloan."

"Do I get to throw things in for you?"

"I guess, if you feel like you have to."

"Then I'm adding all the pain Crawford caused you. Into the cauldron with all that."

"I'm adding any feelings of rejection you might have from the demise of your marriage."

"What feelings of rejection? You mean the ones from my husband trading my middle-aged ass for a shiny new girlfriend? That feeling of rejection?" Jenny said. She laughed and lifted a bubble on her palm. "What makes you think I have any of that?" she said, then blew the bubble off her hand.

"Oh, sorry. I was thinking of someone else."

"Okay, I'm tossing on your behalf again," Jenny said, splashing water in my direction. "All your hyper-independence, into the pot. Also your reluctance to lean on Porter because you think he's going to disappear like everyone else in your life. Oh, and your blindness to the fact that David and Porter and I aren't going anywhere—not intentionally, anyway. Into the pot, all of it."

"I think the cauldron just overflowed. We may need to pace ourselves."

Jenny shook her head and scooped more bubbles onto her arms. "Plenty more room. And once something's in the cauldron, you can't take it back out. Those are the rules."

I dog-paddled over to the wall and reactivated the bubbles as the timer ran out. When I resumed my position on the ledge next to Jenny, I said, "I wish it was that easy. I wish there was a real pot where you could just toss the emotions that aren't working for you. All the fear and anxiety and bullshit."

Jenny nodded. "Me too. But then we'd be way too well-adjusted. I mean, look at us, Bits. We'd be perfect, and everyone knows perfection is boring."

"That's so true," I said. I looked at the water churning around us. "I feel like pasta, sitting in here."

"Oh stop. You're just being fusilli."

I groaned. "You have to walk home," I said, stretching out on my back and letting the water percolate around my head. "That was terrible, Jen. I want a new best friend."

Marco was waiting outside when we emerged from the spa. He had parked the cart alongside the road and was leaning against it with his glasses on, reading the newspaper. When he saw us come out, he dropped the paper onto the front seat of the cart, flipped his glasses onto his head, and called out, "My darlings, you are radiant!"

"Oh my God, I love him so much," Jenny said.

"Of all the thorns in my side, he's definitely my favorite."

Marco held the door for us as we piled in with our tote bags of wet bathing suits. Then he rolled down the thick plastic curtains that zipped to the sides of the cart and took his seat in the front. We zoomed out the arched stone gate that marked the edge of historic Assisi and headed into the countryside. I was very content to just sit and watch the scenery go by, and I think Jenny was, too, but eventually Marco pulled off the paved road.

"Where you want to go?" he asked me.

Jenny turned toward me. "Is it okay if we do a little shopping?"

"Of course."

She looked at Marco. "Can you take us to the jewelry store near the basilica?" She held up her left hand. "I've got to buy a ring."

Twenty-Five

After Jenny left, things calmed down quite a bit.

I finished the article on the pagan church conversions and sent it off to a couple of journals to see if it might land anywhere. The piece on Paolo Franceschini, the conductor, that I'd submitted for the special music issue was accepted. Porter and I watched the Dante documentary one night, and the next day I was able to reach out to the actor who played Dante, Antonio Fazzini, and arrange an interview. Porter and I stuck to our vow to stop day drinking, which made the evenings—when we settled onto his couch in front of the fireplace with a glass of wine—even better.

We stayed pretty close to home, save for a trip to Montepulciano to restock Porter's wine cellar with Avignonesi Nobile, and invited Darren and Dean over for Thanksgiving pasta. A week or so later, we got a tree, and I dragged all the boxes of Christmas decorations I'd stashed in Porter's closets into the living room.

I was contemplating how I wanted to decorate the tree the next morning when Jenny called.

"Yo, Bits. Whatcha doing?"

"I was thinking about decorating the tree, but since you called, I'm gonna sit on the couch instead. How are you? Why are you up so late again?"

"Insomnia. But hey, I got a job."

"Jenny! Congratulations!"

"Wait until you hear what I'm doing. I'd make you guess, but you'd never get it. I'm the new guidance counselor at Saint Francis de Sales Catholic School. I start in January."

I laughed out loud. "You're not! That's so great, Jen. I'm so proud of you."

She held her hand in front of the camera and showed me the ring she'd bought in Assisi. "Honestly, Bits, when I get freaked out, I just look at this ring and think, 'Okay, I can do this. In the grand scheme of things, this is just a blip in time, and things won't always be this way.' It's like a talisman or something. And guess what? I started going to the Episcopal church downtown."

"St. Paul's, right? That place is gorgeous."

Jenny nodded. "It's really beautiful."

"David will be delighted. I'll have to call and tell him you've been converted."

"Not officially yet, but I have to say, I'm thinking about it. I love St. Paul's. They're good people, and I don't feel judged for getting divorced. I went to a support group there and everyone was just incredible."

"I can't believe you're working at our school! Sister Mary Michael must be dancing in her grave," I said. "She would be so happy that at least one of the Fife children has a relationship with God."

Jenny laughed. "Father Declan certainly failed with my brothers. Pack of degenerates and heathens, all of them."

We'd been on the phone for almost an hour when I checked my watch. "Hey Jen, I've gotta get cleaned up and dressed. It's Porter's birthday and I'm taking him to see the mummies in Ferentillo."

"That's a totally normal thing to do on your birthday, go see dead people."

"It was his choice! It is cool, though. The mummies aren't embalmed or anything. They're naturally mummified."

"Again, totally normal birthday trip. Don't stay down there too long, though. Mummified isn't a good look. Will you tell Porter I said happy birthday?"

I promised I would, and then we hung up. I ran upstairs to take a quick shower and pull on jeans and a sweater, then walked out to the barn to find Porter.

Ferentillo is tucked between two mountains, with a river winding through the valley. It was cold out when we arrived and there were numerous fires going, giving the air a delicious smoky smell. Porter and I spent an hour looking at the mummies in the crypt of the San Stefano church, then went for a walk around the tiny town.

"Those mummies are the craziest thing," Porter said. "The brochure said that there's something in the combination of oxygen and the components of the soil that mummified all those people."

"Can you imagine going down to the crypt expecting to find bones and seeing those mummies instead?"

Porter laughed. "It would be shocking, to say the least."

"I read that there's a group of people who think the Holy Grail is in the church of Santa Maria here."

"What makes them think so?"

"I can't remember exactly. Something about the saints that are painted on the walls of the church. Their initials spell out *Santo Graal*, I think."

Porter put his arm around me and kissed the side of my face. "My life would be so much less interesting without you," he said.

"Oh stop. You're just buttering me up for birthday sex."

He threw his head back and laughed. "Busted."

"So what is your birthday wish?" I asked.

"A green cashmere sweater and a new cappuccino maker."

"Yeah, but both of those things benefit me too. The sweater matches your eyes and makes you look even more handsome than usual, and I'm assuming I'll get an occasional cappuccino. What do you want that's just for you?"

Porter looked at his watch. "Can I tell you in a couple of hours?"

"Sure. Does that mean you're ready to head home or do you want to see something else?"

"I'm about ready to head home."

"Let me just pop into the bathroom at the bar."

When I came out, Porter was typing on his phone. He looked up and shoved his phone into his pocket.

"Just replying to a birthday text. Ready?"

As we pulled into the driveway at home, Porter said he had to pee really badly and ran into the house as soon as he shut the car off. I pulled the keys out of the ignition and grabbed our coats and scarves from the backseat and followed him inside. Oliver didn't greet me in the kitchen, which was very strange.

"Oliver?" I hollered.

I heard him whine, but he didn't appear.

"Ollie? Where are you, pup?" I called, walking into the living room.

I stopped in my tracks. The Christmas tree was lit with hundreds of tiny white lights that made the dozens of painted ceramic ornaments seem to glow. A whole army of poinsettias, their bases wrapped in gold foil, were gathered under the tree and on the mantel, and a bottle of champagne was chilling in an ice bucket on the coffee table. There was a fire crackling in the fireplace, candles glowing on every bare surface, and the whole room smelled like a pine forest. As I stood there with my mouth hanging open, music started playing from the speakers mounted around the room—the Dolly Parton and Julio Iglesias duet Porter had sung to me in the bathtub. Our song.

I looked at Porter, who was on one knee in front of the fireplace. Oliver was sitting next to him wearing a red plaid bowtie instead of his collar.

"What is all this, Porter?"

"It's what I wanted for my birthday. Well, almost."

"But how did you do all of this?"

"I had help from Double D."

"It's amazing," I said, turning in a slow circle. "Look how beautiful the Christmas tree looks. And all the candles and poinsettias . . ." I caught sight of a vibrant green bowl filled with red ornaments sitting on the side table. "The bowl from Gubbio! Wait. Porter, what's happening?"

"It's a present for you."

"But it's your birthday, not mine."

"I know. Hey, listen, can I say what I need to say? My knee is really killing me."

"Oh, sorry. Yes, of course."

He reached across Oliver's back and extracted a small black box from behind a couch pillow.

"Here's the thing," he said. "I'm in love with you, Jean Pearson. And I don't want to spend any more time looking for you in airports or thinking about you when I'm playing tennis and giving speeches about real estate."

I'd been tearing up but had to laugh at that. "No more magical thinking?"

Porter shook his head. "No more. I've been in love with you my whole life and I want the world to know." He opened the box. "We've been through so much, Bethy. And I'm hoping you'll accept this ring for the second time and give me the only thing I really want for my birthday."

I was full-on crying at that point and couldn't talk.

Porter looked down at Oliver. "She's not answering."

"I'm sorry. Yes! Yes, I'll accept the ring, and yes, I'll marry you." I dug a tissue out of the pocket of my jeans and wiped my nose. "I'm assuming that's what you're asking?"

Porter looked up at me and cleared his throat. "Uh, actually, no. No one said anything about getting married. I was just asking if you wanted this old ring I found."

It took me a minute to realize he was joking, and then I started laughing for real.

"Help me up?" Porter asked.

I held out my hand and pulled him up. When he was on his feet, Porter wrapped his arms around me. "I love you. I always have."

"I never stopped loving you, Porter."

"I hate to break up this beautiful moment, but can we come out of the closet now?" a voice called.

Porter let go of me. "Come on out, guys."

Darren and Dean emerged from the closet in the hall. "Congratulations!" they shouted.

"How long have you been in there?" I asked, giving each of them a hug.

"We've been over here all day setting up. We only got in the closet when Porter ran in," Darren said.

"I swore I'd never go back in the closet once I came out," Dean said. "Only for you guys."

"We're very happy for you," Darren said.

I snaked my arm around Porter's waist. "Thank you so much," I said to Darren and Dean. I looked up at Porter. "You really pulled this off, Haven. I had no idea anything was going on."

"Double D did all the hard work." He picked the ring box up off the coffee table. "Okay, so about this," he said. "If you want something different, I'll get you something different. This one has sentimental value, but I want you to have something you love."

I pulled the ring out of the box and slid it onto my finger. "It's perfect. Just like I remember."

After Dean and Darren admired the ring, Darren cleared his throat. "Come on, poppet," he said to Dean. "Let's leave the lovebirds alone and head home."

"No champagne?" Dean asked.

"Oh! Stay for a glass of champagne," I said. "I can't believe you did all of this. It's incredible."

"Dean did set design for years," Darren said. "Our living room is full of the plaster guy's stuff, so it was nice to come over here and let him do his thing."

Porter opened the champagne and the four of us had a celebratory drink together, then Darren forced Dean to put on his coat.

"Enjoy your night," Dean said. He winked at me. "Don't do anything I wouldn't do."

"Those are the widest possible parameters, Dean."

"Come along," Darren said, adjusting Dean's scarf. He took Dean's hand and began to pull him out of the room. "I'll let you put Christmas lights up in our bedroom."

"Darling, I can light up the bedroom without any help," Dean said as the kitchen door closed behind them.

Twenty-Six

"I still can't believe you're finally going to marry Porter," Jenny said on FaceTime a few weeks later. She sighed audibly. "It's my favorite love story."

"I'm just glad the ring still fits," I said.

"That's another thing. Who holds on to an engagement ring for thirty years?"

"Porter Haven, apparently. I can't believe I never found it. He said it was in the box with the magical thinking story. I got distracted by that, I guess, and just never finished going through the box."

"So much for your sleuthing abilities," Jenny said, shaking her head. "You'd be a lousy Nancy Drew."

I laughed. "I was really shocked. I did not expect him to propose at all."

"Bits, be real. He wanted to lock that shit down, no cap."

"Excuse me?"

Jenny laughed. "I have a whole new vocabulary from working with teenagers all day."

"How do you like being a guidance counselor?"

"It's early days, but I actually love it. And you won't believe how much the campus has changed. Remember our crappy science room that reeked of formaldehyde? Now we have a science lab with more equipment than you can imagine."

"Does the lunchroom still smell like barf?" I asked, getting up from the kitchen table.

Jenny shook her head. "It smells like sunshine. And get this—there's a salad bar! With edamame and tofu squares."

"You cannot be serious."

"Dead serious. There's also a coffee station with a milk frother and shakers of cinnamon and four different kinds of sugar."

"Spoiled brats." I reached in the refrigerator to grab a bottle of San Pellegrino. "We had a senior smoking lounge, though."

"It's gone. You can't even vape on campus, although the little darlings do try."

"All I really want to know is what the PE uniforms look like."

"Cotton shorts and T-shirts with the school logo. Sweatpants for winter. And don't even think you're not getting a St. Francis de Sales hoodie for your wedding."

"It's the whole reason I'm getting married."

Jenny picked up a can of paint. "Okay, moving along from your prenuptial bliss. I'm trying to avoid thinking about Valentine's Day by staying busy and you inspired me with the colors in your house. This is choice number one," she said, holding the can up to the camera so I could see the dot of color on the lid. She set it down and picked up another can. "And this is choice number two. Which do you think?"

"Both. Put the pale blue on the walls and the darker blue on the cabinets."

Jenny nodded. "That's what I was thinking too."

"How does it feel to have your own place for the first time in your life?" I asked, pulling a glass out of the cabinet.

Jenny looked around her kitchen. "Incredible, actually. I can do whatever I want in here." She leaned forward and wiped the countertop with the sleeve of her sweatshirt. "Except clean, apparently."

"How's everything else? Have you gone on any more dates?"

Jenny shook her head. "I decided over Christmas that I'm just going to focus on me. I spent my whole childhood being ordered around by five older brothers, and then I got married and tried to do what was best for Scott and the kids. Now it's my time. Welcome to the Jennifer Fife Show. All Jenny, all the time."

"I think that's awesome, I really do. I know when Mia died and things with Crawford fell apart, I didn't have a clue who I was outside of being a mother and a wife. It took a lot of retraining my brain to start thinking of myself as a whole, worthwhile person all by myself. I had to get to know who I was again."

"Do you think you know who you are now?"

"Most of the time, yeah. Which is the reason I said yes to Porter. Well, that and the hoodie you're going to give me."

Jenny checked her watch. "I guess I should get painting. That's one benefit of the three and half feet of snow we've had this week; I'm not tempted to go outside. What are you doing the rest of today?"

"Reading an email from David and then giving Oliver a bath. I don't know what he rolled in, but he had to sleep in the barn last night. I'm going to have to use the hair dryer on him so he doesn't get doggy pneumonia."

"Give him some extra ear scratches for me and tell him I love him. He's my forever Valentine."

"I'll tell him."

"Will you tell Marco I said hi the next time you see him?"

I nodded. “He’s pretending to be distraught over the fact that I’m engaged. He said he’s going to bring a *lupara* to the wedding and object.”

“I’m not sure he’s pretending. Is he really coming?”

I shook my head. “I doubt it. Porter said he doesn’t care, but I can’t imagine Marco making the trip. And I sure don’t want his psycho girlfriend there if it’s during one of their reconciliation phases.”

“No kidding,” Jenny said. “Well, I guess I should get to work and put some colors on these walls. Thanks again for the flowers, Bits.”

“I just wanted you to know you’re loved.”

“I appreciate it. Okay, go be romantic. I’ll call again when I’ve managed to get some of this paint on and show you how it looks.”

When I hung up with Jenny, I put the kettle on and made myself a cup of tea, then sat down to read David’s email. I’d sent him the finished article about pagan church conversions, which was scheduled to be printed in a theological review’s summer issue.

Dear Beth,

Another home run, kiddo. I thoroughly enjoyed reading this and learned a lot too. The little I knew about these churches followed the thinking that the conversions were motivated by Christian fervor, but gradual conversion out of necessity makes a lot more sense.

I’m not sure if you know this, but I’ve always loved illuminated manuscripts. The idea of all of those monks adding decorative flourishes and paintings in the margins is just so glorious! And given how costly parchments were, and how common it was to reuse them, I have to think that many of the illuminated manuscripts I’ve admired over the years were palimpsests—something I hadn’t considered before. So the palimpsest motif you used in the article to represent the evolution of the pagan churches resonated deeply with me.

It also got me thinking that a palimpsest is the perfect metaphor for the human experience, what with the constant rewriting that time and experience do to all of us. Every experience, every emotion, every encounter is inscribed on the parchment of our lives, and none of them ever gets erased completely. Those individual moments and memories are the layers of our life stories.

Of course, there are paragraphs in everyone's life that one wishes to have scrubbed from the final record—things we wish we had done or left undone, things we wish weren't recorded for posterity, things we wish we'd said or left unvoiced. But not every passage in our lives can be illuminated. The contrasts are necessary—between illuminated and plain text, between good times and bad, between light and dark, joy and sorrow, rejoicing and regretting. It's the contrasts that reveal who we really are.

Maybe the true task of being human is to illuminate the palimpsest of our lives as much as possible—to add as many beautiful flourishes and as much color as we can to the story we're writing. If we're lucky, by the time we're done in this life, the palimpsest we leave behind is a colorful, messy, multi-layered, light-filled, scrawled-in-the-margins type affair, full of plot twists and unexpected detours.

There's a sermon in there somewhere. I've got my annual preaching gig in the Outer Banks a week after I come back from Europe, so maybe we can work on developing that theme on one of our train rides. Hopefully my sermon-writing skills haven't gotten too rusty, but if they have, I'm counting on you to pinch hit for me.

I've attached a photo from last week when I met Sloan for coffee. She did a great job presenting her paper at Duke—I was able to sneak in the back and listen for a bit—and we had a nice visit. She told me you've been extremely helpful editing her dissertation, which I don't doubt.

You're a wonderful niece, Beth. I probably haven't told you that enough, but it's true. You've definitely illuminated the manuscript of my life and I'm forever grateful I took a chance and brought you into my home—even if you did have to suffer a paisley comforter! My life would have been a lot less colorful without you, in ways I can't imagine and don't want to contemplate.

Keep decorating the margins, kiddo. Keep illuminating the pages.

I love you. You're in my prayers, as ever.

Your favorite uncle,

David

"Beth?" Porter called from upstairs. "Can you give me a hand?"

I closed the lid of my laptop and headed for the stairs.

"Whatcha doing?" I asked as I stepped into the hallway.

"This is the last one," Porter said, gesturing to a beat-up cardboard box. "I want to get rid of some of this and make more room for your stuff. Will you help me go through the closets?"

"You're actually going to get rid of something? I don't believe it."

"I don't need all this stuff now. It's from another lifetime."

"You sure?"

"I'm sure," he said, nodding. "Artifacts of the past. Hey, I don't know if you heard, but I'm actually marrying the girl I went to all those concerts with."

"I hadn't heard! Mazel Tov. Who is she?"

"Famous author," he said, taping the top of the box closed. "She wrote the sexy sheep story Netflix just turned into a movie."

"Lucky her."

"It was a little weird, though—she insisted on having Robert Duvall play Brutus." He shrugged. "Kind of strange casting, but what do I know?"

"Robert Duvall can play anything, Porter. Even a lovesick sheep."

Porter laughed. "Anyway, I don't need all this stuff anymore. I've got the real deal."

"Lucky you," I said, leaning over to kiss his cheek. "Let me go get some trash bags and I'll help you sort. Any chance there's another Head Teddy in there?"

Porter shook his head. "There will only ever be one Head Teddy. He's an original."

"The Robert Duvall of decapitated bears."

As Porter and I sorted through the closets and made piles of stuff to donate and to throw away, I thought about David's email.

He was right about all the layers of experience, and how they never really go away. I will never get over losing Mia, the same way I'll never totally recover from the breakdown of my marriage or the death of my parents. But the pain recedes and the moments of illumination become more frequent. The trick, as David so often says, is to stop casting a shadow on our own lives. Get out of our own way and let the light in.

Things in our little patch of Italy are remarkably peaceful these days. Sloan emailed a thank you note when she got home, then followed up with a question asking my advice about structuring her dissertation, and we've had a lively email correspondence ever since.

She and Porter also email occasionally. He was hesitant at first, but as Sloan and I became friends, his willingness to engage with her grew.

"Just don't make me deal with Libby," Porter said when I first broached the subject of inviting them to our wedding. "Seriously, Beth, I can't handle her cereal box psychology."

"You're just offended that she said your aura was dark," I teased.

Porter rolled his eyes. "If I have to hear her talk about opening my third eye to the consciousness of the universe again, my aura's going to be black as night, I promise you."

It was Sloan who'd wanted to meet David. I was surprised when she emailed to ask if that would be okay with me, but she explained that when I talked about David, it was obvious that he was someone special, and since they lived so near to one another, she wondered if they might meet. I gave David a heads-up, then Sloan reached out to him and they met for coffee a few times. David knows a lot about the Taizé community, and is also friends with several professors at Duke, so they had lots to talk about right off the bat. I was looking forward to having all of them at the wedding, even if Porter continuously threatened to have Libby carted off if she so much as mentioned his chakras.

After a couple hours of work, we'd sorted through all of the boxes and made room in both of the upstairs closets.

"You ready to be done?" Porter asked.

I nodded. "I was going to give Oliver a bath, but I think I'll wait. I'm worn out."

"He's happy out in the barn. I think he'd live out there if we let him."

"Who wouldn't? It's like a Mexican *telenovela* out there with all the sheep drama."

"You know what I'd like to do? Take a hot bath and then watch a movie. I'll get the fire going and we can just chill."

"I'd love that."

"Help me up?"

I stuck out my hand and hauled Porter to his feet. He wrapped his arms around me and I leaned against his body, breathing in the scent of him.

The smell of the woods and tobacco and wine and something deliciously smoky and spicy I've never been able to identify in the thirty-plus years that I've loved Porter.

The smell of home.

Acknowledgments

First and foremost, a huge thank you to Cristen W. Matilainen for being my Jenny all these many decades. Thanks to Lisa P. Hodges for her relentless friendship and willingness to read early drafts, and to Kelly Antonio, Sonja Smith, and Amy Britt for their willingness to drink the margaritas and slay the ghosts. *Vielen dank* to my spirit animal, Walker Antonio, whose painting made the treehouse a home—and the target of would-be art thieves. Thanks to Alan Hastings for letting me borrow Head Teddy and telling me the best way to approach a climb. To the wickedly talented Bess Auer, what can't you do?!

Sadie Hassman, your editorial eye and creative mind inspire me, and I'm so grateful for your input, support, and the side chats that keep me laughing. A million thanks to Travis Ables—an incredible writer, excellent editor, and all-around mensch—for his invaluable counsel. Massive thanks to Susan Lawrence, who taught me to read and love books; to Bo Stewart, who makes me laugh until I tip over like a Tennessee fainting goat; and to Gabe Stewart, who bought ten copies of my first novel just because he loves me.

I'm incredibly fortunate to call Gordon McClellan's DartFrog Books my publishing home. In an industry full of shysters, this talented, dedicated, and ethical team is an anomaly in the best possible way. Suanne Laqueur, your Pings sustain me. G, we're late for Student Council.

In all ways and at all times, my heart belongs to Colburn, Lachlan, Sadie, Ingrid, and Chris. How I got lucky enough to love all of you is one of God's greatest mysteries.

About the Author

Corey Stewart is a writer and editor of books and magazines who loves nothing more than a final boarding call. After nine countries, six states, and approximately forty homes, Stewart prides herself on being able to pack an entire household in two days or less—a talent that has proved useful far more often than you might imagine. Her first novel, *The Wisdom of the Olive Tree*, was a finalist for the 2023 National Indie Excellence Award in Women's Fiction and won the 2023 CIPA Gold Award for Best Women's Fiction. You can find her online at www.coreylstewart.com.